PENGUIN

it's
Complicated

ABOUT THE AUTHOR

Emma Hughes is a freelance journalist who has written for publications including *Time Out*, the *Guardian*, Vogue.co.uk, *Grazia* and *ES*. An early excerpt from her first novel, *No Such Thing As Perfect*, was shortlisted for the 2019 Lucy Cavendish Fiction Prize. She lives in London.

PRAISE FOR *NO SUCH THING AS PERFECT*

'I lost count of the number of times I laughed out loud, I was rooting for Laura from the first page. Tender, funny, smart and brilliantly observed. The perfect blend of uplifting escapism and social satire, an utter page-turner and such a clever, perceptive moving one. I LOVED it!'
Daisy Buchanan

'Brimming with wit and razor-sharp observations'
Sophie Cousens, author of *This Time Next Year*

'Poignant, warm and very, very clever, this is perfect for anyone who thinks they're the only one without the answers. I felt vindicated and lifted after I'd read it!'
Laura Jane Williams

'This is a smart thoughtful romcom with real heart and a deeply satisfying ending'
Red

'A fresh, funny, sexy tale of dating woes, family expectations, technological adventure, and loyal friendships, this book will make your world a brighter place'
Katherine Heiny

'It is so funny (properly laugh-out-loud funny) and smart and full of characters I feel like I know'
Laura Kay

Also by Emma Hughes

No Such Thing As Perfect

it's complicated

Emma Hughes

PENGUIN BOOKS

PENGUIN BOOKS

UK | USA | Canada | Ireland | Australia
India | New Zealand | South Africa

Penguin Books is part of the Penguin Random House
group of companies whose addresses can be found at
global.penguinrandomhouse.com

Penguin
Random House
UK

Published in Penguin Books 2023
001

Typeset in 10.4/15 pt Palatino LT Pro by Jouve (UK), Milton Keynes
Printed and bound in Great Britain by Clays Ltd, Elcograf S.p.A.

The authorised representative in the EEA is
Penguin Random House Ireland, Morrison Chambers,
32 Nassau Street, Dublin D02 YH68

A CIP catalogue record for this book is available from the
British Library

ISBN: 978-1-529-15886-1

www.greenpenguin.co.uk

MIX
Paper | Supporting
responsible forestry
FSC® C018179

Penguin Random House is committed to a
sustainable future for our business, our readers
and our planet. This book is made from Forest
Stewardship Council® certified paper.

For Julia Beck and Edward Williams

Hanwell, West London

2006

It was a sunny Thursday in May, and Dee Jensen was hiding behind a tree.

The tree in question was the fallen oak by the viaduct in Brent Lodge Park, a meadowy stretch of green on the edge of Hanwell that doubled as St Jude's School's unofficial recreation area. It was thirty feet long but only three feet high on its side, which meant that Dee, who was nearly six feet tall, was having to squat. It was an undignified way to spend her lunch break, but she had no choice – she couldn't show her face until Nat Flynn and his new girlfriend Sophie had finished snogging on the path in front of her.

She stuck a hand in the pocket of her blazer and felt for the Twix wrapper that she knew was in there, closing her fingers around it like a protective amulet.

Nat had arrived at St Jude's the previous September: he'd been at a private school before, but his parents couldn't agree who was going to pay the fees so he'd had to leave in the middle of his A-levels. Dee had noticed his dark curls and green eyes, but he didn't make a serious impression on her until parents' evening that November. Sitting next to

1

her mum, she'd spotted Nat squashed between his parents, whose hostile body language sent a chill down her spine. Dee knew exactly how it felt to be in Nat's shoes – and judging by the look they exchanged as she was leaving, *he* knew that she knew.

Dee and Nat were in the same English class, and they'd started walking to and from it together, discussing films – Nat was going to be an actor – and their families. Nat listened sympathetically, shaking his head when Dee told him that her dad had forgotten her birthday. And Dee in turn had nodded when he'd talked about his mum's awful new boyfriend, even though her own newly acquired stepmum was the opposite of awful. Nat would always stop and buy a Twix from the vending machine outside the cafeteria, which he'd then open and offer half of to Dee, nudging it through the gap in the wrapper like Humphrey Bogart offering a cigarette to Lauren Bacall. The day after she'd told him about her forgotten birthday, Dee found one from him hidden in her school bag. Its wrapper was the one she was touching in her pocket now. She was very glad she'd kept it all this time – it was proof that she hadn't just imagined the whole thing.

'OK, the coast's clear,' Dee's best friend Roo called from above her head. 'You can come out now.'

Dee hobbled out from behind the tree, rubbing her calf where it had started to cramp. On the last day of the Easter term she and Nat had sat on the front step of his mum's house, listening to Massive Attack and watching a young family playing frisbee in the park over the road. *Maybe that'll be you and me one day*, Nat had said, pointing at them. Then he'd looked at Dee in a way that suggested he was assessing her willingness to be a part of this plan. She'd thought he might be about to kiss her, but he hadn't. Despite this Dee had floated home, allowing herself to daydream of the future she longed for but which always felt out of reach. But her joy was short-lived: Nat had kissed Sophie at a party the following weekend, and by the start of the summer term they were officially a couple. Dee, mortified by how badly she'd misjudged the situation, had avoided Nat ever since then. There were less than two months left of school, she reminded herself now as she wiggled the pins and needles out of her feet, and then she'd never have to see him again. It should have been a comforting thought, but it wasn't.

'How bad was it?' she asked as she climbed up on to the tree to join Roo, feeling like someone had replaced her heart with a lead weight. 'On a scale of one to *I might as well go and throw myself in the river.*'

'Seven? Maybe an eight.' Roo, who was going to be a doctor, pulled the face that Dee imagined her making in the future when she had to tell someone that they were going to lose a leg. 'I can't see the point of kisses that go on and on like that,' she continued, flicking her plaits dismissively over her shoulder. 'I'd have thought the optimum length of time for a kiss is between five and ten seconds. Surely things start getting repetitive?' Seeing Dee's anguished expression, she put an arm around her. 'Look, I know it hurts right now,' she said with as much patience as she could muster, patting Dee's back. 'But you have to focus on all the bad stuff, Dee. He strings you along, then gets together with Sophie and acts like nothing ever happened. Do you honestly want to be with someone who treats you like that? Also, when I sat next to him on the bus that time he was such a bore – he kept telling me I ought to watch *Fight Club*.'

Dee let her hands fall and started picking a flake of bark off the tree's trunk. She'd accepted that Roo, who was unsentimental at the best of times and positively allergic to feelings when they concerned Nat, would never see what she saw in him. Although they'd been best friends since their first day at St Jude's, there were bits of her that Roo couldn't reach. Bits that Nat *had* been able to.

'He's just . . .' She looked up at the cloudless sky and sighed. 'We have this connection, Roo. We come from the same place. We want the same things. It's hard to explain.'

'I think right now Nat mostly just wants to get acquainted with Sophie's Wonderbra,' Roo said huffily, glancing over her shoulder in the direction Nat and Sophie had gone. Then she reached into her satchel and got out the laptop she'd bought with money from her Saturday job at the chemist. 'I know what'll cheer you up,' she went on, creaking the lid open. 'I remembered last night that the deadline for our yearbook entries is tomorrow, so I got up early and typed all the questions out into Word documents.' She tilted the screen so Dee could see it. 'See? One page for each of us.'

Dee peered at it. 'Wait, you already filled mine in for me?'

'I knew you'd never get around to it otherwise. Anyway, I only did the obvious bits.'

Dee leaned across Roo, shielding her eyes from the sun. From the start, Roo had called most of the shots in their friendship – and Dee, whose instinct was always to fit in around other people, was happy to let her. As well as typing in Dee's name, age and Hotmail address, Roo had taken it upon herself to answer several of the personality questions for Dee. Next to *Favourite subject* she'd written *English Lit*, and by *Favourite snack* was *Whatever Roo's brought for lunch*. For *Favourite tune* she'd put down 'Obviously' by McFly, which they'd both bought on single from Woolworths when it came out.

'I'm changing that to "Teardrop" by Massive Attack,' Dee said, reaching over with uncustomary certainty and highlighting the words to get rid of them. Roo snorted.

'That's Nat's favourite song, not yours – you only bought the album because he likes it.' Roo prised Dee's hands off the keyboard and sighed. It looked like she was about to launch into another anti-Nat treatise, but just then the tinkling *moo-moo-moo* of an ice-cream van drifted across the park.

'Twisters?' Dee suggested; she and Roo had been buying exactly the same lollies for seven years.

'I'll get them,' Roo said, handing Dee her computer and hopping off the log. 'Don't drop this, OK? It's got my university accommodation spreadsheet on it.'

As Dee watched her best friend walking purposefully towards the van, a train whooshed past on the viaduct, heading for Paddington. She waited until its roar had died away, then wrenched her brain away from Nat and turned her attention to the computer on her lap. There was only one yearbook question that Roo hadn't answered for her.

When I'm thirty-five I'll . . .

Thirty-five sounded impossibly old to Dee – it was an age by which you'd need to have everything sorted out. Their head of year, Mrs Crisp (the butt of endless snack-based jokes, who didn't exactly help herself by having a crinkle-cut perm), kept telling them they could have it all. Dee wasn't so sure.

She hesitated, then clicked out of the document that Roo had made for her and into Roo's. In the space next to the same question Roo had written: *Be an anaesthetist, with twins and a husband who knows how to stack the dishwasher.*

Dee looked up. Roo had made it to the ice-cream van and was queuing behind a couple and their three laughing, jostling children: two little boys in matching green school uniforms, and a toddler flailing its arms gleefully in a pushchair. The man, she thought, looked a bit like an older version of Nat. She looked back at the screen and lowered her hands on to the keyboard. *When I'm thirty-five I'll . . .*

Have a family, she typed.

The words stared back at her. She deleted them.

Sixteen Years Later . . .

Chapter One

The doctor, who Dee had managed to get an appointment with before work on a Friday at the surgery in Kentish Town, wasn't the same one she'd seen last time.

'I'm Kirsty!' she said as soon as Dee sat down – she had a lilting Scottish accent, squeaky-clean conker-coloured hair and eyes that were a similar greyish-blue to Dee's. 'It's my first day here!'

Dee thought that you probably weren't meant to tell your patients either of those things, but she let it slide; she never liked making a fuss.

'Congratulations!' she said, crossing her legs on the uncomfortable plastic chair and catching the toe of her boot in her dress. She was wearing the white and black spotty Zara one that everyone had bought – she liked the way it drowned her and made her feel less conspicuous – and black tights as a concession to it being late September. Her coat, which had started its life pale pink but was now edging towards grey, was balled up in her lap. Her stubbornly straight, light brown hair had spent the day escaping from the bun that she'd tied it up in; it was now hanging loose around her shoulders, and the elastic was on her wrist. About once every eighteen months she would leave the hairdresser's with a full fringe that she'd allowed herself to be talked into, which she would then spend the next year and a half trying to grow out before repeating the entire cycle all over again.

'Let's get your notes up then, Dee,' Kirsty the GP said, spinning on her chair so she was facing her computer and beginning to click things. There was a pot of half a dozen identical blue biros on her desk, along with a dog photo calendar – this month's model was a golden retriever – and a framed picture of Kirsty and a smiling man on the beach with a toddler sitting between them.

'So, you saw Dr Phillips the week before last for some blood tests because you'd come off the pill a year ago . . .' Kirsty turned back to face Dee. 'Why did you stop taking it, if you don't mind me asking?'

Dee hesitated. The *real* reason she'd thrown the blue blister packs in the bin was because she'd been single for an embarrassingly long time, and it had started to feel like they were mocking her. Then, when her situation had finally changed a few months ago, getting a new prescription had seemed like it would be much more of a scary expression of a desire for commitment than just buying condoms. But she didn't think Kirsty would understand any of that. She was wearing a sapphire engagement ring with a delicate gold wedding band tucked underneath it.

'It wasn't agreeing with me,' she said, avoiding Kirsty's eye. 'But it's been nearly a year and my periods are still quite . . . odd. I don't have one for months, then I get two in a fortnight. They never used to be like that. That's why I had the tests – they said I'd get my results back today when I saw you.'

Kirsty squinted at the screen and then tapped her forehead.

'Ah yes, that's right – sorry, I'm still getting to grips with the system here! Let's call those up for you now.'

She scrolled down, then stopped and frowned.

'I don't suppose you can remember what day of your cycle you had these done on, can you?' she asked. 'Your numbers look a bit off – sometimes testing just before your period can cause that to happen . . . Or it might just be stress. What do you do job-wise, Dee?'

'I'm a copywriter.' Dee decided to stop there, while she still had a chance of convincing Kirsty that her working life was as glamorous as an episode of *Mad Men*. (The reality, sadly, was more like *Men Behaving Badly*.)

'That must be interesting!' Kirsty said brightly. She cocked her head. 'You know what, I think the best thing to do is just to repeat all the tests today, if that's OK?'

The doctor got up and crossed the room to a cabinet on the opposite wall, which she opened to reveal a wall of plastic-wrapped phials and needles.

'Have you got any nice plans this evening, Dee?' she asked as she started taking things out of it. 'I don't know about you, but all I'm good for by the time Friday comes around is crashing on the sofa with a takeaway!'

'My . . . the person I'm seeing is cooking me dinner, actually,' Dee said, trying not to look at the needles. 'We haven't really seen each other much this week – he's an actor, he's got a big audition coming up that he's been preparing for.'

'Goodness!' The doctor was getting an alcohol swab out of a drawer under the cabinet now. 'Roll your sleeve up for me, will you?'

As she fiddled with her dress, Dee found her eyes flicking

11

towards the framed photo on the desk. Could she imagine herself in the doctor's shoes, with a family of her own? *Imagine* suggested a confidence she didn't have. Maybe *hope* was a better word: she hoped for one, and she always had. But the hope was unspoken: none of her romantic relationships had felt serious enough to bring the subject up. During their teens and twenties, when Roo had spoken with confidence about things she would and wouldn't do with her future children (piano lessons were a yes, sugary snacks were a no), Dee had kept quiet – she'd learned that it was generally better not to talk about things you really wanted, even to your best friend. That way, if you didn't get them, at least nobody knew that you'd wanted them and you could keep the disappointment to yourself.

Kirsty had been watching her as she closed the cabinet.

'Sorry, I know this is a *faff*,' she said, giving Dee a misplaced, reassuring smile. 'But I'll ask the lab to fast-track these for you, they should be back on Monday morning. I can give you a call to talk through them if you like? I very much doubt there's anything worrying going on.'

'Sure thing, no problem,' Dee nodded obligingly. She put her arm on the desk, then heard Kirsty unclipping something and looked the other way.

Anvil, the creative agency that Dee worked at, had its office at the top of a shabby building on Poland Street, above a language school that never seemed to have any pupils. As Dee climbed the stairs she felt the familiar combination of dread and anxiety – she didn't like her job but she was terrified of losing it. It had taken her a long time to find, and she couldn't face starting over again. This wasn't a totally unlikely prospect: the increasingly angry rent demands from the building's landlord piling up on her boss Jay's desk spike hadn't escaped Dee's notice.

The agency's longest-standing – and now only – client was a chain of garden centres called Root and Branch. Jay had given them to Dee on her first day, promising her bigger, sexier clients as soon as she'd proved herself by writing the copy for their flyers and catalogues. But the bigger, sexier clients had gone to bigger, sexier agencies, and now Root and Branch was basically all that Dee, who had never managed to keep a plant alive for longer than a fortnight, did. Strictly speaking, she was freelance at Anvil and could come and go as she pleased. In practice this just meant she had all the worst bits of a full-time job with none of the upsides, like paid holiday or any idea where she'd be in a year's time.

Dee pushed the door at the top of the stairs open; the security keypad had stopped working years ago and nobody had bothered to get it fixed. The office was eerily quiet, but that was nothing new. When Jay had hired Dee as Anvil's senior copywriter – she hadn't realised until she arrived that she was only senior because there weren't any others – there had been four other people at the agency. Now, as she made her way across the tatty carpet to her desk she could only count two heads: Jay's in the glass box of his office-within-an-office, and Hiro the designer's.

Hiro swivelled in his chair as she approached. He bought and sold second-hand clothes in his spare time, and was a walking advertisement for his business: today he was wearing a pair of bright green acid-washed dungarees over a black lurex rollneck. He spent most of his time at his fiancée

Poodle's place – she was a burlesque artist, one of whose acts involved dressing up like Oscar the Grouch and leaping out of a bin – and not long after Dee had started at Anvil he'd suggested that she could rent his flat in Kentish Town for a big discount, as long as she didn't mind sleeping on the sofa whenever he needed to come back. It wasn't exactly how she'd hoped to be living in her mid-thirties, but Dee had jumped at the chance: she had far more space at Hiro's than she'd ever have been able to afford otherwise, and the flat even had a tiny balcony.

'Our favourite people called,' Hiro said laconically. 'They've emailed you some pictures of their brand-new leaf blower. Bet you're excited.'

'Not as excited as you'll be when you're spending hours cutting them out on Photoshop,' Dee shot back – joking around with Hiro was one of the few things she actually enjoyed about her job. She enjoyed writing too, but it was hard to feel good about the sort of writing she did for Root and Branch. She picked at the sticky strip of loose trim around the edge of her desk as she sat down. It was the sixth she'd sat at since she moved back to London after finishing her degree, but they'd all ended up looking the same – she'd carted the same fuzzy miniature cactus and Penguin Classics postcards between them every time. *This is it*, they whispered now. *This is as good as it gets.*

Hiro cracked his knuckles and leaned back in his chair. 'Oh look, there goes our glorious leader now,' he said with deep disdain.

Jay had emerged from the glass box of his office-within-an-office. He'd started in advertising in the nineties and dressed like he was still there: baggy suits, bright colours, thick-framed glasses with a yellow tint like something from *Trainspotting*. Striding through Soho with his phone clamped to his ear, he looked as dated as a pickled shark. Hiro always said that Jay was the world's most divorced-seeming man, but he was actually married to a much younger model-turned-nutritionist called Bizzy, and together they had a six-year-old daughter named Persephone.

'Wotcha, Big D!' Jay called out to Dee now as he swaggered towards the kitchen. He was chomping furiously on the nicotine gum that seemed to be permanently lodged in his cheek; he'd been sober since 2013 but still gave the twitchy impression of just having emerged from the toilet at Chinawhite. 'How's it hanging? All good?'

'It's hanging!' Dee confirmed. She reluctantly woke her computer up and saw she had a Google Chat message from Minnie, who had appointed herself to the position of Dee's joint best friend a few years earlier. A party planner who mostly worked in the evenings, Minnie liked to message Dee across multiple platforms throughout the day, updating her on things like *The Real Housewives of Salt Lake City* and what she was having for lunch. This message was about the foxes that kept getting into her bins. Dee sent a suitably sympathetic reply to her, then opened the email from Morag Craggs, Root and Branch's head of marketing. As well as clogging up Dee's inbox with high-resolution leaf-blower photos, she'd rejected the coverlines Dee had suggested for the autumn brochure. *Could we revert to last year's?* she'd written. *And hero the products?* Morag was always wanting to hero things, or circle back, and there was a disconcertingly robotic tone to all of her messages. Sometimes Dee wondered if she was actually corresponding with a supermarket self-checkout machine. The only upside was that Morag had never shown any interest in talking on the phone or, worse, on a video call – Dee had never actually spoken to her, or even seen a photograph of her opposite number.

She sighed.

'I don't get it,' she muttered to Hiro, clicking out of the email. 'They're paying an agency to come up with new angles, but all they want is the same old stuff. Why don't they just save their money and do everything themselves?'

'People like the *idea* of change,' Hiro said solemnly, 'until they realise it means *they're* going to have to change.' He looked across at Dee. 'Ah hah, you're wearing your date-night dress . . . Does this mean you're seeing Britain's hottest up-and-coming young actor this evening?'

In spite of everything, Dee couldn't help smiling. 'Maybe,' she grinned. As she waited for the leaf-blower photos to download she allowed herself to drift off to a happier place.

On the way back to her flat Dee stopped at the wine shop on Kentish Town Road to buy a bottle. The shop had a little counter in its window with two stools where you could sit and drink, and this was where she and Nat (yes, *the* Nat) had met for their first, magical drink two months ago. They weren't officially boyfriend and girlfriend yet – Nat had told her he wanted to take things slowly, and that he didn't want any drama – but Dee was starting to cautiously relax into the idea that they were *seeing each other*.

Dee and Nat hadn't stayed in touch after they'd left school, but Dee had silently followed his life on Facebook. He'd gone to RADA and roles had followed in *Midsomer Murders*, *Holby City*, *Grantchester* and *Downton Abbey*. Her career hadn't been anything like as exciting as his, and her romantic life was bruising. She'd always hoped that the right relationship would unlock the sense of security that had always eluded her, so she had dutifully joined all the apps. She'd stood on touchlines in the rain and traipsed round record stores and cooked countless Nigella-approved pasta dinners for the men she was seeing. But it didn't seem to matter how hard she worked, her relationships always felt precarious and confusing. And they always ended after weeks or months, leaving her no closer to finding what she was looking for. Her most recent not-quite-boyfriend had broken up with her by voice note, and the one before that had ended things because he'd fallen for a middle-distance runner with too many teeth called Henrietta.

Then, two months ago, Nat had sent Dee a message out of the blue on Facebook. It had come through while the triathlon-obsessed management consultant Dee was struggling through a first date with was in the bathroom of the noisy pub he'd chosen.

So I went for a walk in Brent Lodge Park the other day and you popped into my head, he'd written very casually, as though it had been days, not years. *Fancy a drink?*

A quick google and a trawl through a *Downton Abbey* fan forum had confirmed that Nat was recently single, having split up from the set designer he'd been seeing. Dee had managed one more pint with the management consultant, composing a reply to Nat in her head while he went on and on about Half Ironmans and clip-in pedals. *Yes*, she saw herself typing. *Yes, yes, yes.*

They met four days later. Nat arrived after her, tanned from a long weekend at a festival, wearing a white T-shirt over vintage jeans and apologising profusely for being late. They'd had a bottle of wine with a funky label that he'd chosen and the years had melted away. Nat had asked her lots of searching questions – this almost never happened on dates, Dee had found – and given thoughtful answers to hers. He'd been honest with her about his romantic history and Dee had paid forensic attention, mapping a course around Nat's likes and dislikes. The set designer, he'd said, had been a planner, which meant that Dee would always go with the flow. A make-up artist who he'd had a fling with had been too keen to put a label on things, so Dee resolved to use only the most abstract of nouns to describe their situation if it ever turned into anything – which, judging by the way Nat kept letting his hand brush against hers, it actually seemed like it might.

'This kind of feels like . . . coming home, doesn't it?' Nat had said as he got up to order another bottle of wine. And all Dee had been able to do was nod, stunned. That was exactly how it felt. She'd never let herself believe in happily ever afters – but if she had, this was what hers would have looked like.

When she got to Hiro's flat with the wine she'd bought for them, Nat was sitting on the wall outside, wearing a linen shirt over his jeans and a scuffed pair of suede boots. He looked up and waved and Dee's heart did an Olympic gymnastics routine. She remembered to let her hip go slack. She was taller than him – he'd never commented on it, but it made her self-conscious. *You need to get better at taking up space, darling,* her mum had always said to Dee. *Those Viking genes of yours aren't going anywhere.* It wasn't the most tactful way of putting it, she thought – she took up space whether she wanted to or not.

Nat stood up, then clapped a hand to his forehead.

'Shit, I just remembered – I was going to cook tonight, wasn't I?' he said apologetically. 'Sorry, Dee, I forgot to go to the shop on the way . . .'

'It's totally fine,' Dee said quickly, even though she'd been looking forward to it all day, 'you've had a lot on your mind. We can just get a takeaway or something.'

Nat's face broke into a grateful smile. 'You're amazing,' he said, closing the distance between them. He put a hand on the small of Dee's back and pulled her towards him, and they kissed. Nat was very, vey good at kissing.

Hiro's flat was on the top floor, overlooking Camden Road. Dee had done her best to make the kitchen-slash-living room homely by putting a throw over the sofa and sticking photos to the fridge, but there wasn't much room for personal touches, what with the rails of second-hand clothes that Hiro was getting ready to sell and Poodle's costumes.

Once they were inside Nat kicked his boots off and stretched out on the sofa while Dee went to get two glasses out of the cupboard. She watched him stifling a yawn and pushing his hair off his face. He deliberately kept it quite long, he'd told her once, in case he had to audition for a period drama – casting directors wouldn't wait for your hair to grow. Being an actor, Dee was learning, meant that both you and the people around you lived in a state of suspended

19

animation where it was almost impossible to make firm plans. Right now Nat didn't even have a place to live: he was splitting his time between his mum's house and various friends' spare rooms. If Dee was being honest with herself, she found the uncertainty difficult. She and Nat never talked about the future, and they rarely made plans beyond the following week. But it wasn't forever. And there had been enough of what she thought of as 'Twix moments' to make up for it.

As she gave the glasses a rinse under the tap Dee's stomach rumbled; she was still feeling a bit light-headed after the blood test. There was half a block of Cathedral City in the fridge but she didn't like the idea of Nat seeing her hungry, overwhelmed by need.

'I got us this,' she said, turning back to face Nat with the glasses in one hand and pulling the bottle of wine she'd bought out of her bag with the other one. 'It's the same one we had on our first . . .' She stopped herself from saying *date* just in time; the word felt a bit relationshippy and she didn't want to look presumptuous. 'The first time we met, remember?'

Nat sat up and rubbed his eyes. 'You're so sweet. Come here, you . . .'

He swung his legs around and patted the sofa. Dee brought everything over and sat down next to him. Nat stroked the back of her hand with his thumb.

'Hey, before we order dinner, would you mind if we just run through my scene for the audition?' he asked. 'I'm just a bit worried, I really need it to go well . . .'

'Of course.' Dee squeezed his hand. It was a Friday night, which meant that whatever takeaway they got would take the best part of an hour to arrive – she tried not to think about how hungry she was. Anyway, that wasn't her most urgent concern right now. She was worried too, but for different reasons to Nat.

The audition – the first Nat had actually had since they'd started seeing each other – was for a part in Netflix's epic fantasy show *Dragon Quest*. He was spending tomorrow packing, before flying to Romania, where the show was filmed, to read for a part in the next series. Dee was experiencing deep, consuming anxiety about what this meant for them – if he got the part he'd be spending months at a time living thousands of miles away from her – but she hadn't said anything to him. The most important thing in all of this, she kept telling herself, was for her to be supportive: this was the opportunity of a lifetime for him. And anyway, she was meant to be going with the flow.

Nat had reached into his satchel and got out a dog-eared script. He passed it to Dee.

'So, the scene I'm going to be doing in front of the director is the one where Olric Longblade – that's who I'm in the running to play – and Agnes are in prison,' he said, rolling his shoulders as though he was limbering up to put on a suit of armour. 'They've both been captured by General Veritas's army, and now they're chained up next to each other in his castle. There's been this tension between them ever since they fell into an enchanted river together, so Olric decides to finally tell Agnes how he feels.' He pointed at a line at the top of the page. 'Let's take it from here – you go first, OK?'

Dee glanced down at the stage directions, trying to keep her face absolutely still. Agnes was a beautiful nun-turned-archer played by Lulu Hartley, an actress who occasionally modelled for Burberry. *Agnes's tunic is torn in several places*, she read silently with dismay. *As she speaks her chest heaves.* She put a hand over her own distinctly unheaving chest and cleared her throat.

'Are you afraid, my lord?' she asked, trying to copy Lulu's plummy delivery. Nat's piercing green eyes were fixed on her. His posture, the way he held himself – everything was subtly but definitely different. He was capital-A Acting.

'Of dying, you mean?' His voice was deep and firm. 'No, Agnes. I . . .' He paused, and Dee felt the energy between them change as he snapped back into being just Nat. 'Sorry, can we try that once more? Something just felt a bit off.'

'Sure.' Dee's stomach rumbled again. She pulled a cushion over it, hoping Nat hadn't heard, then went back to the script. 'Are you afraid, my lord?'

This time Nat exhaled before he spoke. 'Of dying, you mean? No, Agnes. I have no fear of death – only gratitude for the life I have lived.' He tipped his head back and sighed as though he really was staring at the ceiling of a prison. 'If this is indeed the end, I have only one regret.'

A bead of sweat trickles slowly down Agnes's neck, the stage directions said. 'And what is that, my lord?' Dee asked with a sinking heart.

Nat looked straight at her. 'Not claiming you for my own the very first time I set eyes on you,' he said in a voice that cracked with emotion. Then he reached across, slipped a hand behind her head and kissed her.

They sank back into the sofa together. Nat moved his arm under her legs and brought them up on to the cushions – Dee dropped a hand to move the wine glasses out of the way before they could get knocked over, not wanting to break the spell.

'Is this in the script?' she asked as Nat slid his hand under her dress and up her leg, kissing her neck as he moved.

Nat stopped. 'It definitely isn't,' he said, looking up at her with a grin.

While Nat's attention was elsewhere Dee quickly reached into her sleeve, peeled off the plaster in the crook of her elbow and pushed it under the cushion behind her head. She had decided not to mention the blood tests.

Minnie:
Hiiiiiiiii
Who's up for breakfast
tomorrow?
I really fancy The Canal Cafe!

Roo:
Tomorrow as in twelve
hours' time?
That's very short notice,
Minnie . . .
I'm going for a run, then
I've got a training course to
prepare for

Minnie:
Boooooooo
Dee?

Dee:
Kdfhththth txbsb&&x*
Sorry, typing in the dark. Nat's
asleep, I'm eating cheese in
the kitchen. Wait, let me put
the cooker light on

I think I'm free! Not sure
when Nat's heading off.
What sort of time were you
thinking, Minnie?

Minnie:
Eleven?
Actually, better make it
twelve – I've got company
tonight, might be a late one
😏

Dee:
Haha, OK, twelve
Roo, I'll see you on Sunday
for cat-sitting at my mum's,
right?

Roo:
You certainly will, it's in the diary

Minnie:
Of course it is
You and your diary 😜

Dee:
Great 😃
Look, I'd better get back to
bed. Love you both

Minnie:
We love you too! Don't do
anything I wouldn't do . . .

Roo:
That doesn't narrow things
down much . . .

Minnie:
😝

Dee:
GOODNIGHT

Chapter Two

When Dee woke up she was alone in the bed, which was technically Hiro's but had the nice Orla Kiely duvet set she'd invested in after her first month at Anvil on it. The first thing she felt when she realised Nat wasn't there was a jolt of panic; she still hadn't quite been able to shake off the fear that he might just evaporate one day while she wasn't looking.

But no, there were his clothes from the night before over the back of the chair in the corner, and she could smell fresh coffee through the open door. Maybe he was going to bring them their first breakfast in bed, she thought hopefully. She rolled on to her back and felt her pulse returning to normal.

Nat's deep voice drifted towards her from the kitchen. It sounded like he was talking to his agent.

'I haven't seen *Seven Samurai*, actually,' he was saying. 'But if you think it's worth me watching it before the audition then obviously I will . . .' There was a pause. 'I'm not at home, no . . .'

Dee waited for him to elaborate, maybe even mention her by name, but the conversation moved on. She tried not to feel disappointed. Of course Nat wouldn't tell his agent he was at hers. Why should he? There was absolutely no need for him to. She stuck an arm out from under the duvet to get her phone and saw she had a telltale bruise coming up in the

26

crook of her elbow from the blood test. She wondered if she ought to put a jumper on to cover it up so Nat wouldn't spot it and ask her where it was from; she couldn't think of anything more offputting than her talking about hormones while they were in bed. She was hopeful that Nat still wanted a family of his own one day too: he had nephews who he adored and he'd once sent her a photo of himself on the set of a TV show about the Blitz hugging the little boy who'd played his son. And of course, her mind kept turning to that conversation they'd had all those years ago on his mum's front step. *Maybe that'll be us one day*, he'd said to her. She hoped more than anything that it would.

The door opened and Nat appeared. He hadn't made breakfast but he was holding a coffee in each hand and he was naked, so Dee really couldn't complain. As he walked round to her side of the bed she allowed herself to stare at his well-muscled chest, his tanned forearms, the tattoo on his inner wrist of a line from *Hamlet* ('This above all: to thine own self be true'). She still couldn't quite believe that some-one as handsome as him was interested in someone like her, whose looks nobody had ever commented on other than to say things like *Wow, you're tall!* and *What's the weather like up there?* The fact that he *was* interested – that he'd looked past what she saw as the mismatch in attractiveness – gave her faith that there really was a deeper connection between them.

'Sorry about all the noise,' Nat said with a grin, passing her one of the coffees. 'My agent called, she's been talking to the *Dragon Quest* casting director and she thinks I'm exactly what they're looking for.'

'That's fantastic!' Dee snuffled her legs up as she took the mug, trying not to think about the distance between London and Bucharest. Nat got in next to her, put his mug down on the bedside table and looped his arm around her shoulders. He hadn't showered before bed and she could still smell the Comme Des Garçons on his skin – in the early days, to her everlasting shame, she'd actually ducked into Liberty on her way to work and surreptitiously sprayed the tester on her own wrist.

'So, what are your plans for this weekend?' he asked her, stifling a yawn.

Dee weighed up her options. Nat's flight wasn't until Sunday morning, and she'd secretly hoped he might suggest they spent the rest of today together. Minnie wouldn't mind postponing brunch, she'd told herself. But Nat hadn't asked her *if* she had plans, he'd asked *what* they were, which suggested that he was expecting her to have some, and that he hadn't been thinking about staying here.

'I'm meeting Minnie for brunch, then me and Roo are looking after Ronnie at my mum and Ines's on Sunday,' she said, resting her head against his shoulder. The steady thump of his pulse was reassuring.

'Nice.' Nat was a good actor, but not quite good enough to sound genuinely enthusiastic. He'd only met Roo and Minnie together once, but the evening hadn't exactly been a success. Dee had invited Roo, Roo's husband Sam and Minnie to Hiro's for dinner with her and Nat – Roo, who'd clearly still not forgiven Nat for his behaviour when they'd been at school, had been in a brittle mood, while Minnie had told everyone the story of how she and Dee had met in the toilets at Gordon's while Dee was banging on the vending machine trying to get a pack of Lillets out of it. *I'd have given her a tampon if I'd had one on me but I almost never do, I've got poly-cystic ovaries you see*, Minnie had announced, making them sound like a must-have accessory, before launching into an eyebrow-raising story about a sword-swallower she'd met on Hinge. Nat had described the meal as 'an experience'.

Nat was looking at her, she realised now – *really* looking at her.

'God, you're beautiful,' he murmured, gently pushing the fringe she'd been attempting to grow out for six months off her face. They kissed. Then he kissed his way down her stomach and between her thighs.

Nat was so good at what Dee thought of as the *choreography* of sex that she sometimes wondered if he'd studied it at drama school, like stage fighting. Not that she was complaining: she was thrilled to be on the receiving end of his skills. She'd never been very confident about all that stuff, so it was great that Nat was confident enough for them both. He hooked his thumbs into the waistband of her pants and slid them off, then pushed her T-shirt up so it was bunched up under her arms. The first time she'd ended up naked from the waist down like this in his company, Dee had joked that she felt like Winnie-the-Pooh. It wasn't a joke she'd repeated – for Nat, sex was a serious business.

Dee adjusted her position, trying to get herself into one that was both comfortable and flattering. Nat had made a point of saying this was one of his favourite activities, and that he could go on 'for hours'. She sort of hoped that he wouldn't – she didn't like being alone with her own thoughts, and when she had nothing to do except lie there her mind tended to wander in unhelpful directions. She hadn't told Nat that though; she didn't want to seem ungrateful.

Nat left about an hour later.

'I'll message you when I'm home,' he'd said, kissing her lightly between the eyes.

After he'd gone Dee decided to cheer herself up by walking to meet Minnie for brunch rather than getting the Overground. It was about an hour's trip east along the Regent's Canal, and the weather was perfect: sunny but with an autumnal nip in the air. Dee pulled on jeans and her favourite jumper – a grey cable-knit one that had originally been her stepmum's – and put her phone on to flight mode so she wouldn't spend the whole walk looking at it.

She cracked as she was nearing King's Cross and switched it back on to normal mode. Nat would definitely be back at his mum's house in the posh part of Hanwell near the station by now, but he hadn't messaged her. Dee took a quick picture of the view from the bridge she was standing on and posted it to Instagram: Nat, she knew, sometimes looked at her Stories, and although it was definitely too soon for her to be messaging him – they'd said goodbye less than two hours ago, after all – this felt like an acceptable form of communication. She was as careful in her messages to him as she was in person, forensically assessing each word's potential to press Nat's buttons negatively. Was three questions in one message too many? Would 'miss you' be read as a demand that he say it back to her? It would be so nice, she thought as she set off again, when they were at the stage where this stuff didn't feel like an elaborately stressful tango. She decided not to dwell on the fact that she had never actually got to that stage with anyone, ever.

The Canal Cafe, which was tucked away along the leafy stretch of water just before Kingsland Road, was an east London institution, with thousands of Instagram followers and a guaranteed place in every best-of article. People thought nothing of spending an hour or more standing in line for the tomatoes on sourdough, the folded eggs and the cheese toasties with dill pickles, all of which were inspired by the decades its chef-owner Angie had spent living in San Francisco. Today it had attracted a long brunch queue that joggers and cyclists were having to weave their way around. Minnie was already sitting at one of the tiny tables outside, surrounded by her Saturday morning essentials: a milky coffee, a pack of Silk Cult and a copy of *Fate and Fortune* magazine. She was wearing high-waisted stonewashed jeans, a cut-off T-shirt and little white ankle boots with a faux-fur bomber jacket thrown over the top. Her bleached curls tumbled over her shoulders, and her perfectly applied lipstick was fire-engine red. She was quite literally turning heads: as Dee approached she saw a cyclist wobble and nearly fall off his bike. Minnie had cartoonishly arched eyebrows and the kind of body that meant she could bring a room to a standstill by picking something up off the floor (which she quite often did, just to get a reaction). She'd been a model as a teenager back home in Leeds, before realising, as she put it, that she 'fucking loved cake and didn't give a fuck about my thighs' and putting on three stone in eighteen months.

'You look FIT,' she hollered across the towpath when she spotted Dee; a flock of coots scattered. 'Check you out!

You're all glowy, must be all the *S. E. X.* you're having with *N. A. T. . . .*'

Dee grinned as she squeezed in next to her. It was hard to believe that Minnie's mum, Rabbi Debbie Marks, was responsible for keeping the congregation at the Sinai Synagogue in Roundhay on the spiritual straight and narrow.

'How was last night?' she asked as Minnie enveloped her in a hug. 'Fun?'

'Oh, *exhausting*,' Minnie replied with relish. 'It was The Admiral, remember him? The one who said "Ahoy there!" the first time he saw me naked? He's just got back from Australia and he wants to rekindle things but I'm not sure I can be bothered, he snores like Concorde taking off.'

'Ah yes, how could I forget.' The Minnieverse, Dee had learned early on, was full of men whose actual identities were lost in the mists of time, but whose nicknames had stuck. There was Big Mac (large, Scottish), News at Ten (worked in local radio) and Lord Voldemort (very tall and bald, but he did have a nose). Minnie had a busy and varied love life, but strictly speaking she'd never really had, or wanted, a serious relationship. She felt about boyfriends how other people felt about pets: nice enough to have around, she said, but they tied you down.

As Dee was putting her phone on the table she deftly switched from Instagram to Twitter. Nat had an account, and in the early days he'd sent a few tweets that had clearly been references to her. There'd been the one he'd posted after they'd walked most of the way around London together, with the verse from *Perfect Day* about the zoo above it. When Dee had asked him if it was about her he'd just smiled

32

enigmatically, but she'd known it was, and felt like her heart was going to burst.

'Give me your phone please, I'm taking it into protective custody,' Minnie said, somehow sensing exactly what Dee was doing. She fixed her blue eyes on Dee; reluctantly, Dee passed her phone over. Minnie dropped it into her tote bag and blew her a kiss.

'Thank you. Now, stop *worrying* – Nat'll be back before you know it, and he's going to spend the whole time he's away thinking about you anyway. Don't pull that face, how could he not? You've got the legs of Cindy Crawford and that fringe makes you look exactly like Jane Birkin, I can't get enough of it.'

This, Dee thought as they turned in unison to look at the blackboard menu behind them, was why people put up with Minnie being late all the time, having a non-existent attention span and constantly flirting: she had a huge, warm heart that she gave everybody equal access to, whether she'd known them for five minutes or five years. It was why Dee, who was instinctively wary of new people, had allowed herself to get so close to Minnie so quickly after their chance meeting five years earlier. And it was why Roo, who was fiercely protective of her and Dee's shared history, had consented to their gang of two becoming a three.

Dee had been incredibly nervous about introducing Minnie to Roo, and the atmosphere while the two of them had waited in the pub for Minnie on the fateful day was uncomfortable – Dee suspected that, while Roo had probably thought about Minnie quite a lot in the run-up to this meeting, Minnie, in the nicest possible way, had barely thought about Roo at all. It didn't help that Roo had just cut her long hair off into a crop that she was clearly feeling uncomfortable about. As soon as Minnie walked in, though, the tension evaporated.

'I bloody love your hair!' she'd called out to Roo as she approached. 'It's stunning!' She was dressed in a denim boiler suit with her curls tied up in a pineapple that bounced as she waved. 'Dee's told me so much about you – I feel like I'm meeting a celebrity!'

Dee had watched as Roo's expression softened into a delighted smile. Faced with both barrels of charm from Minnie, it was almost impossible not to melt.

Roo and Minnie both had strong opinions about most things (especially Dee's life), but that was where the similarities ended. Minnie had a lavishly cracked phone screen and lived on 15 per cent battery, while Roo took a spare power pack everywhere. Minnie lived for late nights, whereas Roo loved nothing more than early bedtimes. They had opposite attitudes to money: Minnie lived in the cheapest place she could find and cut her own hair but was happy to splurge hundreds on a weekend trip, while Roo allowed herself fifty pounds a month for 'Miscellaneous Fun' on her budgeting app. But so far Dee had just about managed to keep their unlikely coalition together.

'Right, I'm starving, let's order,' Minnie said now, suddenly all business. 'You want the toastie right?' She flagged down the smiley, pink-haired waitress. 'Hiya! My friend would like the cheese toastie, please, and could I get the pancakes?'

The waitress flicked her eyes at the blackboard. 'We don't . . . actually have pancakes on the menu, I don't think?'

'Oh, you don't officially, but Angie always makes them for me when I come in,' Minnie said with a megawatt smile. 'We've known each other for ages, I'm Minnie Marks.' A beat. 'You know, like the mouse, but Jewish.'

Dee had heard her use that line before and it normally got a laugh, but not today. The waitress chewed her lip.

'I'll ask,' she said with a grimace. They watched her hurrying towards the kitchen.

'Poor her, maybe it's her first day here . . . Ooh, I totally forgot to tell you, Dee, I have a new flatmate!' Minnie pulled her phone out of her bag. She did some tapping and then handed it to Dee. 'If you click on "Instructors", he's the first one that comes up.'

It was the home page of a gym called Boombox in Shoreditch. The first bit of writing on the Instructors page said 'Jonas Muller: Spin Superhero'. Dee scrolled down, and there was Jonas himself, leaning against a concrete wall in a vest with his arms folded – he had white-blond hair, blue eyes and sharp cheekbones, and was staring smoulderingly at the camera.

'How did you . . .' Dee began, slightly blindsided. Minnie was grinning from ear to ear.

'I know, right? He's from Berlin – I went to one of his spin classes last week, we got chatting afterwards, he mentioned he was looking for a room, one of my flatmates was moving out . . . I'm helping him touch up his roots tonight.'

'I bet you are,' Dee said, giving her a nudge; Minnie shrieked and elbowed her back.

Someone cleared their throat.

Dee and Minnie turned around. Standing just to their right

35

was a tall, fair-haired man in a slightly grimy white T-shirt and jeans with a flour-streaked, navy-and-white striped apron over the top. He was about six foot three, Dee guessed – her *Mastermind* subject would have been other people's heights – but in all other respects he was completely average, with the slightly-too-short haircut and exasperated air of an over-worked secondary school teacher on playground duty. The only really chef-like thing about him were his arms, which were covered in tattoos: a swallow, the outline of a four-leaf clover, a bar of musical notes and some writing just below his sleeve that Dee couldn't read.

Minnie was staring at him. '*You're* not Angie,' she announced with a frown.

'Good observation.' The man had a northern accent but it wasn't anything like Minnie's, which Dee took to mean he was from somewhere in Lancashire. 'Angie's gone back to the USA for the winter, I'm holding the fort here.'

'Oh! Well, lucky her!' Minnie, recovered, gave him her biggest and brightest smile. 'So she always makes me her special chocolate-chip pancakes when I come here, would that be OK? I'm Minnie, and this is Dee. I didn't catch your name, sorry . . .'

'It's Andy,' the man said bluntly. 'And the answer is no. It's just me back there today because my sous chef called in sick half an hour before we opened and I can't be messing around with special orders.'

Dee, who had a lifelong aversion to confrontation of any kind, cringed.

'Oh.' Minnie, who almost never heard the word *no*, looked startled. 'Really?'

'Really.' The man nodded at the blackboard. 'Do me a favour and get the fried green tomatoes instead – I had to wake up at four this morning to buy them and I'm not going to be best pleased if they end up in the bin.'

Minnie looked even more put out. Feeling like it was on her to do something – anything – to lighten the atmosphere, Dee scanned the blackboard.

'Well, I was going to order a latte . . .' she began, looking at Andy. 'But if they're really three pounds fifty here maybe I could just have some coffee beans to chew?'

'Welcome to the Hackney Riviera.' Andy smiled for a nanosecond. 'Now, if you'll excuse me . . .'

Dee and Minnie watched him walking back towards the kitchen.

'Looks like I'm going to have to find somewhere else to come on Saturday mornings,' Minnie said with a roll of her eyes as she turned back to Dee. Then she glanced over her shoulder again. 'Or maybe not . . . Grumpy Andy's quite cute, no? Reminds me of thingy – you know, he was in *The History Boys*, used to be married to wotsit from that TV show, the one who played the Queen . . .'

Minnie's mental Wikipedia of celebrity and civilian men was impressively wide-ranging. She waved her phone – open at IMDb – at Dee, who couldn't honestly say she'd formed much of an impression of Grumpy Andy. For the past two months of her life men had fallen into two camps: Nat and Not Nat, and only the first one was interesting. And even before they'd started seeing each other, Nat had shaped her taste in men – ever since the last year of school, Dee had been drawn to people with his curly dark hair and slight air of melancholy.

'Oh, him, I know who you mean. Hmm, a tiny bit,' she conceded. 'The eyes, maybe. But chefs are bad news. My dad was one when he and my mum met and look how well that turned out. They've all got serious issues.'

'Grumpy Andy's too tall for me, but he'd do for you,' Minnie went on, ignoring Dee. 'You could kiss him without having to stand on something, I'd have to get a stepladder out.'

Before Dee could stop her she'd retrieved Dee's phone from her bag, swiped the screen in a Z to unlock it – Dee cursed herself for being so predictable – and went straight into Instagram.

'There you go, you're following the cafe's account now, you can keep an eye on him.' Minnie blew her a kiss as she put Dee's phone away again. 'Don't look so horrified, there's nothing wrong with keeping your options open. If Nat wants you all to himself he can ask to make things exclusive, can't he? Until then you're a free agent.'

Minnie inhabited a world of infinite possibility in which she was always the chooser, rather than the chosen. To Dee her self-belief was absolutely awe-inspiring. When they'd first met, Dee had been approaching thirty with very few single friends: Minnie, who was always up for going out and having adventures, had felt like the answer to a prayer. She made being unattached seem like an enviable lifestyle choice, and there was nothing second-best about the chaotic but glamorous existence she had built for herself, and she had no desire to change it. But although their lives might have looked similar from a distance – they were both free-lancers who defaulted to singleness – Dee knew they were fundamentally different. Minnie had chosen her life, whereas Dee's had just sort of . . . *happened* to her, like everything else over the years had.

'Blimey, I've owned cars that probably cost less than one of those,' Minnie said, pointing at a woman pushing a hi-tech double buggy along the towpath. She lit up a Silk Cut and sighed. 'For thousands of years raising a child was just a thing you did. Now there's this huge pressure to have the most expensive kind of everything and make every part of it a lifestyle choice. Have you considered what your changing mat says about you? If not, why not? I call it the *parenthood industrial complex*.' She stifled a yawn. 'Must be exhausting, I'm so glad I'll never have to think about it.'

Dee nodded dutifully. The buggies, she knew, would have had the opposite effect on Roo, and Dee in turn would have felt the need to respond quite differently. Shuttling between Roo and Minnie, she sometimes felt as though she was having to switch between two completely different languages, neither of which was naturally hers.

Just then she noticed the inside of Minnie's bag lighting up – it was her phone flashing up a notification. She decided to take advantage of Minnie being distracted by her cigarette and made a grab for it, swiping the screen off lock. Her heart leapt: Nat had replied to her Instagram story.

Missing you already x

Dee squeezed it, hugging the words to herself. It was all going to be OK.

Chapter Three

Time had always seemed to stand still in sleepy Hanwell, where Dee's mum Alice and her stepmum Ines lived. But as Dee walked from the station to Milton Road in the late-afternoon sun on Sunday, she felt as if it had suddenly started to move – fast. There were expensive-looking cars parked all along the streets and 'For Sale' signs had popped up everywhere. A few months ago an estate agent had rung the doorbell and offered Alice and Ines a valuation, which had bothered Dee more than she wanted to admit. After her parents had split up, she and her mum had spent eight years moving around west London before finally coming to rest here at number 67. And although Dee hadn't lived there for fifteen years, she didn't quite feel ready for anyone else to.

Her mum and Ines's house was a well-kept 1930s terrace, with bay windows and a little wooden porch. Dee stopped a few doors down from it to check her phone. She knew from refreshing Skyscanner that Nat had landed in Bucharest at midday UK time, and she'd messaged him two hours ago asking him how the flight had been, but although he'd read it he still hadn't replied. She chewed the inside of her cheek. She'd thought dealing with the long gaps between Nat's messages would get easier with time, but actually the opposite seemed to be true.

'*There* you are!'

Dee looked around to see her mum and Ines walking down the road towards her, wheeling their overnight cases. Dee's mum was wearing a shirt with a sequinned collar under dungarees with her Bettie Page fringe peeping out from beneath a spotty scarf. Dee had always thought that in another life her mum might have been an actress, or maybe a nightclub singer. In this one she'd been a waitress, an artist's model and an assistant manager at Shoes For You in Hanwell, before getting her current job teaching art classes at Ealing Adult Learning. Ines, who had trained as a psychologist and was now a couples' therapist, was still in her work clothes: a white shirt, black trousers and black brogues. From Monday to Friday she saw people who were leaving relationships, thinking about leaving them or doing everything in their power to avoid it, and every third Sunday she ran a community clinic in Acton with peeling walls and lino that was bubbly underfoot (nobody worked in mental health, Ines deadpanned, for the interior design). They were going to Brighton for the night for their wedding anniversary – it was where Ines had lived when she first moved to England from Argentina, and where they'd got married five years ago.

Alice stopped in front of Dee and did a little twirl, her green eyes dancing. It was clearly a good mood day, Dee thought as she hugged her – most of her mum's days were now, thankfully, and they had been for a long time. But still, she worried.

'Good news, darling!' Alice said, detaching herself. 'The London Wetland Centre has started doing sunrise walks again!'

'Um, that's . . . great!' Dee tried not to show that she had no idea what her mum was talking about. This was how conversations with Alice often seemed to go: they felt a bit like switching the TV on halfway through a programme. Dee had always found it a struggle to keep up and match her mum's pinballing enthusiasm for things. Not only did the two of them look nothing alike – Alice was small and curvy with chameleon hair that was currently cherry red – they were poles apart temperamentally. Alice was a gleefully extroverted oversharer who lived in the moment – like Minnie, only more so.

'You used to love going there when you were a little girl,' Alice went on, unperturbed. 'Anyway, I've got the four of us tickets for next Saturday – you, me, Ines and Nat. It's about time we met him, don't you think? He's been your boyfriend for what, two months? Three?'

'Mum, he's not my . . .' Dee's heart sank into her shoes. Her mum had never made a secret of the fact she was desperate for Dee to settle down, and ever since Dee had told her that Nat existed she'd bombarded her with invitations, all of which Dee had declined without even running them past Nat. He hadn't suggested she meet his family yet, and she didn't want to spook him.

Dee gave Ines an imploring look over Alice's shoulder. Ines tactfully made a show of checking her watch.

'We'd better make tracks if we want to catch the train, Al,' she said, stepping forward and touching Alice's arm. She hugged Dee. 'Have a lovely time tonight, Dee-Dee – I'm so glad you and Roo are getting to spend some proper time together.'

For the millionth time, Dee silently gave thanks for Ines.

*

Dee's parents had met while they were working in a restaurant near Piccadilly in 1986. Alice was a nineteen-year-old
waitress applying to art school and Karl was in the kitchen,
working his way around Europe after getting bored of his
sleepy home town in Denmark. Six weeks after they started
seeing each other Alice found out she was pregnant. She
decided to keep the baby, shelve art school and move in with
Karl. By the time Dee was born their relationship was ter-
minally frayed, and the arrival of a child didn't help things.
Their arguments often ended with Karl disappearing for days
at a time. The days turned into weeks, and one day, when Dee
was seven, he didn't come back.

After she and Karl split up, Alice brought home quite a lot
of boyfriends. Dee watched her spending money they didn't
have on new outfits to impress them, using every single pan
in the kitchen to cook them dinners that ended with the
smoke alarm going off, and crumpling when things didn't
work out. The boyfriends either ignored Dee or embarrassed
themselves trying to talk to her about *Top of the Pops*. It was
distressing seeing Alice working so hard to secure the affec-
tions of such mediocre men. Alice, Dee knew, desperately
needed to be loved – it was what kept her together.

Then one day, when Dee was fifteen, Alice came back
from Shoes For You to the house they were looking after for
a friend with armfuls of pasta and a big smile on her face.
She'd just dyed her hair a fluorescent pink, and the starlet
waves she'd set it in bobbed as she talked.

'I met an amazing woman in the shop today,' she said to
Dee while they were making dinner; she was an easily distracted cook, and the tomato sauce had already splattered

43

all over the hob. Dee noticed the water was about to bubble over and turned the gas down. 'She came in looking for suede spray and we ended up having a lovely chat. She's just moved here from east London and bought a place on Milton Road – she's a couples' therapist from Buenos Aires. Isn't that interesting? Anyway, we swapped details. You can never have too many local friends, can you?'

A week later, Dee unlocked the front door to find Alice at the kitchen table opposite a woman she'd never seen before. There was a chessboard in front of them and a chunky aluminium coffee pot on the hob.

'Darling, this is Ines,' Alice said when Dee came in – her voice was merry, and she was wearing a new pink lipstick. 'The woman from the shop I was telling you about, remember? I mentioned to her that I'd never had a proper coffee at home so she brought her Bialetti round. And she's teaching me to play chess!'

Ines got to her feet and kissed Dee's right cheek without making a big song and dance about it like some adults did. She was tall, Dee noted with relief – her mum was barely five foot four, and she felt enormous in comparison, like the BFG.

'Lovely to meet you, Dee,' she said. 'How was school?'

Ines had short, dark hair, and she was wearing black trousers with what looked like a man's shirt and a waistcoat. Dee's mind drifted back to the time she and Roo had watched a group of boys on the bus sniggering over a photo of the singer k.d. lang in a barber's chair, dressed exactly like Ines was, with Cindy Crawford pretending to give her a shave. *Dykes*, one of them had muttered, and they'd hooted like hyenas. Dee and Roo had rolled their eyes, smug in their maturity. But Dee wasn't sure she'd ever met an actual real-life lesbian before – if that was even what Ines was, she thought, rebuking herself for making assumptions. She stared at their grimy floor, worried the visitor could see what she was thinking.

'If your patients come in twos, does that mean you get paid twice?' she asked, instead of any of the more perplexing questions that were actually at the front of her mind.

Ines laughed. 'I wish,' she said; she had a nice, warm voice. 'But no, sadly. Just the once. It's twice as interesting, though – to me, anyway. Relationships always have so much going on in them.'

Alice laughed too. Then she sipped her coffee, leaving a lipstick print on the mug's rim, then glanced down at the board.

'I think it's your move . . .' she said, flicking her eyes at Ines.

Ines became a regular visitor, often popping in for a drink. Dee looked forward to her coming round and found her presence reassuring: here, finally, was someone who seemed to have been given the instruction manual for life. One time the three of them went to Hanwell Zoo (Alice's idea) and fed the alpacas. As they were tossing hay into the enclosure Ines told Dee quite matter-of-factly that her own mum had died when she was a baby, and that she hadn't spoken to her dad since she was a teenager. When she was nineteen, she'd explained, she'd had a summer job helping a neighbour look after his horses. She and the neighbour's wife had started seeing each other in secret, except it hadn't stayed a secret for very long. When her father had found out he'd thrown her

45

out. She'd got on a flight to Amsterdam, where she'd stayed for a few months before coming to England. Then she'd changed the subject, and Dee, who dreaded pushing people who were important to her – as Ines had become – beyond the point where they were comfortable, hadn't pressed her.

Then, about six weeks after Ines had first come round, Dee got back early on a Sunday morning from staying at Roo's to find the curtains in the living room drawn, two empty wine glasses on the carpet at either end of the sofa and Ines's coffee pot on the stove in the kitchen. She stared at it for a long minute, trying to find a way of not coming to the obvious conclusion, then ran out of the house, slamming the front door behind her.

The park was quiet. Dee headed for a grassy hillock near the gate and sat down with her back against the far side. Her mum had never been with a woman before – or maybe she had, and she'd just kept it a secret. And if that was the case, what other stuff was there in the back of the cupboard, waiting to explode out and turn her life upside down? Even the ground she was sitting on felt suddenly unstable, like all of its atoms were shifting dangerously underneath her.

After a while she heard a cough. There was someone standing in front of her: Ines, in jeans and one of Alice's jumpers (the arms were too short), holding out a steaming mug.

'Your mum's gone to the station to look for you – I told her I'd try here,' she said in a soft voice. 'We're so sorry you found out like this, Dee, it wasn't what either of us wanted. We thought you were staying at your friend's for lunch.' She crouched down, as though Dee was a frightened animal who might bolt. 'I made you a coffee. It's cold out here.'

We're so sorry. Us. Alice had never been part of a *we* or an *us* with anyone, and even though Dee had been secretly desperate for someone sensible to step in and take the pressure of looking out for Alice off her, the speed with which it seemed to have happened behind her back made all the blood rush to her head.

'I don't like coffee,' she snapped – she wanted to lash out, make Ines feel exactly as bewildered and hurt as she did. 'Especially if you've made it.'

Ines didn't react in the way her mum would have, with theatrical tears or accusations. She just put the mug down on the grass, positioning it carefully so it wouldn't fall over, and straightened up.

'I'll be over there,' she said gently, pointing at a bench.

Dee stared angrily at the grass between her trainers, trying to work out what to do next. As the minutes wore on she felt the thawing frost starting to soak through her trousers – she'd left her denim jacket behind in the house, and the cold and the damp were starting to get uncomfortable. Had Ines just been nice to her to get to Alice? She really didn't seem like the sort of person who'd do that.

She risked a glance at the bench. Ines wasn't actually looking at her, but Dee had the sense that she was being thought about.

'You're still here, then,' she said sarcastically. Ines looked back at her and smiled, taking all of the wind out of her sails.

'I told you I would be, didn't I?' she said.

Three months later Dee and Alice moved for the last time, into Ines's house on Milton Road – which then became their house too. Ines gave up smoking because Alice hated the smell of tobacco, and Alice gave up Nescafé. There were lots of things that Dee realised she could simply stop thinking about now that Ines was there all the time. Things like making sure Alice ate properly when she was having a low day, and secretly checking the strips of Citalopram and lithium that she kept next to her toothbrush to be sure she was taking them. Ines had joined her in looking out for Alice, and the relief of no longer being alone on the mission was life-changing.

When Dee started university, Ines got the train with her to Edinburgh to settle her into halls – her mum, who had a terrible cold, was in tears as she waved them off at King's Cross, but Dee felt guiltily relieved that it would just be the two of them. You always knew where you were with Ines.

'That your daughter?' someone's dad had asked chummily while they were queueing to pick up the keys. Ines had smiled.

'Nine-tenths,' she'd said, squeezing Dee's hand.

Ronnie Biggs, who'd been given his name by Cats Protection after spending years on the run, was stretched out on the living-room sofa, taking up almost half of it. Dee grinned when she saw him; she still found it hard to believe that this magnificent beast was the same cat as the scrawny stray that Alice had brought home in a cardboard box from the shelter eight years ago. Within months Ronnie's body weight had doubled and his grey fur had thickened out into a lustrous mane and lynx-like ear tufts. Now, to put it mildly, life on Milton Road revolved around him. He had a bed in every room and three different cat trees, all top of the range. Unlike his namesake, Ronnie wasn't violent, at least not intentionally. But he was massive, the size of a corgi, and clumsy with it. He also had an unpredictably sensitive stomach, a drug dependence to rival Sherlock Holmes's and insisted on sleeping in Alice and Ines's bed. These quirks just made Dee adore him all the more, though. Besides, coaxing him into eating his hated hypoallergenic food would give her something to worry about other than Nat's trip.

Dee put her bag down on the carpet, dumped the Twiglets she'd bought for Roo (who loved anything salty) on the coffee table and squeezed herself into the space next to Ronnie. The cat opened one eye, then the other, and yawned lazily.

'Tired, Ron?' she asked, tickling him under the chin. 'Same here.'

Ronnie answered by heaving himself upright, waddling across the sofa and flopping back down across Dee's legs. Once his purrs had turned into snores, Dee gingerly reached over him to get her phone out of her bag. It was coming up for six: Roo had messaged her at half past saying she was setting off from her house in Ealing and that she'd be with Dee at five to, so she didn't have long. She was about to quickly read Nat's last message again when a knock on the living-room window startled her. She looked over her shoulder and saw Roo standing on tiptoes in the gravel outside.

'Don't move him, it's fine,' she called through the glass. Dee watched her fishing the spare key out of the pot of lavender on the window ledge. A moment later she heard the front door open and close, and there was Roo in the hall, unlacing her shoes and lining them up neatly against the wall just like she had the very first time she'd come to Dee and Alice's old flat after school for tea.

'I swear he's grown again,' she said, pointing at Ronnie, who was still fast asleep; she was in her weekend uniform of navy trousers and a pale-blue crew-necked jumper. Dee patted the sofa next to her; Roo sat down and they hugged.

'Mum sent me a list of everything we need to do. Apparently, he doesn't like the new dishwasher so we can't switch it on when he's in the kitchen, but if we accidentally do there's a YouTube bird-video channel that calms him down . . . He's on some kind of cat-sitters' blacklist; I can't think why.'

Ronnie woke up and fixed them both with a stare that suggested he knew exactly what they'd been saying but couldn't be bothered to do anything about it.

'Drink?' Dee asked, giving him a conciliatory stroke; Ronnie closed his eyes again with a huff. 'There should be some of that non-alcoholic beer you like, or there's usually white wine in the . . .'

'Wine, please,' Roo said firmly, and Dee felt a cloud settle over the evening. Roo had given up drinking when she and Sam started trying for a baby, but as time had worn on she'd begun giving herself the night off if she'd just got her period, as a kind of faint consolation prize. This meant it had been yet another disappointing month.

'I'm really sorry, Roo,' she said quietly, putting a hand on Roo's shoulder; all the muscles in her neck felt tense. 'Do you want to talk about it?'

'No.' Roo stood up and set off for the kitchen. 'We're looking at doing something called IUI. It's where they shoot sperm straight into your womb to maximise the chance of an egg being fertilised each month. Pretty romantic, right? I just really don't want to do IVF if we can possibly avoid it – stabbing myself in the stomach with a syringe full of hormones every evening isn't my idea of fun.'

Dee performed a practised forklift manoeuvre with her arms, sliding Ronnie off her lap on to the sofa so she could follow Roo into the kitchen. 'Wait, what? You're an anaesthetist: you love injections . . .'

'They're my job, not my hobby. Anyway, it's different when you're doing it to yourself, trust me,' Roo said, opening the fridge and taking the wine out. 'Also you have to have been trying for two years before you can get help on the NHS, and it's only been eighteen months for us.' She sighed. 'It feels like so much longer – time really doesn't fly when you're not having fun . . .'

Back in the living room with the wine, the glasses and a bowl for the Twiglets, the two of them assumed their traditional positions on the sofa. Roo curled up at the end nearest the window next to Alice's drinks trolley and Dee sat at the opposite one, covered in the crochet blanket. Ronnie stretched out on his back between them, exposing his plush tummy. Dee checked her phone – Nat still hadn't replied to her message, but there was a new one in her and Roo's group chat.

'Minnie's sent us this week's horoscopes from her astrology app,' she said to Roo, who was raking her fingers through Ronnie's fluff, eliciting rumbling purrs. 'Mine says, "In order to be heard, you must speak louder." Yours probably says you're going to order a really horrible pizza tonight that's mostly anchovies.'

'For once that would be accurate . . .' Roo made a show of

rolling her eyes, then allowed herself a whisper of a smile. 'She always puts the lady doctor emoji after mine, it's very sweet. Although obviously I disapprove of the whole concept of star signs.'

'Obviously.' Dee went back into her chat with Nat: still nothing. She could feel Roo watching her.

'How's Nat?' Roo asked carefully – she'd never actually spelled out that she didn't approve of Nat, but Dee had known her for long enough that she didn't need to. Ignoring this fact was starting to take its toll, and even though she'd never known Roo to change her mind about anything, Dee really hoped she would at some point.

'He's fine, he landed a couple of hours ago.' She didn't let on that she only knew this because of Skyscanner. She glugged some wine into Roo's glass and nudged it across the table towards her. 'I really, really hope this audition goes well. It's so hard for actors, most of them don't know where they're going to be next week, never mind next year.'

'And what about you, Dee?' Roo put a hand on her knee, suddenly serious. 'Where do *you* want to be in a year? If Nat gets the part he'll be moving to another country . . .'

'I'm – we're just taking it one step at a time.' Dee tried not to let Roo see that she'd poked a sore spot. Roo had met Sam in her first week at Oxford, she reminded herself, and she'd never even been on a proper date, let alone spent half her life swiping through apps. She had no idea what dating in your thirties was like, how many compromises it called for.

'Hmm,' Roo said. She didn't look convinced. 'Did you get your blood test results back by the way? Your appointment was, what, two weeks ago?'

'Not yet.' Dee helped herself to a fistful of Twiglets. 'Well, no – they've come back, but I saw a different doctor and she said they looked funny so she redid them all. I'll get the new ones tomorrow.'

Roo frowned. 'Funny how?'

Dee shrugged. 'I didn't ask. She didn't seem worried, I don't think it's a big deal.'

'Well, you don't know that,' Roo said without a trace of malice. 'It might be.'

Roo had always been blunt and bossed Dee around. They never really argued, though, especially about personal things – it just wasn't something they did. And Dee didn't want to spoil one of their rare solo evenings with a disagreement: this was the first sleepover they'd managed in months. Even as a teenager Roo's diary had been ridiculously full, with CV-boosting activities scheduled for before and after school and a part-time job at the weekends. As a married adult who gave at least sixty hours a week to the NHS she was even harder to pin down

'Come on, Roopa Gill,' she said, getting up. 'Let's order pizza before it gets too late.'

They got the same ones they always did from Santa Maria in Ealing and ate them in front of the TV. Ronnie lumbered up the stairs after *Strictly Come Dancing* and flopped down in the middle of the bed in the spare room. It had once been Dee's bedroom, and if she looked carefully at the wall behind the bed she could still see the quartet of shadows left by the Blu-Tack that had once held up her *Pulp Fiction* poster (she had still, to this day, never actually seen the film).

Dee and Roo slotted themselves in around the cat, being careful not to disturb him. Between Roo and Ronnie there was only about a square foot of mattress left for Dee. They were about to put the light out when an alarm went off on Roo's phone. She swiped it away, then produced a plastic pill bottle from her overnight bag.

'Folic acid, it makes me feel revolting if I have it in the mornings,' she said, trying to get the top off. 'You're meant to start taking it just before you try for a baby, but me being me I factored in a six month buffer just in case, so I've been taking it for nearly two sodding years. If Boots does a Nando's Black Card, I'm owed one.' She gripped the lid tighter, gritting her teeth as she finally managed to pop it off. 'This thing has a child-proof cap, can you believe it. The irony.'

A bittersweet memory rushed at Dee as she watched Roo shaking out a tablet on to her palm. The two of them had taken drugs together exactly once, when Roo had come to visit Dee in Edinburgh at the end of her first term, and they'd planned the night with military precision. After several failed attempts Dee had managed to obtain a single pink pill from a third-year chemistry student called Timothy who referred to himself as The Wizard of Ounces, while Roo printed off fifteen pages of guidance from the website FRANK about hydration levels and blood pressure. They smuggled Dee's loot into a club and took it in turns to nibble its edges in a toilet cubicle. Neither of them was convinced it had actually done anything (*It was probably just the world's most expensive Feminax*, Roo had grumbled as they traipsed across the Meadows the next morning with their shoes in their hands) but that hadn't felt important. They had been living hundreds of miles apart for the first time in their lives, and the experience had reassured them both that they could cope with being long-distance best friends. Suddenly, more than anything, Dee wanted to feel like she and Roo were properly sharing a universe again, even if it was only for a few seconds.

Roo, like most doctors, could fall asleep at the drop of a hat, and it wasn't long before her breathing started to slow. Dee could still feel the tension in her body, though. There was so much she knew Roo wasn't saying.

Roo had always seemed to have all the answers. She'd approached having a baby in the same way that she'd gone about getting her place at medical school and becoming the youngest ever consultant anaesthetist at St Thomas's: in the sincere belief that if she just made a detailed plan, then worked hard enough and for long enough, it would happen. It wasn't just her hopes for a family that were being tested to breaking point right now, Dee thought as she reached past snoring Ronnie to stroke Roo's hair – it was her entire understanding of how the world worked. This wasn't how her story was supposed to go.

'Roo?' she whispered.

Silence. Dee lifted her head off the pillow and listened – Roo was gone.

Dee reached for her phone, turning the brightness all the way down so she wouldn't disturb Roo or Ronnie, whose pudding-like paws were twitching in his sleep. She had a message from Nat.

All good. You'd love Bucharest. Night you x

Her scalp prickled; the relief of knowing he hadn't forgotten about her was enormous, and even though they'd never talked about her coming out to visit him if he got the part, the second sentence felt like a promise that he'd show the city to her one day. She typed out a reply, then scheduled it to send in an hour's time so he wouldn't think she'd been lurking in their chat waiting for him.

Chapter Four

The next morning Dee woke up much later than she'd meant to after a restless night full of strange dreams. She found Ronnie licking condensation off the inside of the window and a note from Roo on the pillow saying she'd had to leave for work. After chasing Ronnie around for half an hour – he was shockingly agile when it came to avoiding his eye drops – it took a bath towel and half a packet of Dreamies to subdue him enough to administer them.

Once she'd cleaned up the claw-scratches on her arms and made herself a coffee, Dee went and got her phone from upstairs. There was nothing from Nat, but her Gallery had sent her a notification.

On this day five years ago . . .

It was the video she'd made after Alice and Ines's wedding in Brighton. The other guests had all gone home, and there were five of them in it: Alice, Ines, Dee, Roo and Minnie, who despite only having known Dee for six months at that point had invited herself along. (Roo had been furious about this until Ines diplomatically asked her to be the ring bearer.) The ceremony was at the Pavilion, then they all went for dinner at a pub. At closing time, after many hours and even more drinks, it was decided that they'd get fish and chips on the seafront. In the clip they were all queuing outside Captain's.

'Don't suppose you have a lighter?' Minnie was saying mock-flirtatiously to Ines; she'd relaxed her curls for the occasion and was wearing her hair over one eye. 'I seem to have mislaid mine . . .'

'Minnie,' Dee groaned from behind the camera. 'Please. They've literally just got married, can you not?'

Alice chuckled. 'Honestly, this happens all the time,' she said to Roo, who was still gripping the bag that the rings had been in. 'Women who've never so much as thought about another woman before meet Ines and completely lose it. I think it's the suits.'

'Well, you would know, Al,' Ines said, kissing her on the cheek. 'You were one of them.'

Alice accepted the kiss, scrunching the velvet of Ines's lapel.

'I most certainly *had* thought about women before, thank you very much – I just hadn't actually . . .'

'You guys are ADORABLE!' Minnie exclaimed with a squeal, just in the nick of time. 'Was it love at first sight?'

'Hah! No, not at all.' Ines shook her head. 'When I met Al the absolute last thing on my mind was a relationship. I'd literally just bought my first house – as far as I was concerned, I was going to live there by myself and have a nice, quiet life. That was the plan.' She smiled ruefully. 'Also, I thought she was straight. But she invited me round for coffee and I thought, well, why not? We could be friends.'

'It crept up on me too,' Alice began, slipping her arm under Ines's jacket so she could put it around her waist. 'And you know what, girls, I . . .'

Dee stopped the video, smiling like she always did when

she watched it. Her parents had never actually got married – the fact that her mum and Ines *had* meant more to her than she allowed herself to admit. Marriage had meant a lot to her mum too; she guessed that was why Alice – who'd been a protest-attending, zine-reading 1980s feminist in every other respect – had suggested to Karl that Dee take his surname when she was born.

By the time she got to work Dee was running even later and starving. She would log on, she decided, then sneak out to the cafe on Wardour Street for a four-cheese panini. This plan was dashed when she saw Jay lurking by her desk.

'Big D!' he called out across the office; he was looking like a human yacht-rock playlist today in an oversized suit with big shoulders. 'Mind if we have a quick natter?'

Dee's stomach flipped. She followed Jay into his office, feeling sicker with every step. The moment she'd been dreading had clearly arrived: she was about to lose her job.

Jay sat down in his Eames chair behind his desk, which had a framed photo of him and Linda Evangelista at the Met Bar on it. The pile of rent demands on the spike had definitely grown.

'Agility is one of our core values here at Anvil, right, Dee?' Jay said, lacing his fingers together while doing everything in his power not to look at her.

Dee nodded, trying to remember what the others were. Bringing in cake? Replacing the toilet roll if you finished it?

'So, er, I was hoping that you might be prepared to be a bit agile this Friday night,' Jay went on. He met her eye for a second, then grabbed a discarded Pret a Manger napkin off his desk and blotted his top lip with it.

Was Jay . . . hitting on her? No, that was impossible: for all his lads' mag bravado he was happily married, and also secretly terrified of women. Maybe he wanted her to work on a pitch for a new client. But it was more likely to be a repeat of the time he'd turned up with burritos from the Mexican restaurant on Poland Street to make up for the fact their salaries were going to be delayed that month.

'Um, I'm not sure yet, why?'

'Ah, great!' Jay looked relieved. 'So, er, Bizzy and I are meant to be going out – but our usual babysitter just cancelled, and you wouldn't believe how hard it is to find someone who doesn't have plans on a Friday night . . . I was wondering if you fancied keeping an eye on Persephone for us? We'll probably be back quite late, so you'd be welcome to crash in the den if you wanted.' He paused. 'We'd pay you the going rate, obviously.'

Given Jay's attitude to Anvil's payroll this actually wasn't at all obvious. Dee weighed up her options: she wasn't massively keen on the idea of spending the night at her boss's house, but this coming Friday was a designated sofa-sleeping evening as Hiro was going to be back in the flat. And she could definitely do with the money. Hiro was pretty chilled out as landlords went, but he had a mortgage to pay, and things were very tight even with the discount he was giving her. Earlier in the year, after Jay had decided to give them both an enforced week off for cashflow reasons, she'd had to borrow her rent money from Roo, and then borrow even more from Minnie to pay Roo back. And it wasn't like she had plans, anyway: Nat wasn't due back until Sunday.

'Sure!' she said brightly. 'Looking forward to it!'

When she got to her desk she found Hiro staring at his screen with a half-eaten vegan sausage roll in his hand and an unreadable expression on his face.

'I take it you've seen this?' he asked.

Dee hadn't.

It was a *Mail Online* article that had gone live that morning, with a big photo at the top of Lulu Hartley brandishing a longbow in *Dragon Quest*. Next to it was a paparazzi shot of her and Nat on a cobbled street corner.

The first few paragraphs read:

She's best known for playing *Dragon Quest's* sexy nun-turned-archer Agnes. But yesterday Lulu Hartley swapped chainmail for knitwear as she stepped out in Bucharest with Nat Flynn – a fellow actor who's in town to audition for a part in the series.

The pair were snapped late on Sunday afternoon in Bucharest's picturesque Old Town. Petite blonde star Lulu, 34, was sporting her trademark pixie crop as she showed Nat the sights of the Romanian capital. She looked cosy and casual in furry boots, leggings and a mint jumper, which she paired with an adorable matching bobble hat. Meanwhile, handsome Nat, 35, looked brooding in a dark overcoat, scarf and boots.

Perhaps they were discussing fiery developments in the next series of *Dragon Quest* – or were things hotting up between them?

There were so many photographs. In one Nat looked like he was picking a bit of fluff – possibly from the adorable matching bobble hat – off Lulu's gilet. In another they'd stopped in a square, and Lulu was gazing up at him with what looked very much like fascination: her head was level with his shoulder in a way that Dee's could only have been if she amputated both her legs at the knee.

'Everyone knows they just make stuff up . . .' Hiro said, not entirely convincingly. He held out the sausage roll. 'Look, do you want the rest of this?'

Dee accepted it wordlessly. She took a bite, chewed and swallowed. Then she ran to the toilet and threw up.

As she walked back to her desk after swilling her mouth out under the tap she felt like she was on an airport travelator; the floor seemed to be moving beneath her. It wasn't like Nat was kissing Lulu in the pictures, she told herself. Or holding her hand. Or doing anything, really. But there was nothing stopping him from doing all of those things if he wanted to: they'd never spoken about it. And that really bothered her, far more than she'd allowed herself to admit. But Nat had specifically told her that he wanted to take things slowly; if she said something, she feared, things would simply fall apart. She reminded herself of his comment about the make-up artist he'd been seeing before her – she'd been too keen to put a label on things. All she could do right now was try very hard to be patient.

'Really sorry if this tips you over the edge, Dee, but Morag just emailed,' Hiro said as she was sitting down. 'Looks like a real doozy . . .'

Dee logged on and opened Morag's message. It was about something called a Mulchomatic.

Morning, Dee! Pics and specs attached. Shoptimisation-wise this is low-hanging fruit for us – we see this as a chance to

lead the pack with some really dynamic proprietary content.
Could you get calls to action back to me by end of play?

Someone was calling her from a landline number that she
didn't have saved. Dee was about to let it go to voicemail –
the last time she'd picked up that kind of call she'd been
stuck on the phone to a market research company for twenty
minutes – when she remembered. Today was Monday, which
was when she was meant to be getting her test results. This
was probably Kirsty the GP calling with them.

'Hello, K— I mean, Dr Stewart?' She stood up. 'Sorry, let
me just go somewhere a bit quieter—'

'Actually, Dee,' the doctor cut in, and the way she said
Dee's name turned her spine to ice. 'I was wondering if you'd
mind popping down to the surgery?'

Kirsty the GP swivelled her computer's screen so Dee could
look at it. Her whole demeanour was totally different today.
Even the golden retriever on her desk calendar looked sad.

'So, the tests we did were looking at the levels of a couple
of different hormones in your blood, Dee,' she said with a
solemn new intonation, pointing to letters and numbers. 'The
first is something called anti-Müllerian hormone, which is
produced by the follicles in your ovaries. It tells us how many
potential egg cells you have left, basically. A normal range for
a thirty-four-year-old woman is between seven and forty-
five – yours is just three point five.'

She scrolled down.

'Then there's oestrogen, which controls your cycle, and
follicle-stimulating hormone, which takes care of ovulation – I

always think of it as being a bit like the gas pedal on a car. At your age we'd expect your oestrogen to be high and your follicle-stimulating hormone to be low – if you have a lot of it that can mean your body is having to work really hard to release any eggs, like it's got its foot flat on the floor.' She cleared her throat. 'But as you can see, your oestrogen is pretty low, and you've got about three times as much FSH as you should, which is . . . well, quite concerning.'

Dee knew it was her turn to speak, but she couldn't – her mouth had gone dry.

'What does that mean?' she managed to ask. 'Am I . . . infertile?'

'Not just yet, no,' Kirsty said in what was clearly meant to be a comforting way. 'But if you *do* want a family it looks like that's something you'll need to get on with pretty soon.'

Years ago, Dee remembered, she'd slipped while she was doing the washing up and sliced right through the pad of her thumb on a knife. She remembered seeing the blood as she lifted her hand out of the water and thinking *ouch*, but she hadn't actually been able to feel anything. This was the same. She gulped down a breath.

'How soon is soon?' she heard herself saying.

'Oh, just as soon as you can, really,' Kirsty said blithely, as though she was reminding Dee to take the bins out. She took a leaflet from a stack next to her keyboard.

'This goes into a bit more detail about your options,' she said, passing it across the desk to Dee. She turned the leaflet over and pointed to a little box at the bottom. 'And look, here's a helpline you can ring if you have any questions.'

Out of the corner of her eye Dee could see Kirsty's family

photo next to her computer. She felt light-headed; she couldn't remember the last time she'd actually taken a breath in.

Kirsty suddenly leaned forwards and dispensed a very undoctorly pat on the knee.

'Us girls are all in this together, aren't we?' she said. 'It can be so hard.'

She was just trying to be nice, Dee told herself as she numbly accepted the pat. But it was a lie. The only thing the two of them had both been in was the surgery's overheated waiting room.

Chapter Five

*Normally, your ovaries will release an egg each month until they start to shut down as you go through the menopause in your fifties. Sometimes, though, that shutting-down process begins much earlier. If you're under forty when it does, you're experiencing what's known as **premature ovarian failure**. Although it's irreversible and there's no treatment to stop it, a specialist can talk you through your family planning options.*

Dee clicked out of the NHS article, which she'd already read so many times that she could probably have reproduced it from memory, feeling numb. *Options.* First the leaflet the doctor had given her, and now this – why did everyone keep pretending she had any? As far as she could see, her only options were to start a family now, or not at all. Both of those were impossible for a million and one reasons – and that was before she'd even got to the question of Nat.

It was six o'clock that same day, and she was sitting on a bench by the Regent's Canal towpath, just before the turning for Minnie's street. As soon as she'd left the surgery she'd messaged Roo and Minnie, who had swung into action – Roo had cancelled her gym class and Minnie had offered to cook dinner for the three of them so they could have a crisis summit. She'd been in a such a daze that she'd allowed twice as long as she needed to get to Minnie's from work – so here she was, sitting on a bench trying to type *mid-thirties bad fertility cure* into Google yet again. Her fingers wouldn't co-operate with her brain, though, or maybe it was the other way around: she kept mangling the words and having to delete everything. Not that it really mattered, the same results kept coming up.

Dee was one of life's overthinkers. But her fertility, ironically, wasn't something that she'd thought that much about. Of course, she was aware that she was coming up to an age where getting pregnant could get more difficult – it was hard not to be, what with the drip-drip-drip of newspaper scare stories illustrated with cliff-edge graphs and pearl-clutching opinion pieces about a generation of selfish 'career women' (visions of Sigourney Weaver in *Working Girl*) missing out on the joys of motherhood. Being a woman in your mid-thirties, she'd often thought, was like having a permanent, low-level headache. Just the other morning she'd heard an embryology professor on the radio with a name reminiscent of an indigestion remedy bemoaning the fact that what he called 'females' were putting off trying for a baby until it was too late because they 'wanted to have fun'. Professor Pepto-Bismol had suggested a campaign to remind young women that their fertility was going downhill. But absolutely nobody, Dee had wanted to shout at him, was putting off starting a family because they thought they had all the time in the world – and she definitely wasn't. For her it was just that the whole project felt impossibly, depressingly out of reach. Financially, of course – Roo was a doctor and Sam wrote computer games and *they* could barely afford the childcare they'd need to both keep their jobs – but emotionally too.

As the child of a single parent who'd struggled painfully with single parenthood, Dee had never felt like deliberately choosing that path was an option. So first she would need to meet someone she really liked, and who really liked her back: that was step one. Then they'd have to figure out if the two of them were compatible in all the thousands of big and small ways that determined whether they would make each other happy or slowly ruin each other's lives. Then, and only then, could they start thinking about becoming parents. Dee had spent most of her adult life stuck on step one, and after twenty-odd years of that, getting all the way to the parenthood stage with anyone felt about as likely as her climbing Everest. So she'd just done her best not to think too much about it – and while she'd been busy looking the other way, the whole thing was being decided for her.

'It's Dee, isn't it?'

Dee's head snapped round. Standing behind her was the chef from The Canal Cafe – Andy – holding a black bin bag in each hand. He was smiling at her. It was an objectively nice smile: it made him look much more approachable than he had on Saturday when he'd come to talk to them. But right now it was about as welcome as someone putting the *Macarena* on at a wake.

'Sorry, I didn't mean to make you jump – I've just locked up and I'm taking these out. They're only kitchen waste, I'm not a murderer.'

Dee stared at him, her ears ringing. Andy, whose smile was fading now, put the rubbish bags down.

'You all right?' he said, sitting down at the other end of the bench. He'd left a big gap between them, as though he was worried she might bite.

She still hadn't actually said any of it out loud, Dee realised as she shook her head – she'd told Minnie and Roo over WhatsApp. *I have failing ovaries*, she'd typed into the group chat, and for a mad second she'd felt the urge to add a 😊 at the end, as though she was telling them her train had just been cancelled or she'd locked herself out of the flat. She didn't especially want to confide in Andy, but she was going to have to start somewhere, she supposed.

'I got told by a doctor today that if want a family I need to get on with it, like, now,' she heard herself saying in a hollow voice. 'Unfortunately my life is a mess, my boss pays me in burritos and I don't even own my own bed, plus . . .'

She stopped herself; she couldn't go there. Andy was now wearing the panicked expression of a man who'd waded into deep water before remembering he couldn't actually swim.

'Really sorry to hear that, Dee,' he said in a stiff voice. 'That's shit.'

Dee experienced her usual urge to say something like *Oh, it's fine* or *Don't worry about it*, but her tongue had gummed up. They sat there in uncomfortable silence as a barge glided past. Then Andy cleared his throat.

'Look, I don't know if this makes you feel any better . . . But I'm sort of in the same boat. I was with someone for a long time who didn't want a family, and I thought I didn't either. Then we broke up, I went travelling and I realised that actually, I really did. But dating for basically the first time in my adult life has been a total nightmare, I've given up on it to be honest. It turns out there isn't a massive amount of demand for forty-year-old men who work antisocial hours and aren't bankers. Among sane people, anyway. And us blokes don't really have the option of having a child by ourselves, unless you're incredibly well off – which I'm definitely not.' He shook his head. 'I don't want to be pushing my kid on the swings and worrying about putting my back out. I even found myself looking at this website where you're meant to be able to find someone to team up with platonically, but it was even more depressing than Tinder.'

As she listened to him talk, Dee felt like she was having an out-of-body experience. This was the point where she would normally have made sympathetic noises or asked polite questions, even though he'd just mansplained both dating and parenthood to her. But instead, something snapped. She had spent the afternoon cycling through the stages of grief, and the wheel had just landed on anger.

'Except it's not the same boat though, is it?' she said sharply. 'You can have a child with someone in their twenties when you're ancient like Mick Jagger if you really want to, there's nothing actually stopping you.'

Her pulse was banging in her ears as she stood up.

Minnie's flat was on the ground floor of a house off Kingsland Road. The walls were filigreed with damp and the shower curtain had a sexy sloth in a bikini being showered with dollar bills on it. Through the grimy kitchen window Dee could see Minnie's white Volkswagen, which had so many dents in it that everyone called it the Golf Ball, parked haphazardly outside.

'Personally I hope Pound Shop Tom Hiddleston stays in Romania and falls victim to Dracula,' Minnie said breezily, standing in front of the hob. 'What was he *thinking*? Quite apart from anything else I saw Lulu Hartley in the street once and she's not that hot up close. Nose like a builder's elbow.'

'He wasn't actually doing anything with her in those photos . . .' Dee protested weakly, feeling like she ought to at least try to defend Nat. It didn't even sound convincing to her – and it definitely didn't to Roo, if the incredulous noise she made was anything to go by.

'Sorry, Dee, but Sam and I have been married for eight years and I don't pick fluff off his clothes like that.' She was sitting opposite Dee at the table, drinking a Capri-Sun from Minnie's personal stash. 'I hope you're going to give him a piece of your mind when you next speak – you've got to tell him that he needs to pull his finger out if he wants to be with you. In sickness and in health, remember? Speaking of which . . .'

'What about if Dee freezes some eggs?' Minnie butted in. 'My cousin Essie did it years ago and she's got a kid now. He's a complete pain in the arse but I don't think that has anything to do with how he was conceived.'

Roo shook her head emphatically. 'Dee doesn't have many good eggs left, that's the whole point. It would be like . . . oh, I don't know, putting food that's about to go off in the freezer.'

'Lovely bedside manner you have, Roo.' Minnie raised her eyebrows as she glugged sunflower oil into the pan in front of her.

Roo decided to ignore this interjection. 'Anyway, even if Dee did go down that route, there's the cost to consider – she wouldn't be able to get it on the NHS. It's at least five thousand pounds per cycle and she'd probably need at least three cycles to get enough good eggs for it to be worth it.'

Minnie whistled. 'Well, I think that absolutely stinks,' she said, transferring dollops of mixture from the bowl to her left into the pan. 'It's not like Dee would be doing it for a laugh, is it? OK, first batch of these babies coming right up . . . Argh, sorry, Dee, forget I said babies. Sorry, sorry.'

Dee drained her third gin and tonic. So far the crisis dinner had been all crisis and no dinner: Dee and Roo had arrived at seven o'clock to find Minnie elbow-deep in a pile of grated potatoes watching *Selling Sunset* on her iPad, which had flour all over the screen. Now Roo was looking at the cat-shaped clock above the door, which had a pendulum for its tail – it was coming up for eight thirty.

'Minnie, is there anything we can do to help?' she asked, completely failing to sound relaxed.

'No, you just sit back, you've had a long day at the hospital!' Minnie looked over her shoulder: tonight she was dressed like Velma from *Scooby Doo* in a tangerine jumper, a red mini-kilt and red T-bar shoes with ribbed orange tights. 'These'll be worth the wait, I promise . . .'

Minnie was the opposite of observantly Jewish. She ate pork and shellfish like they were going out of fashion, spent her Friday nights getting sweaty at gigs and told anyone who'd listen that there was no God. But she'd hung on to an affection for childhood special-occasion dishes, and she loved cooking them for other people. Tonight she was making latkes topped with sour cream, apple sauce and – because this was Minnie – edible gold glitter she'd saved from a hen week-end she'd organised.

Roo glanced down at her lanyard: *Roopa Gill, Anaesthetist, St Thomas's.* 'It's just that I'm going to have to leave soon – I've got a full day of surgery tomorrow and I need to be getting scrubbed up by seven. That means leaving the house at five thirty a.m., which means being in bed by nine thirty tonight if I want to get eight hours' sleep . . .' She turned to Dee, who still hadn't actually said anything. 'Have you told your mum and Ines yet, by the way?'

Dee shook her head – it felt much too heavy, like a balloon on a stick. 'I can't face it. Ines would be great but Mum would completely freak out.'

'She probably would, to be fair,' Roo nodded. 'And Nat? I'm guessing the answer is no.'

Hearing his name made Dee's stomach turn a somersault. She stared at the scuffed floorboards; she really didn't want to have to spell it out.

'Not yet, he's got his audition tomorrow . . . He's got a lot on his plate, Roo.'

'Dee, *you* have got a lot on your plate,' Roo said firmly. 'And if Nat finds strutting about in chainmail stressful I'd like to see him cope with a Saturday night shift in A & E. Anyway, he ought to be supporting you through this – what's the point of being in a relationship if you don't do that for each other?'

'I'd say it's more of a *situationship* right now, to be honest.' Minnie flipped the latkes over with a stray fork, then tore open a bag of parsley. 'But Roo's right, Dee, you need to send him a message,' she went on, sticking a pair of scissors into it and snipping the contents up. 'Not least because he owes you an explanation for those photos. Come on, we'll write it together.'

'I'll write it with Dee, you focus on dinner,' Roo said firmly; Minnie huffed and went back to the parsley. Roo picked up Dee's phone and positioned it on the table between them. 'Why don't you just say something like *Hi Nat, hope all's well, I wanted to let you know that I got some news from the doctor today.* Then send him a link to that NHS article you sent us both earlier.'

'*Hope all's well*,' Minnie snort-whispered. '*Kind regards.*' She fished the latkes out of the pan, transferred them to a wire rack to stop them going soggy, then bobbed over to the table and refilled Dee's glass with a fifty-fifty ratio of gin and tonic. 'Tell you what we need,' she said as she poured. 'A nice treat, all three of us. How about that Saturday afternoon yoga class I got the flyer about? Don't make that face, Roo, it'll be fun. And it'll take Dee's mind off everything. Come on, get that impeccably colour-coded diary of yours out.'

Roo grumbled a bit, but she did it. Dee didn't move.

'Well, the last week in October is no good . . .' Roo said, scrolling through her calendar. 'I'm going to the Isle of Skye with Sam's family, remember? They've rented this falling-down farmhouse with actual bunk beds. Not really my idea of a holiday, but marriage is all about compromise.'

'And that's one of the many reasons I'm never getting married . . .' Minnie shuddered. 'OK, how about Saturday the seventh, Dee?'

'Works for me, let's pencil it in,' Roo said, nodding, before Dee could answer. She looked back at the cat clock and shook her head. 'I've really got to go, I'm sorry, Minnie – it takes me an hour to get home from here . . .' She pushed her chair back and got to her feet, then glanced down at Dee. 'How are you getting back? I'm worried about you, I don't think you should be alone tonight.'

'She can stay here if she wants,' Minnie said cheerfully. 'Plenty of space in my bed. Here, hang on a second, Roo . . .'

She tore a strip of kitchen paper off the roll next to the microwave, carefully placed three golden latkes on it and folded it into a parcel for Roo. As she handed it over Roo's cheeks flushed.

'You're sweet, you know that?' she said, putting the parcel in the pocket of her waterproof jacket. 'Thanks, Minnie.'

'I *do* know it. I do.' Minnie kissed her on the cheek. 'Good luck tomorrow, hope you don't kill anybody by mistake. The front door's a bit stiff, remember, you'll need to give it a good yank.'

Dee let Roo hug her, and tried to hug her back – it was an effort to raise her arms, which felt like they'd had lead poured into them. Thirty seconds later she heard Minnie's front door creak open, then slam. Minnie wandered over to the fridge, stopping to peer at Dee's phone as she passed it.

'You've got a voice note,' she said. 'Karl Jensen – that's your dad, isn't it?'

Before Dee could stop her she'd pressed play.

'Hey there, kiddo . . .'

Dee's dad's voice, still slightly American-sounding from the four years he'd spent in New York after he'd left London, filled the kitchen. Karl had changed his WhatsApp profile photo since he'd last messaged her – the new one showed him in overalls, proudly holding up a giant bunch of soil-covered leeks. The blond curls she dimly remembered tugging as a toddler were grey now and his face was lined, but he was still a handsome man.

'So, it's sunny out here on the farm today, and I'm check-ing on the potatoes,' Karl went on. 'They're not going to be harvested for another couple of weeks, but it's good to show them some love, I think. Then I'll—'

Dee cut him off mid-sentence. When his US visa ran out her dad had packed up his chef's knives and gone home to Denmark. He'd ended up buying a smallholding in the north of the country, and he and his wife Sofia (who'd been a lawyer in Copenhagen, and who'd paid for it) turned it into a B & B. They grew all their own vegetables, kept floppy-eared pigs and had twice been glowingly profiled in *Condé Nast Traveller*. On their website they described themselves as 'homemakers'.

She put her head in her hands.

'Urgh, he keeps leaving me these long voice messages. And he won't stop sending me memes.'

'Oh no, not memes! How awful!' Minnie teased, getting a tub of sour cream out of the fridge. 'He probably just misses you. Come and help me top these.'

'Trust me, he doesn't. We used to go for months without speaking, it never bothered him before. The last time we were meant to see each other he didn't even bother to turn up.' Dee got up, taking a proffered teaspoon from Minnie. As she fumbled it into her right hand she realised she was really quite drunk.

Minnie nudged the tub of cream down the worktop towards her. 'I find it so bizarre that I've never met your dad. What's he like?'

'Unreliable, mostly.' Dee couldn't quite stop the old

bitterness creeping into her voice. 'He can be really fun, but if you're not literally right there under his nose it's like you don't exist.'

'Sounds like someone else we both know . . .' Minnie raised her eyebrows. 'Except Nat's not fun. Kidding, kidding.'

It was a source of daily astonishment to Dee that Minnie, the most tactless person she had ever met, had a psychology degree. She moved to give her boot a whack with her shoe, but instead she felt her eyes starting to brim.

'Dee! Oh no, please don't cry!' Minnie dropped her own spoon and enveloped her in a hug, her blue eyes huge with sympathy. 'I'm sorry, that was really shitty of me, I shouldn't have said it. Look, maybe this whole thing will be a turning point for you and Nat. Maybe he'll realise how much you mean to him and ask you—'

They heard the flat's front door open again, then shut. Somebody whistled their way down the hallway and into the living room.

'Ooh, Jonas is back early from the gym!' Minnie exclaimed, dropping Dee. 'Come on, let's go and say hi.'

The mysterious Jonas was lying on the sofa in the living room in shorts and a tight white T-shirt, drinking a protein shake and reading a book. His bleached hair was damp from the gym shower and his icy blue eyes glittered.

'Hey, *roomie*,' Minnie said, arranging herself against the door frame. 'This is Dee, she's staying tonight in my room. Be right back, I'm just going to get dinner – and a nice strong cup of tea for you to help with the shock, I think, Dee.'

Jonas turned to Dee. 'Good evening,' he said, giving her a polite wave. He had a deep voice and a German accent. Dee shifted her weight from foot to foot, trying not to sway, and stared at various things in the room that weren't Jonas. He was terrifyingly attractive, a living Diet Coke advert.

'What are you reading?' she managed to ask, nodding in the general direction of the book. Jonas held it up obligingly.

'*Brideshead Revisited*,' he said. 'Do you know it? It is my second time reading it – so I suppose you could say that I am revisiting it, in fact.'

'Jonas is doing a literature degree at Queen Mary!' Minnie interrupted, reappearing with a plate of fully loaded latkes and a mug of tea for Dee. 'That's why he's working at Boombox, to pay the fees.'

Jonas smiled; his teeth were blindingly white. 'People are often surprised,' he said. 'They don't expect me to be smart.'

'I'm not surprised!' Dee said, many decibels too loudly. How did Minnie cope with sharing a bathroom with him? She took the proffered mug gratefully, even though she wasn't a tea drinker.

Jonas's smartwatch started bleeping. 'Ah,' he said, reaching for the remote control on the coffee table; all the muscles in his back rippled as he moved. 'My show is on. It is a documentary about Evelyn Waugh, actually, on Sky Arts.'

'Mmm, I *love* her,' Minnie purred. 'Budge up.'

Jonas made space for Minnie, who plonked herself down about two inches away from him. There was technically room for Dee too, but not really – she perched uncomfortably on the arm of the sofa, watching Minnie munching on latkes, and Jonas watching Minnie eating.

'What *is* that on the top of them?' he asked her, frowning at them. 'They are sparkling.'

'Edible glitter.' Minnie wiped her hand across her mouth, her eyes twinkling. 'Want one? Go on . . .' She picked up a latke and zoomed it towards his face, making airplane noises. Jonas laughed as he swatted her away.

'Minnie, you are mad,' he said, shaking his head. 'Please, no glitter. But the carbohydrates are good – we have our first run together tomorrow, remember?'

'I can't wait!' Minnie swung her legs across his lap and jammed a latke into her mouth, then launched into a story about a TV chef she knew who liked women to wear his aprons in bed. The programme was a lost cause, but Jonas didn't seem to mind. Dee tried to focus on the screen but her vision was blurry at the edges and her brain was too loud. She put her tea on the floor.

'Back in a bit,' she whispered to nobody in particular. Neither Minnie nor Jonas seemed to have heard her. She quietly stood up and tiptoed out of the living room. She paused for a second by the front door after getting her coat off the peg, listening to the jazz from the TV and Jonas laughing at something outrageous that Minnie had just said.

It had suddenly got cold outside. Dee sat down heavily at the top of Minnie's steps, pulling her coat around her. The gin was making her head swim. She got her phone out and googled 'situationship'.

When one person is in love and willing to do the work to make a relationship happen and the other doesn't feel the same way but will still have sex with you, the Urban Dictionary said.

Suddenly feeling unnaturally calm, Dee clicked out of the page and turned the brightness all the way down on her screen. Then she went into her address book, found Nat's number and called it.

He answered just as she was about to hang up.

'Dee?' She could hear music down the line, and voices. 'Hey! So I'm actually just . . .'

'Nat, what are we doing?' Her timing was off – she could hear how clumsy her interruption was, how badly this was already going, but there was nothing she could do about it now. 'Us. This. What are we?'

There was a long pause. The music got quieter; Dee imagined Nat walking away from whichever bar or club he was outside, mouthing an apology to someone. Normally she'd have been mortified by the idea that she was inconveniencing him. But she couldn't do normal any more.

'I mean, do we have to *be* anything?' His voice was light, but there was a definite edge to it. 'We're having fun, aren't we?'

The whoosh and honk of the traffic on Kingsland Road seemed to fade away. Dee felt like she'd passed through intoxication, emerging in a still and silent place where everything was suddenly very clear.

'Is that what you were doing with Lulu Hartley yesterday?' she heard herself asking, dropping the words like rocks. 'Having fun?'

'Christ, Dee . . .' Nat let out an exasperated sigh. 'There is absolutely nothing going on with me and Lulu – she was just showing me around. That's allowed, isn't it? I don't see what the big deal is.'

Dee scrunched the corner of her coat up in her free hand. A cold emptiness was creeping upwards from her feet, like icy water.

The silence went on for what felt like years. Then Nat exhaled heavily again.

'Look, I'm sorry, but I absolutely can't handle this right now, OK? I've just got too much going on. Whatever happens with the audition tomorrow, I think I'm going to stay out here for a bit longer. Maybe it's for the best if we . . . I don't know. Take a break. Or whatever.'

Chapter Six

Dee spent the rest of the week in an entirely robotic state. She went to work and performed tasks for eight hours. Then she came home and got into bed with a plate of toast, which would go cold as it got dark outside on Camden Road and car headlights drifted across the ceiling. Although Nat's silence – and the fact he was suddenly popping up on Lulu Hartley's Instagram – made it clear that it really was over, all the roads in Dee's brain still irreversibly led to him. Every time she picked up her phone she felt as though someone was pouring drain cleaner into her chest.

On Friday morning Dee varied her zombie routine by packing an overnight bag, then getting the tube to Chalk Farm after work to look after Persephone, Jay's daughter. Jay and Bizzy lived in Primrose Hill (of course they did), at the end of a row of pastel-painted houses that was mobbed by tourists in the summer. The fairy-tale loveliness of the scene was smothering: as Dee dragged herself over the railway bridge it seemed to be taunting her, deliberately rubbing its happily-ever-afterness in her face. The sky was cloudless, birds were chirping and there were couples holding hands everywhere she looked. It all felt like a horrible joke at her expense.

It would be hard, she reflected as she turned the corner on to Jay and Bizzy's road, to design a worse weekend for a heartbroken, reproductively challenged woman than babysitting here in Richard Curtis Central followed by an early morning tour of a wildlife sanctuary. Roo had volunteered to take Nat's ticket for the Wetland Centre, but Dee still hadn't told her mum that he wasn't coming – she just couldn't face Alice's reaction to the loss of yet another future son-in-law. And that, she knew, would be a drop in the ocean compared to how her mum would react if she found out about Dee's test results.

She would get Ines to do it, she decided – that was the best way. She'd actually avoided the subject of Nat with her stepmum while they'd been seeing each other: given her job, Ines was annoyingly good at asking the kinds of questions that Dee preferred not to contemplate. But she was endlessly kind and patient, and a world expert at handling Alice.

Dee stopped by a magnolia (it wasn't in bloom thankfully; that would definitely have pushed her over the edge), got her phone out and texted her stepmum.

> Looking forward to seeing you tomorrow morning! Nat and I sort of . . . aren't together right now. So he isn't coming. I've invited Roo instead, hope that's OK. But I'm worried about how Mum's going to react when she finds out, you know how excited she's been about meeting Nat . . .

She left it there, hoping Ines would take the hint. Ines did. She replied straight away; she must have been between patients. The relief was immediate: Dee had never really known the meaning of 'a problem shared is a problem halved' until she'd met Ines.

Ines:

Hello Dee-Dee

Don't worry, leave it with me –

I'll talk to her

Sorry to hear about Nat

I'm here if you want to chat

about it x

Dee:

Thanks, Ines, you're the best x

Jay and Bizzy's house was painted pale purple, with neat lavender-filled window boxes to match. Dee had only been here once before, for the first Anvil poker night (which had also been the last, on account of Jay losing repeatedly and humiliatingly to Hiro). She climbed the steps and rang the bell with a heavy heart, wishing she was anywhere else – then she remembered she had nowhere else to be.

Bizzy opened the door with a flourish. She was wearing a turquoise silk kimono over a pair of jeans that were artfully frayed at the ankles, and a pair of red backless slip-on flats that completed the look perfectly, but which Dee suspected would make her look like an actual clown if she wore them. She had a salon-fresh blow-dry and her tanned skin glowed: it was hard to imagine her ever lunching, as Dee had that day, on a microwaved frozen pain au chocolat she'd found entombed in the depths of the office kitchen freezer. Dee knew from a profile piece she'd read while swotting up for her Anvil interview years ago that Bizzy wasn't that much older than her – she was barely into her forties. That fact hadn't made much of an impact on her at the time, but it certainly did now.

'Dee!' Bizzy exclaimed, leaning forward to kiss the air next to Dee's cheeks; she was positively fizzing with energy. 'Jay's just doing his hair, he won't be a minute – come in, come in! Ooh, you've got crumbs on your top, what have you been munching, you naughty thing?'

The hall felt like an extra-large branch of The White Company: everything was cream and made of nubbly wool, and the walls were a soothing (and clearly expensive) greyish beige. Even the toys that were scattered around looked like they'd been positioned by a stylist: there was a wooden rocking horse at the foot of the stairs and a trio of teddy bears going up them in height order. And there were family photos everywhere, black-and-white studio shots. It was all far too much, complete smugness overload – but as Dee followed Bizzy inside she felt the same twinge she'd had when she'd spotted Dr Kirsty's photo. It wasn't the stuff that she envied: it was the stuff *under* the stuff. However objectionable and ridiculous Jay and Bizzy were, they seemed to be a genuinely happy family.

'Guess who stayed up to say hello to you . . .' Bizzy pointed to the top of the stairs. In the middle of the landing was a pyjama-clad little girl with bobbed hair and Jay's thick, dark eyebrows, holding a soft-toy rabbit.

'Say hello to Dee, Seffy!' Bizzy prompted.

Persephone stared at Dee with narrowed eyes.

'You're tall,' she said with the withering diction of a Hollywood villain, twisting the rabbit's ears. 'Really tall.'

'That's right!' Dee smiled maniacally; it was very important, she reminded herself, to be body-positive around children. 'I am!'

'Taller than Daddy,' Persephone went on, getting louder

as she warmed to her theme. 'Taller than *everyone*. You're like the *EMPIRE STATE BUILDING*.'

'Seffy!' Bizzy tutted affectionately. 'Honestly! What have we said about not commenting on things that people can't change about themselves?'

Persephone scowled. Then she stomped down the stairs and straight past them, into the living room to their right. Bizzy laughed, then gave Dee an expectant look.

'I'll, er, just go and keep an eye on her,' Dee said, picking up on her cue.

The living room was bigger than Dee's entire flat. A huge quilted and tasselled ottoman in the centre of the room was covered in lifestyle magazines that looked like they'd never been read. There was a pink velvet love seat in one corner of the room, and Persephone was furiously tending to a wooden play kitchen in the other, banging pans around. Dee watched from the doorway, trying to summon the courage to actually go inside.

'That looks really good, Persephone!' she said loudly, walking over to join her. She sat down cross-legged on the carpet, picking up a wooden fried egg from one of the pans and pretending to bite it. 'Mmm! Yum!'

Persephone looked up at her like she was an idiot.

'It's not real,' she said.

Dee put the egg back and rubbed her stomach, which had been grumbling ominously all afternoon. The pain au chocolat had been a bad choice.

Persephone was watching her. 'What's wrong?' she demanded. 'Are you ill?'

Honesty was the safest policy here, Dee decided. 'A bit,'

she admitted. 'I ate something strange for lunch and it's made me feel poorly.'

Persephone thought about this. 'Was it organic?' she asked.

'No, it definitely wasn't.' If anyone was in need of adult supervision around here, Dee decided as she attempted to discreetly de-pastry herself, it was her.

Persephone pulled a *well, there you go* face.

'Right, we're off!'

A camel coat-wearing Bizzy had appeared in the doorway with Jay hovering behind her; he gave Dee an uncharacteristically subdued wave over her shoulder. 'We'll be back around eleven but you've got our numbers if you need them. Grab whatever you like from the fridge except for the chia seeds, they haven't finished sprouting. Oh, and I've popped some Sauvignon Blanc in the door for you – I remember what it was like being in my twenties!'

'I'm thirty-four,' Dee said. Bizzy looked mortified.

'Oh!' She stifled a nervous giggle. 'From the way Jay talks about you I just assumed you were younger . . . Well, we'd better get going, hadn't we? Seffy, it *really* is bedtime now, come on . . .'

Five hours later Dee was lying diagonally across the sofa bed (was this just her life now, sleeping on other people's sofas?) in what Jay called 'the den' next to the kitchen, drinking warm Oyster Bay from a Nutribullet cup. Bizzy had left her fifty pounds in cash in an envelope, twenty of which she'd spent on Deliverooing herself a very small amount of sushi; twenty pounds, it turned out, didn't go far at all in Primrose Hill. Amazingly, Persephone had stayed in bed the whole time Jay and Bizzy had been out. Dee had held back on the wine until they got home – things were bad, but not drunk-in-charge-of-a-child bad – but now everyone was in bed there was nothing stopping her from trying to drink away the pain.

The den seemed to be the only room in the house that Jay had been allowed to decorate, and it felt like walking into a back issue of *Loaded*: the Union Jack cushions had punky safety pins through their corners and there was a framed poster on the wall for a Sex Pistols gig that Dee was certain Jay hadn't actually gone to.

Her phone was propped up on her knee and she had WhatsApp open. Her chat with Nat had fallen down the list, but it was still there at the bottom of her screen. Her finger hovered over it for a moment – then she tapped. A second later she felt a cold hand squeeze her heart. *Online*, the italics under Nat's name said. He was talking to somebody. Just not to her.

Roo and Minnie, meanwhile, weren't holding back in their three-way group chat: the notifications were popping up faster than Dee could swipe them away.

Roo:
I know I swore an oath to do
no harm
But I could cheerfully push
Nat off a cliff
This is EXACTLY what he
did to you at school, Dee
He strings you along and
then whoosh, gone

Minnie:
No jury would convict you,
Roo
Also *Dragon Quest* is such a
stupid show
Even *I* know they didn't
have thongs in the Middle
Ages
Are you back on any dating
apps yet Dee?
Best way of getting over
someone is to get under
someone else 😜

Roo:
The priority has to be Dee
deciding what she's going to
do fertility-wise
Dating can wait
Sorry, bedtime here, early
start tomorrow x

Dee sloshed some more wine into her cup and started typing.

Dee:
Dating can't wait though,
can it?
If I want to do the whole
family thing I need to find
someone to do it with

Minnie:
It's 2022, Dee . . .
There's no shame in being a
single parent

Dee:
Yes, I know that
But there's no way I could
afford to do it by myself
Anyway, I remember how
hard it was for my mum

Minnie:

The den's door creaked open and a pyjama-clad Persephone appeared, holding her rabbit.

'Hi Persephone! Everything OK?' Dee instinctively hid her cup behind a cushion; nothing sobered you up like having a six-year-old's eyes boring into your soul.

'If I get up in the night Mummy and Daddy let me have a coconut yoghurt to help me go back to sleep,' Persephone said with a straight face. She held Dee's gaze for a second longer, then stared at the ceiling shiftily.

'Hmm, do they really?' Dee raised her eyebrow with her index finger.

Persephone stifled a giggle, then chewed her lip. 'No,' she conceded. 'But can I have one?'

'Will you go back to bed really, really quietly afterwards?'

Persephone nodded, and Dee heaved herself off the sofa. 'Then yes. I'll come with you and sit with you while you eat it, OK?'

They tiptoed out of the den together, Persephone's small, warm fingers curled around Dee's in a surprisingly firm grip. They were in sight of the kitchen – which looked like a cross between an organic farm and a polished chrome spaceship – when Bizzy appeared at the top of the stairs, swaddled in a fluffy cream dressing gown with a silk eye mask around her neck.

'Seffy, what are you doing out of bed? It's the middle of the night . . .'

Persephone looked from Bizzy to Dee, then back at her mum.

'Dee asked me if I wanted a yoghurt,' she said calmly, showing a readiness to push someone else under the bus that Dee felt would probably see her seizing control of a FTSE 100 company before her twenty-first birthday. Luckily, Bizzy didn't seem annoyed.

'Angel, it isn't good to snack after you've brushed your teeth. Come on, let's tuck you up.' She gave Dee an apologetic smile. 'I envy you not having to deal with this sort of thing, Dee!' she said in the exact same voice that couples who were holding hands at weddings always seemed to use to tell her they missed being single. 'Make the most of those unbroken nights!'

As Persephone allowed herself to be led back to her bedroom she turned to look over her shoulder and gave Dee a comradely nod.

Walking back to the den alone, Dee felt an absurd sense of pride at having apparently won over the most terrifying child in north London. And then she felt very, very sad.

Minnie had messaged her again while she'd been away.

Minnie:
Oh before I forget!
I saw Grumpy Andy earlier
I was walking past the cafe
and he asked after you
He said you had an
argument!?!?!?!

Dee:
Oh God . . .
I bumped into him on my
way to yours on Monday
I told him everything, I think
I was still in shock
He basically told me how
much worse men have it
I sort of bit his head off

Minnie:
Really?
That doesn't sound like you,
Dee . . .
Well he said he was going to
message
He just seemed worried
about you tbh

Dee:
I'm worried about me . . .

Dee checked Instagram – sure enough, there was a message

in her inbox from The Canal Cafe's account. *Hi Dee, Andy here, hope you're doing all right. Just wanted to apologise for upsetting you on Monday, I was trying to help but I know I didn't.*

As she read it Dee felt guilt prickling at her. Saying exactly what she was feeling had been an unusually liberating experience, but maybe she'd been a bit harsh on Andy. Perhaps he really had just been trying to cheer her up. And the message he'd sent her was genuinely nice. She typed a reply – *Thanks for messaging, Andy. Don't worry, I was upset already!!! Hope your Friday night's going better than mine* – then let her phone drop on to her chest, defeated. The cracks on the ceiling made a bleak kind of map, covered in roads going nowhere. What Bizzy had said earlier about her seeming younger than she was had really hit a nerve. She *was* far too old to be drifting like this, not anchored in place by anything. But she had no idea how to change that: the harder she tried, the less possible it seemed. Unless she did something dramatic soon, she thought, she was going to be like this forever.

Minnie had sent a voice note to their group chat, she saw.

'OK, sooooo guys, I've been reading this article about websites where you can find an 'intentional co-parent' to have a kid with,' she began excitedly. 'They're for people who want a family but aren't looking to have a romantic relationship with the other person. It's totally kosher, no sex, turkey basters all the way . . . There's one called It Takes Two Dot Com. Great name, right?'

A link popped up in the chat and Dee clicked on it.

A slick photo slideshow appeared immediately: a good-looking, smiling man and a woman pushing a toddler on a swing; another equally attractive and happy-looking pair walking in the park with a slightly older child holding their hands; a third couple reading a sleepy little boy in pyjamas a bedtime story. Then some text appeared.

> *Reaching career security, getting on the property ladder, finding love: these things can take a while. But although our lives are very different to what they were a hundred years ago, our bodies aren't. If you're worried you're running out of time to start a family with a romantic partner but would rather not be a solo parent by choice, platonic co-parenting can be a great solution. Your baby gets a ready-made family, and you get to share the highs and lows of raising a child with another committed adult . . .*

Andy had replied to her message on Instagram.

I'm actually deep-cleaning
the fridge
So yeah, a massive Friday
night here
How about you?

'Hah,' Dee said out loud. Maybe it was the fact she'd drunk the best part of a bottle of wine on a nearly empty stomach, or maybe it was just a case of misery loving company, but she was starting to revise her opinion of Andy. He

94

was all right, really. Not unfunny. She hesitated, then started typing a reply to him.

> Dee:
> So weirdly Minnie's just sent
> me a link to this website
> called It Takes Two . . .
> Was that the one you were
> telling me you'd joined?
> The platonic co-parenting
> one?

The Canal Cafe:
That's the one
To be clear though, I didn't
join it
I just set up a profile and
then wished I hadn't

> Dee:
> What's so bad about it?

The Canal Cafe:
It's just bizarre and
depressing
Like a dating site without the
dates
The first profile I looked at
just had a picture of a car
on it

Dee:
Was it an estate car?

The Canal Cafe:
Hahahahaha
What difference would that
make?

Dee:
The person might have been
trying to show how family-
friendly they were . . .

The Canal Cafe:
Hah!
I think it was a Vauxhall Astra
Like I said, very depressing
Anyway, good luck if you do
decide to join

Dee:
I definitely won't be after
this conversation

Dee put her phone down and shook the last of the Oyster Bay haphazardly into her cup. She leaned down to put the empty bottle on the carpet, levered herself upright again – and just then an idea danced butterfly-like into her mind. It seemed no better or worse than any other idea she'd ever had. She watched it hovering there for a moment, beckoning her to follow it. Then she went back into Instagram and started typing.

Dee:
Maybe we should just cut
out the middleman . . .

Chapter Seven

Roo was somehow managing to keep a straight face.

'Well . . .' she said, giving Dee her phone back in London Wetland Centre's car park. 'It could have been worse.'

'How? How could it have been worse? I suggested to a man I've met twice that we have a child together, Roo . . .'

Dee took a sip from the bottle of Lucozade that Roo had insisted she buy from the kiosk at Barnes station 'for the electrolytes' and grimaced, trying very hard not to look at her screen. Not that it made a difference: what was on it had been burned permanently into her brain. There was the message she had sent Andy the night before – *Maybe we should just cut out the middleman* – and underneath it, *Seen*. So he'd read it, but he hadn't replied. And who could blame him, Dee thought as a fresh wave of shame crashed over her. How could you reply to a message like that, other than with a restraining order?

Roo gave her back a pat. She was wearing her weekend uniform and the blue duffel coat that made her look like Paddington Bear over the top. It was a cold morning, and her breath steamed.

'Come on, let's sit down over there,' she said in her best doctor voice. 'You look a bit green. We've still got a few minutes until we're meant to meet your mum and Ines.'

Dee allowed herself to be led to a bench next to a notice-board. The Lucozade was helping her hangover but that wasn't necessarily a good thing – at least when she'd been concentrating on not being sick on the train here from Water-loo she hadn't been able to think about anything other than that. With her head starting to clear, the full hideousness of the situation was revealing itself. She was going to have to leave London, and quite possibly the country.

'God, Roo, what am I going to do?' she groaned, putting her head in her hands.

'Just message Andy in a bit and say that you'd had a lot to drink and aren't in a great place right now,' Roo shrugged. 'With a bit of luck you'll never have to see him again.'

Dee shook her head. 'I bet I will – Minnie goes to the cafe where he works all the time, they're practically neighbours.'

'Well, why don't you go there after this and explain in person, then?' Roo sounded slightly exasperated. She sighed. 'Dee, it's *fine* – it was the wine, not you. Everybody does silly things when they're drunk, it doesn't mean any-thing. Andy'll understand that.' Case apparently closed, she turned around to look at the noticeboard. 'Hmm, it says here that the Wetland Centre is home to nationally significant numbers of gadwall, wigeon and teal. Did you know that? I didn't.'

It was the wine, not you, Dee tried to tell herself, staring into the middle distance. But in her heart of hearts she knew that wasn't true. It *had* been her. She'd never in a million years have made the suggestion to Andy if she'd been sober – it was an absolutely insane idea – but that didn't mean there weren't real feelings behind it. The whole mortifying episode had proved to her how much she wanted a family of her own. And there was precisely nothing she could do about that.

Something caught Roo's eye in the distance. 'Ah! There's your mum and Ines walking into the visitor centre,' she said, pulling Dee to her feet. 'We'd better get going. Oh, wait – before we go in, I had a chat with a gynaecologist I know from medical school when I got home last night. She's at the Whittington, your local hospital. They run this fertility counselling service for people who are having various kinds of issues – the waiting list's months long, obviously, but she said if they get a cancellation she'll book you in. Anyway, I've given her your details.'

Alice was inside in the gift shop, dressed in wide-legged burgundy corduroy trousers and a purple top, both with paint smudges on them – if she wasn't teaching on Saturdays she liked to spend them doing what she called 'daubing' in the shed at the bottom of the garden that doubled as her studio. She was talking animatedly to a bashful-looking man in a Wetland Centre polo shirt and a bird-shaped badge that said *Marcus, Volunteer*. There was no sign of Ines.

'. . . and the populations of gadwall, wigeon and teal are actually nationally significant . . .' Marcus the Volunteer was saying as he fiddled nervously with his badge.

'How *fascinating*,' Alice mused. She tailed off when she spotted Dee and Roo and called out to them at top volume. 'Darling, you're HERE! Ines told me about you and Nat, you POOR THING . . .'

Dee's hangover roared back with a vengeance.

'Um, Mum, where's Ines?' she asked as she gave Alice a perfunctory hug, trying to keep the desperation out of her voice.

'Oh, she's over there talking to someone,' Alice said airily. 'Probably something to do with work, she always seems to be on call – they want to make her the clinic manager at Relate, did I tell you? She wouldn't want us to hang about I'm sure, she'll catch us up.'

Dee looked where Alice was pointing. Ines, dressed in the off-duty version of her usual look (black trousers and a white shirt, but with a jumper on top) was in the corner of the gift shop on her phone, her palm covering her other ear so she could hear over the noise. Dee found herself feeling childishly annoyed: she'd really been counting on Ines smoothing things over today.

'Come on!' Alice said, brandishing their tickets in one hand and grabbing Dee's with the other. 'Last one to the otters loses!'

The visitor centre opened out on to a courtyard full of tables where you could have a picnic when the weather was nicer. Beyond that was the wetland itself: the archway that led into it was frosted with dew and the air was alive with hoots and splashes. Alice went ahead down the wooden-planked path with Marcus the Volunteer, who'd somehow been swept up in the plan. Dee held Roo back.

'How can I stop my mum going on about Nat?' she whispered urgently. 'I can't handle it, Roo, not today . . .'

'Ask her when she went through the menopause,' Roo suggested. Dee elbowed her. 'No, I'm being serious! It would be a helpful thing for you to know, Dee, sometimes there's a genetic element to what you're dealing with. Go on – I'll distract Marcus.'

Before Dee could stop her she'd marched off. 'Excuse me, Marcus, I just have a question about ground-nesting birds . . .' she called out, steering him over the bridge they were coming up to.

Alice had stopped at the foot of it to wait for Dee.

'Isn't this magical?' she sighed. 'I'm so happy we're all here together, darling.' She *did* look genuinely happy, Dee thought guiltily as she got closer. And wasn't that the most important thing? Hadn't it always been?

'It really is,' she agreed. 'Um, Mum, bit of a strange question, but when did you . . .' A moorhen was staring at her in a very judgemental way; she lowered her voice. *'Go through the menopause?'*

Most people would have blanched at this. But Alice wasn't most people.

'Hmm, let me see . . .' She started breezily counting on her fingers. 'So I met Ines when I was thirty-five. You went off to university when I was thirty-eight, and around the time you finished there I went to the doctor because I hadn't had a period for yonks. They did some tests, and I was told I'd been lucky to have you when I did because everything down there had been tumbleweed for years – it had happened without me even realising. Typical!'

'So you were forty-two when you saw the doctor, but it could have happened before then?' Dee did some maths of her own; her chest felt tight. 'That's young, Mum. Like, really young.'

'Yes, I suppose it is,' Alice said mildly. 'Oh, darling, you look sad! Don't be, it didn't stop me doing anything – it never crossed mine or Ines's mind to have another child. It was so much more of a faff back then for two women to get pregnant, we'd have had to jump through so many hoops.' She put her head on one side. 'Why do you ask?'

How could it not have occurred to Alice that this might be relevant information? Why, in thirty-five years of constant oversharing, was this the one thing that she'd kept to herself? Dee breathed in, held the breath for several seconds, then let it out. For a mad moment she actually considered telling her mum everything. But what was the point? Alice would only get upset, then she'd feel terrible and spend the rest of the morning apologising. And even if she *had* known that her mum had been through the menopause very young, would it have changed anything? It wasn't like her twenties and thirties had been an endless series of opportunities for serious relationships that she'd walked away from to drink cocktails by a swimming pool.

'No reason,' she said with effort. 'Oh, look – the otters are on the other side of the bridge, shall we go and see them?'

The otters had their own pond surrounded by bullrushes and logs. There was a Perspex screen separating the path from the water with an illustrated information display on it.

'Todd and Honey are Asian small-clawed otters,' Alice read, leaning down and squinting. 'Todd is five and Honey is nine, they're a "bonded pair" and apparently Honey makes all the decisions for the two of them. That sounds very sensible to me.'

Dee glanced across at Alice, clocked her mum's expression and realised, with a sinking feeling, exactly what was coming.

'It makes you think, doesn't it?' Alice sighed. 'At the end of the day we're all just mammals. And there's no getting around how important pair bonds are—' She gave Dee a pointed look. 'Do you think you and Nat will be able to sort things out? I hope so, you were so excited about him.'

A horrible image of the most recent picture of Nat that Lulu had posted on Instagram (he was in a Bucharest dive bar with the top three buttons of his shirt undone, giving the camera – or whoever was behind it – a smouldering look) flashed through Dee's mind.

'We . . . want different things,' she mumbled, avoiding her mum's eye – and even though she'd just said the first thing that came into her head, she realised that it was true. She wanted to be with Nat, and Nat didn't want to be with her – at least, not enough. That was what it boiled down to, what it had always boiled down to. The thought made her want to go and lie in the pond.

Alice, oblivious, waved a hand. 'Sometimes you just have to get on with it and worry about how it's all going to work later. If your dad and I had gone back and forth this much you wouldn't be here, would you?' Before Dee could reply she'd switched tack. 'I don't suppose you remember me pushing you around this place in your buggy when you were little, do you?' she said with a smile, sweeping an arm across the view. 'The man on the desk used to pretend to be reading the paper when he saw me because he knew I didn't have the money to pay to get in. We had fun in those days, didn't we?'

There *had* been fun bits: nobody else Dee knew had eaten all their meals off disposable barbecues for three weeks (marshmallows had featured heavily), or been encouraged to potato print an entire wall in their rented flat because it was about to be knocked down. But that wasn't the whole story – there had also been Alice's lurching moods, and all the times she'd sent Dee to fob off irate landlords, and the whole weekends that she spent in bed sobbing inconsolably. And how on their first Boxing Day after Karl had left, Alice had swallowed an entire bottle of sleeping pills. She'd called an ambulance and left Dee with a neighbour, who'd told Dee that Alice had accidentally eaten a drawing pin and was going to be fed cotton wool sandwiches by the doctors. (For several years Dee had innocently repeated this story to people.) Alice was referred to a psychiatrist, who eventually diagnosed her with something called cyclothymia. Dee, who'd overheard her mum using the word on the phone when she was ten, took herself off to Ealing Library and looked it up in a medical dictionary. *A depressive illness that causes sudden and unpredictable mood change, from cheerfulness to misery,* she read. The next sentence made her blood run cold. *Without the right support people with cyclothymia are at increased risk of developing bipolar disorder.*

Dee had already seen enough of Alice's dealings with the receptionists at the local surgery to know that *the right support* wasn't going to come from there. And Dee's grandparents – her mum's mum and dad – definitely wouldn't provide it. They had so disapproved of teenage Alice having a baby with a man who she had no intention of marrying that they'd wondered aloud if she ought to put Dee up for adoption – a suggestion which ended in Alice cutting off all contact with them and tearing up the pointed little cheques for twenty pounds that came with a Derbyshire postmark once or twice a year. Alice had lots of friends, she made them everywhere – people always seemed to be flattered that someone so beautiful and gregarious was taking such an interest in them. But most of them came and went, drawn in and then driven away by Alice's stormy moods. And none of them, Dee was sure, could be there for her mum in the way she really needed. As she closed the dictionary she felt certain that it was all going to be down to her.

Today, Alice talked cheerfully about what she called her 'silliness' – she even joked about it sometimes – but Dee still felt the shadow of it whenever they were together. It meant she'd never really felt able to come to her mum with any of her own problems in case they tipped Alice back into despair. And it made it almost impossible to argue with her, however aggravating she was being: the sight of Alice in tears made Dee feel ill. So she bit her tongue to keep the peace, always.

They caught up with Roo by the main lake, which had kingfishers zipping around above it. The sunlight flashed dazzlingly on their wings.

'. . . people think they're the same animal, but actually a stoat's tail has a black tip and a weasel's is brown . . .' she was saying to Marcus the Volunteer, who looked extremely relieved when Alice dragged him off to look at the bitterns ('Do they *actually* boom? I've always wanted to know!')

'How did you get on?' Roo asked when they were alone again on the path. 'Did you find out anything useful?'

'You were right, Mum was really young when she went

through the menopause.' Dee slowed down so she and Roo were in step with each other. 'That's bad, isn't it?'

'I mean, it's not *good* . . .' Roo was really trying hard not to do anything with her face. 'But honestly, Dee, gynaecology isn't a very well-funded area of research, and there's still so much that we don't know about all of this stuff. Things might go the same way for you that they did for your mum, or they might not – all we know for sure is that they're not going in a very positive direction.'

'Wow, thanks, Roo – sometimes I regret asking to borrow your protractor in 2001,' Dee muttered. Roo put a hand on her arm.

'Sorry, Dee, I just . . . don't want you to bury your head in the sand about this, it's too important.' She got her phone out. 'On a lighter note, Minnie's just sent us this,' she said, turning it around so Dee could see the screen. It was a photo taken by Minnie of her and Jonas doing calf stretches in their running gear, with their arms draped across each other's shoulders. *Just eaten a fry up*, Minnie had written underneath. *Hope I don't barf in the canal!*

Roo raised an eyebrow. 'You don't think those two are . . . you know. Do you?'

Dee shook her head vehemently. 'She'd have told us if they were. Also she's actually really sensible about stuff like this, and sleeping with your flatmate is the world's worst idea. Apart from asking strange men if they want to have a baby with you, obviously . . .'

'Darling!' Alice's voice drifted towards them from around the next corner. 'Come and look, they've got mallard chicks!"

Dee was extremely grateful to see Ines walking towards

them along the path from the visitor centre. She watched as her stepmum rolled her shoulders forwards then backwards like she was trying to get something out of them.

'You're just in time, Mum's been giving me the birds and the bees chat but without the bees . . .' Dee called out. She waited for Ines to smile or laugh. But Ines did neither of those things. Somewhere deep in the back of Dee's mind, an alarm bell started to ring.

'Are you . . . OK?' she asked when Ines caught up with them, suddenly not sure whether she wanted to hear the answer.

'Oh, fine, fine,' Ines said quickly, giving her a distracted smile. 'Just a tricky call. Come on, let's go and find Al. And you need to fill me in on everything that's been going on in your life, Dee-Dee . . .'

The shutter was down at The Canal Cafe when Dee got there. Although she'd told Roo when they said goodbye that she was going to come straight here, Dee had actually gone back to Hiro's and spent several hours doing laundry in the hope that she'd run out of time and wouldn't have to talk to Andy. It looked like her plan might actually have worked. The outdoor tables were gone and the waitress with the pink hair who'd taken Dee and Minnie's order was locking up.

'I'm looking for Andy, is he around?' she asked as casually as she could. The waitress shook her head.

'You've just missed him, sorry, he left five minutes ago.' She finished locking up and dropped the keys into the pocket of her denim jacket. 'Want me to pass on a message?'

Dee let out the breath she'd been holding in. The decision

had been taken out of her hands, and she was off the hook. The relief of having dodged an excruciating conversation was making her feel light-headed. Or – her stomach rumbled – maybe she'd just been on too many trains today and needed to eat something to put this hangover to rest. She smiled at the waitress.

'Where would you say the best place around here would be for me to buy a *lot* of chocolate with no questions asked?'

The waitress grinned back. 'Try the Tesco Express on Southgate Road, they've got all the Ritter Sports.'

'Perfect.' Dee started backing away. 'Could you let Andy know that Dee came to apologise? Thank you!'

The Tesco Express didn't disappoint. Standing under the bracing air conditioning in the Sweets and Chocolate aisle, Dee created a three-course Ritter Sport menu for herself (Cornflake, Cocoa Wafer and Strawberry Yogurt to finish), composing an update for Roo and Minnie in her head. She'd done her best to sort things out with Andy but the universe had intervened – neither of them could argue with that. Satisfied, she stuck her headphones in and put on Madonna for her walk home. 'Papa Don't Preach', she noted with grim amusement, was the first song on the playlist. She turned up the volume as loud as it would go and set off for the till.

She was so caught up in the music that as she turned the corner at the end of the aisle she walked straight into a man carrying a bag of crinkle-cut McCain's. The man, she realised as she looked up, their eyes met and her heart plummeted into her shoes, was Andy.

'Dee? What are you doing here?' He was wearing a parka with a furry hood like a cartoon of a man from Manchester and looked as though he'd just seen a ghost.

'What are *you* doing buying oven chips?' Dee blurted out in a panic; for someone who'd constructed her entire personality around avoiding confrontations she certainly seemed to be having a lot of them with this man. 'I thought you were meant to be a chef.' She fumbled with her phone to pause Madonna, her hands trembling. She hadn't actually been sick yet today but she had a horrible feeling that might be about to change.

'I am, but I've got better things to be doing on a Saturday night than peeling potatoes.' Andy paused. 'Actually, no, I haven't, but the kitchen situation in my new place isn't that conducive to creativity. Most of my stuff's in storage still.'

What was she doing critiquing his frozen-food choices? She was lucky he hadn't staged some kind of intervention on her, Dee told herself as she attempted to get her breathing back under control. She'd come here to apologise – now she actually needed to do it.

'So, um, I was actually at the cafe just now,' she said, trying to get the words out as fast as possible so it would all be over quickly. 'I wanted to say sorry for sending you that incredibly weird message last night, I was really drunk and as you know I'm dealing with some stuff at the moment, but that's no excuse. Anyway, I'll let you get on.'

She turned to go.

'Dee, wait . . .'

Andy didn't look angry or alarmed or any of the other

things she'd thought he might. She couldn't make his expression out at all.

'Maybe we should . . . keep talking about it?'

Dee's face caught fire. 'No, I really don't think we should ever talk about the most embarrassing night of my life again.'

'Not that – I mean . . .' Andy dragged his hands through his hair and stared at the ceiling. 'God, this is hard. OK, look – I'm forty, and if I'm going to be a dad I'd like to do it before I get much older. You're up against a deadline too, and it doesn't seem to be working out for either of us the old-fashioned way. So bearing all that in mind, what if we just . . .'

Dee felt like a computer with too many browser tabs open.

'I'm sorry, are you actually saying we should go ahead and . . .' She checked over her shoulder to make sure nobody was listening, then lowered her voice to a whisper. '*Cut out the middleman?*'

Andy shook his head vigorously. 'No, no. Christ, absolutely not. At least, not any time soon. But I don't see any harm in us finding out a bit more about each other, do you? If nothing else it's good to talk to someone who's going through similar stuff to you, right?' He cleared his throat. 'This would be as friends, just to be clear – I'm absolutely not asking you out or anything like that.'

In spite of the multiple bomb blasts that were currently going off in her brain, Dee felt herself bristle. Who did he think he was, Ryan Gosling?

'Don't worry, you're quite safe with me,' she said, crossing her arms. 'You're very much not my type.'

'Good to know,' Andy said dryly, swapping the chips into

his other hand. 'Believe it or not, romance isn't on my agenda here either.'

A thin ray of clarity broke through the fog in Dee's mind. Yes, Andy could do with spending several terms at charm school and seemed to be in the middle of having some kind of midlife crisis. And he was a chef, and as a group they were notoriously bad news. But he was right: where was the harm in talking to someone who was trying to figure out the same sorts of things as her? It wasn't as though she had any other options right now. She blew out her cheeks.

'All right, then,' she heard herself telling him. 'It's a deal, Andy . . .'

'Jones. Andy Jones. It's a very, very boring name, I'm afraid. We should swap numbers, shouldn't we?'

As Dee typed hers into his phone – an iPhone that was almost as bashed about as Minnie's – a voice she knew she really shouldn't be listening to piped up in her head. The man standing in front of her with a bag of chips under his arm was the opposite of Nat in every way: tall where Nat was not-quite-tall, fair where Nat was dark, borderline rude where Nat was softly spoken. According to the laws of the universe, opposites attracted. And if she threw herself into . . . whatever this was with someone who was the reverse of Nat, it whispered, karma might bring a new, improved version of Nat back.

Roo:
How are you getting on,
Dee?

Dee:
Fine! Back at Hiro's now,
having a beer in the bath –
hair of the dog and all that

I talked to Andy
We're exploring the
possibility of platonically co-
parenting together

Roo:
Um, what? Dee, are you OK?
How much have you had to
drink?

Dee:
Just one beer. I've got some
breadsticks too though,
don't worry

Roo:
That wasn't really the bit I
was worrying about . . .

Minnie:
OMG GRUMPY ANDY,
Dee!!!! TELL US EVERYTHING

Dee:
Look, we're just talking, OK?

Roo:
Dee, where would you
live? Would Anvil give you
maternity leave?

Minnie:
Oh Roo, don't be such a
party pooper. You and Andy
would have a cute baby, Dee!
I mean, it would be massive
obviously. What with you
both being so tall. But cute!

Roo:
I'm sorry, but this is insane
You've only met him twice!

Dee:
Three times actually

Minnie:
I say go for it, Dee! What's
the worst that can happen?

Roo:
Where do you want me to
start . . .

From: Roopa Gill
To: Dee Jensen
Subject: Things you and Andy need to think about
Monday, 2 October, 08:03

I've been looking at that website Minnie was telling you about – it has a list of questions for potential platonic co-parents to ask each other. These are just for starters . . .

1. What are your beliefs?
2. What are your career plans?
3. Where would you like to live?
4. How will you divide up the childcare?
5. What will happen if one of you meets someone?

I still can't tell if you're actually serious about this whole thing, Dee, or if it's just a hysterical reaction to the whole Nat situation – but if you are, you and Andy really need to go through these ASAP.

From: Dee Jensen
To: Roopa Gill
Subject: RE: Things you and Andy need to think about
Monday, 2 October, 09:47

UNSUBSCRIBE

From: Roopa Gill
To: Dee Jensen

Subject: RE: Things you and Andy need to think about
Monday, 2 October, 09:52

I mean it, Dee! Leaving aside the fact that this is an obviously insane idea, this stuff is really important. You wouldn't go into business with someone without working through every detail of how your company was going to run, would you?

From: Dee Jensen
To: Roopa Gill
Subject: RE: Things you and Andy need to think about
Monday, 2 October 10:27

You wouldn't be sending me emails like this if I was married and thinking about having a child the old-fashioned way . . . Actually, who am I kidding – you definitely would.

From: Roopa Gill
To: Dee Jensen
Subject: RE: Things you and Andy need to think about
Monday, 2 October, 10:32

I'm only doing it because I care x

From: Dee Jensen
To: Roopa Gill
Subject: RE: Things you and Andy need to think about
Monday, 2 October, 10:51

I know x

Chapter Eight

The man sitting in the security box at the entrance to New Covent Garden Market was frowning.

'I'm not being funny,' he said, peering at Dee over his glasses in the milky early morning light, 'but are you *sure* you're in the right place?'

Dee had been asking herself exactly the same question all the way to Vauxhall to meet Andy for the first of their getting-to-know-each-other outings, shivering in a bobbly jumper and skirt that weren't nearly warm enough for this time of day. Somewhere around Oxford Circus the question had taken on an existential dimension. What the hell *was* she doing?

It had been just under a week since her and Andy's conversation in Tesco Express. Seen through the blurry twin lenses of a hangover and despair, their agreement hadn't seemed entirely ridiculous. In fact, Dee had walked back to Hiro's with a bit of a spring in her step that afternoon, buoyed by the unusual feeling of having any kind of plan at all. But in the cold, unforgiving light of today the whole thing struck her as being – as Roo kept telling her – completely and utterly insane. She just wanted to turn around and go back to bed. But she knew that if she left now the only thing waiting for her at Hiro's was last night's washing-up and the TV. And right now the Netflix *Are you still watching?* prompt could probably inflict a lasting psychic wound.

It didn't help that trying to work out what she and Andy were going to do and when they were going to do it had been a toe-curlingly awkward nightmare; as yet *Time Out* had no section entitled 'Things To Do With Your Potential Platonic Co-Parent'. He had rejected all of her suggestions and she'd rejected all of his. At least there seemed to be an unspoken agreement between them that arranging any kind of activity specially would feel too much like a date. This meant that one of them was going to have to tag along with the other for something they were already doing. Andy had suggested Dee come shopping for the cafe with him before he started his Saturday shift; Dee resented the implication that his working life was more interesting than hers, but given her days were spent writing about compost bins it probably was. So here she was, about to go and look at cour-gettes in the middle of the night with a man she barely knew and wasn't even sure she liked as a person, who she might or might not decide to have a child with at some extremely distant, hard-to-fathom point in the future. Except it couldn't be *that* distant, because she didn't actually have that much time left. Round and round it went, her brain churning away like a washing machine.

Out of the corner of her eye she saw a 156 bus pulling up at the stop on Nine Elms Lane. There was a *Dragon Quest* banner on its flank, featuring the whole cast. Lulu, who wasn't lacking in the cleavage department to start with, had been Photoshop-inflated in her chainmail to look like Bayeux Tapestry Barbie. It had been nearly a fortnight since Dee had called Nat outside Minnie's, and she still hadn't heard from him. The silence was both a horrible shock and not a shock at all – she'd always worried that Nat would just disappear one day, and that was exactly what had happened. No, she told herself as she watched the 156 pull away, going back to the flat would be an even worse idea than sticking this out.

The security guard was staring at her.

'You do realise this isn't the Covent Garden with all the nice shops, don't you?' he said, raising his voice and speaking more slowly, as though he suspected that English wasn't her first language. 'This is the market where all the chefs come first thing to buy stuff to cook with.'

'Yes, I'm meeting a chef here, thank you,' Dee heard herself saying primly. 'Which way's the Market Cafe, please?'

The security guard jerked his thumb towards what looked like a series of aircraft hangers. 'Go straight on until you get there – mind the lorries.'

'Thank you.' As she set off, Dee looked again at the not-at-all helpful instructions Andy had sent her – *Go in through the main entrance, I'll meet you at the Market Cafe* – then reread the messages that Roo and Minnie had sent her the night before to try to make herself feel a bit more normal.

Minnie:
Have fun at the market
tomorrow with Grumpy
Andy, Dee 😄 😄 😄

Roo:
Minnie, we talked about this
Dee's not going on a date
with Andy, they're just . . .

I'm actually not sure what
they're doing
But it's not a date

Minnie:
When's Andy's birthday,
Dee? I want to check your
astrological compatibility.
Not in a lovey-dovey way!
Just in a normal way 😊

Roo:
I'm not sure there is a
normal way . . .

Minnie:
Dee, don't forget to take
that cute bag I lent you!
C'est très marché
Also DON'T BE SCARED
I'm sure Andy's way more
nervous than you are
Like bears are with humans!

Roo:
Oh my God, Minnie . . .

Dee had actually brought the bag – a bucket-shaped
wicker one with EN VACANCES embroidered on it in loopy
script – because she couldn't face telling Minnie she hadn't,

but she felt deeply uncomfortable clutching it, like she was in Minnie-drag. The skirt was a paisley one with knife pleats that Hiro had given her years ago, which she'd hoped suggested vintage cool but now looked more Angela Lansbury in *Murder She Wrote*. It was completely wrong for today, but she also had no idea what right would be: when Andy had asked her how she was with early starts it hadn't crossed her mind that she'd be getting out of bed at five o'clock in the morning to buy vegetables on the other side of London. And all the fashion Instagram accounts she followed were mysteriously silent on the question of what to wear on a pre-dawn visit to a windswept industrial estate with a man you had nothing in common with apart from the fact you were both, apparently, desperate.

It was definitely rush hour in New Covent Garden Market. Beeping trucks were reversing into loading bays, and teams of men in green overalls were heaving crates of fruit and vegetables off them. Looking through the market's website the night before, Dee had discovered that this was where basically every restaurant, cafe and bar in the south of England got its fresh produce from: if you were a chef you could either call up at the crack of dawn and put in a delivery order or, if you were in London, come and do the shopping yourself. She wasn't sure why Andy hadn't done the former; he must be a masochist. The tarmac was strewn with runaway cauliflowers, abandoned cardboard boxes with tyre tracks across them and sad, squashed tomatoes.

As she picked her way around the spoils Dee started to feel clammy with nerves. The humiliations of all her and Andy's interactions so far were piling up on top of each other in her mind, and she was beginning to irrationally resent him for making her feel that way. Right on top of the heap, obviously, was the message she'd sent him suggesting they – she still couldn't think about it without feeling like she'd eaten something she shouldn't have – *cut out the middleman*. Then there was the fact he'd gone out of his way to make it clear that he didn't fancy her, the way she'd flounced off after they'd spoken by the canal . . .

By the time she managed to find her way to the Market Cafe – a serving hatch with some seats outside it at the end of a man-made wind tunnel between two of the market halls – Dee was nearly rigid with cold and embarrassment. She scanned the crowd of traders for Andy, spotting him eventually at the edge with a rucksack between his feet. He was in jeans, Converse and his parka, holding two steaming Styrofoam cups of tea.

'You found it, then,' he said as she approached. Judging by his expression he was even less enthusiastic about being here than she was.

Dee managed to stop herself from saying *no thanks to you*, but only just. She nodded, trying to stop her teeth chattering. At least she might die of hypothermia before she cringed herself to death. Andy passed her one of the cups – although she'd never liked tea she took it, partly out of temperamental politeness and partly because her hands felt like they were turning blue.

'Right, shall we?' He picked his rucksack up and shrugged it on. 'The market closes at six, we need to get a move on or there won't be much left.'

One good thing about Andy, Dee thought as they doubled

back on themselves and he opened what looked like the door to a multi-storey car park's stairwell, was that she didn't have to slow down the way she did with most people: she actually had to speed up to match his pace.

'You've got your jumper on the wrong way round,' he said abruptly as he held the door open for her, and the tiny spark of goodwill she'd been kindling was snuffed out. She took a sip from her cup and tried not to grimace at the bitter taste.

They emerged into a glass-roofed hall laid out like an arcade, with a long row of shops along either side. The signs above them were faded and the names in curlicued writing felt like stills from an old film – *Grapelli's Fine Foods, Knockbeg's of Grantham, P. Albert & Sons* – but the shops themselves were a riot of colour. Dee watched as a man with a clipboard in white gloves ran his hand appraisingly over a pallet of ruffled lettuces, and another buffed ranks of cucumbers with a duster.

Andy pulled a receipt out of his pocket, with a shopping list scribbled on its back in biro.

'We're looking for corn cobs, heritage carrots, more of those sodding green tomatoes . . .' he read without enthusiasm as they walked. 'Oh, and edible flowers. Which never actually get eaten, I've noticed, so they're a complete waste of money – but God forbid the brunching masses of Hackney should have to behold a plate of French toast that doesn't look like something off *Gardeners' Question Time*. If it was up to me I'd scrap them but unfortunately I can't change Angie's menu while she's away.' He put the list back. 'There's quite a lot about this job that I find frustrating, as you may have gathered.'

'Why did you take it, then?' Dee asked, surprising herself with her own bluntness. Andy's was contagious, clearly.

He shrugged. 'I didn't have much of a choice. I've been cooking since I was a teenager, but the older I got the harder I found it: the hours are absolutely brutal, everyone's running on class As and self-loathing, you never see daylight in the winter and the only friends who'll put up with you are in the same line of work. That just wasn't the kind of life I wanted. So a few years ago my ex and I moved out of London and set up this consultancy business: she'd been a general manager and we'd help new restaurants with their recruitment, training, menu development, all that kind of stuff. I say we – it was very much her company and her money behind it. So when we split up just over a year ago, it made sense for me to be the one who moved on to pastures new. I went travelling, found myself and all that – but I realised the only pastures I'm good for involve spending twelve hours a day in a kitchen, which is exactly what I was trying to get away from.'

He stopped in front of a stack of wooden crates overflowing with tomatoes and crouched down to find a price tag. As she watched him Dee felt her attitude towards him softening slightly. They might have next to nothing in common, but they both knew what it was like to be stuck in jobs they didn't want to be doing. That was a start.

'I'm really sorry that happened to you, Andy,' she said. 'It must have been hard.'

'Such is life.' Andy straightened up, shaking his head. 'Six pounds a kilo for those, they must be joking. I don't miss being a consultant, it wasn't as glamorous as it sounds – I mostly just told people to stop serving chips in those stupid little metal baskets. Anyway, what do you do?' He made a face. 'Sorry, it feels weird to be asking you that now – it's like we're doing everything back to front.'

He'd said what she'd been thinking, Dee thought. 'So I'm a copywriter at a creative agency called Anvil . . .' she began. She considered trotting out her usual misleading speech about it being Soho, but she decided she was too tired and cold. What was the point? 'It's pretty bad, to be honest with you,' she went on. 'My boss is an idiot and the pay is terrible but there are so few jobs out there. And in terms of glamour, I raise you our one remaining client, Root and Branch, and their patented leaf-waste-processing machine, the Mulchomatic.'

Andy snorted. 'You just made that up, didn't you?'

'I wish I had . . .' Dee got her phone out, making a mental note to switch it on to airplane mode so any inappropriate messages Minnie might send wouldn't pop up, and found the Mulchomatic on Root and Branch's website. Andy shielded the picture from the neon lights overhead with his hands. They were flecked with burns – the paint-splatter kind you got from boiling oil spitting at you, plus a thin white strip on the back of one near his wrist where he must have touched a hot grill while taking something out of an oven.

'I take it all back.' Andy took his hand away from the screen, then looked down at the cup in Dee's hand. 'You haven't had much of your tea.'

'Oh – no.' Dee pulled a face. 'I'm not really a tea person, actually.'

'Really?' Andy frowned. 'Why did you take it, then?'

He sounded genuinely confused. Dee wasn't really sure how to answer him: it felt like someone asking her why she was breathing. The list of things she'd done over the years because other people were enthusiastic about them was long and varied, ranging from eating oysters to canvassing for the Liberal Democrats. She always said yes because people liked yeses, and she wanted people to like her. But what did she actually have to show for it? And here, now, with Andy, she really didn't have to pretend to be anything she wasn't. They weren't on a date, they never would be on a date, there was no need to worry about trying to present the most appealing version of herself.

'I don't really know,' she said, giving Andy the cup back.

He took it from her without making a big deal about it, and Dee felt a tiny bit more of the tension that had been knotted up inside her start to loosen. The morning wasn't turning out to be quite as bad as she'd been expecting. She wrestled with her jumper so it was the right way round.

'These'll look lovely on some French toast, I think,' she said, pointing at a rack of plastic boxes filled with pansies, snapdragons and cornflowers. Andy laughed.

'Won't they just.' He glanced across at Dee's borrowed wicker bag. 'And we should probably get you a string of onions to put in that thing . . .'

Once they'd found everything on Andy's list they went back to the Market Cafe for floury, ketchup-splattered bacon rolls and walked across the car park with them in paper bags. There was a grass verge at the edge of it, just below the railway line that ran into Waterloo – Andy sat down in a sunny patch, stretching his legs out in front of him, and Dee followed gratefully. They ate their rolls in a silence that felt if not quite companionable, then at least not uncomfortable.

'How are you holding up?' Andy asked when he'd finished. 'I'm used to the early starts but I sometimes forget that not everybody is.'

Dee opened her mouth to reply and a yawn came out. She clapped a hand over her face; they both laughed.

'It's fine, I'm meant to be doing a yoga class after this with Minnie and my other best friend Roo – you know, the one I was telling you sent me all those questions – so hopefully I'll get to have a lie-down then.'

'Whereabouts?' Andy checked the time on his phone. 'We open at ten and I've got about six thousand sweetcorn fritters to prep before then, but if you're going north or east my car's just down there, I can give you a lift.'

His phone's background, she saw, was a photo of a black and white tuxedo cat with Proustian whiskers and a mournful expression. More common ground, Dee thought.

'Is that your cat?'

'He was.' Andy gave her a slightly sad smile. 'He's not dead or anything, I just mean he lives with my ex – his name's Sylvester. He's twelve now and he'll only eat sardines because his sense of smell's gone, so I used to have to take the bins out twice a day. To be honest he's a pain in the arse – but he was my pain in the arse.'

'He sounds a bit like Ronnie, my mum and stepmum's rescue cat – my mum actually cooks for him . . .' Dee got her own phone out and found the video that Alice had sent her the night before, which showed Ronnie sitting sphinx-like on

Ines's laptop, his massive bulk spilling over the sides ('It's fine, Ronnie, I don't need my keyboard. Or my screen,' Ines's resigned voice came from somewhere out of shot).

'Christ, what are they feeding him, fertiliser?' Andy grinned. 'I'm joking, he's gorgeous. And good on them for giving him a home.'

'I don't think my stepmum had much choice, really – Ines always says that she wanted a dog and mum wanted a cat, so they compromised and got a cat. She's so great with Ronnie, though, she's an incredibly caring person.' A note of pride always crept into Dee's voice when she talked about Ines. 'Sorry, I never thanked you for offering me a lift – I think the place I'm meant to be going to is behind Oxford Circus, but let me check . . .'

She was scrolling back through her chat with Roo and Minnie to find the address when an email notification popped up at the top of her screen. *Karl Jensen*, it said. Her stomach turned over and she groaned.

Andy gave her a concerned look. 'Everything all right?'

'Sorry, it's just my dad.' Dee put her phone away, hoping Andy couldn't see how rattled she was. 'Him and my mum split up when I was really young and we didn't see each other for ages, but he won't leave me alone now.'

'Doesn't sound so bad to me.' Andy balled up the bag his bacon roll had come in.

In spite of how well they'd been getting on just now and the growing sympathy she'd been feeling for him, Dee bristled. She couldn't stop herself thinking back to all the conversations she'd had with Nat about their families – whatever his faults he'd understood, and Andy obviously didn't.

'I'm guessing your parents never got divorced, then,' she said tartly.

Andy gave her a look she couldn't quite decipher.

'You're right, they didn't,' he replied very slowly. He chucked the balled-up bag into the bin to their left. 'They never got the chance to, because my dad died when I was thirteen.'

Dee wished the ground would swallow her. How could she have played the tiny violin like that about her parents when one of his was actually dead?

'I'm really sorry, Andy,' she said quietly, her face burning up. 'I'm an idiot.'

'It's all right, my tragic childhood was a long time ago.' Andy got to his feet. 'And you're absolutely not an idiot – everyone's dealing with something, aren't they? Sure I can't give you a lift? You can choose the radio station so long as it's Radio 2.'

Dee, still cringing with every muscle in her body, mumbled something that made no sense about wanting to stay here for a bit.

'Sure? All right, well, we should get something else in the diary, shouldn't we?' Andy ran a hand through his hair; in the week since they'd last seen each other it had lost its awkward, just-cut look. 'You can plan our next outing if you like.'

Dee felt her pulse returning to somewhere more like normal. 'I'm not sure how I can top a picnic next to a railway line, but I'll try.'

'Just as long as it doesn't involve edible flowers . . .' Andy grinned. 'All right, I'll message you when I get off work later. Good luck with yoga.'

As she watched him walking back towards the car park the sun came out from behind a cloud, and the warmth on her skin was so unexpected that it made her feel for just a second like she was on holiday. A very strange, stressful, sleep-deprived sort of holiday – but a holiday nonetheless. She waited until Andy had disappeared, then got her phone out again and opened her dad's email.

Hey there, kiddo! Thought you might enjoy this photo of yours truly back in the day. I'll tell you the story behind it when we next see each other, which I hope will be soon. Dad x

Dee's finger hovered over the delete icon. She came within a couple of millimetres of pressing it, but didn't.

After her parents had split up, Karl had gradually disappeared from Dee's life. But it hadn't been a smooth fade-out, like someone dialling down the colour saturation on a digital photo. There had been periods of weeks or months before he left the country when he and Dee had seen a lot of each other: they would do touristy things like riding around on an open-top bus and eating roasted nuts out of paper cones on Waterloo Bridge. But every time, just as Dee was starting to relax into the rhythm of seeing him regularly, Karl would disappear again, hollowing out Dee's weekends and leaving her to pick through her memories of their outings like an archaeologist, wondering what she'd done to drive him away. Then he'd reappear with enthusiasm but no explanation or apology, and the cycle would repeat itself.

On the day Karl had told her he was moving to America he'd given Dee one of his T-shirts. It had a laughing cartoon hamburger on it and smelled of him: when Dee pressed her face into it she could almost feel his hand resting on the top of her head at Paddington station when they'd been waiting for the train back to Hanwell. She'd kept it under her pillow for weeks, only to come home from school to find that Alice had stripped the entire bed and unknowingly put everything – including the T-shirt – in the wash. When Dee got it back the smell had gone. And this time, Karl really had too.

They didn't really speak for years. Then, on Dee's eighteenth birthday, an enormous bunch of hothouse flowers arrived for her at Milton Road, with a card from him. Ines said maybe he was trying to turn over a new leaf, but Dee found it impossible not to be cynical. Of course her dad wanted her back in his life now – she was an adult, which meant that (in theory, anyway) she didn't actually need anything from him. He could do bugger all without feeling guilty about it.

Still, she went along with his suggestions to meet up whenever he was in London. Just like they had when she was younger, they did touristy things: they took a Thames boat trip and went round Borough Market, eating as many samples from the stalls as they could get away with. Karl had a talent for having fun, but Dee couldn't honestly say that was how their time together felt: she was always on edge around her dad, waiting for history to repeat itself. Karl didn't seem to notice her discomfort – he was an eternal optimist, and his optimism made him careless. He breezed through life never looking back and just expected everyone else to do the same.

It had almost been a relief when their last planned meeting had gone so wrong. It was a week before her thirtieth birthday, and Karl (who was visiting to speak at a sustainable festival) had suggested dinner at The Shard. He still had connections in the London restaurant world, he'd boasted, and he could get them a table right by the window. Dee had never been to The Shard, and in spite of herself she felt excitement bubbling up as the lift whisked her to the thirty-first floor. Karl had indeed managed to get a table next to the window, and there was a frosty glass of champagne waiting for her on it.

Half an hour passed, then an hour. Dee sat with her drink getting warm in front of her, an old, familiar sickness brewing in the pit of her stomach. Eventually someone with a badge came and crouched down next to her: if the other person wasn't joining her, perhaps she could eat at the bar? There was a queue of walk-ins and they really needed the table. Dee paid for the champagne and left. Karl left her a voicemail later that night, full of apologies – he'd been on a train that had broken down, his phone had run out of battery, he hadn't been able to charge it. After she'd deleted the message, Dee changed his name in her phone's address book from 'Dad' to 'Karl Jensen'. She did it to prove to herself that she didn't care about him any more. But she knew it really just showed how much she still did.

Chapter Nine

'Look, you keep telling me I need to make a plan, that's all I'm doing,' Dee whispered to Roo as they sat cross-legged at the back of the yoga studio later that afternoon.

'I'm not sure that going shopping with this man counts as a plan, Dee.' Roo manoeuvred one leg to the front of her mat and aggressively stretched it like she was about to run a marathon. 'No offence to either of you.'

'None taken,' Dee muttered, although actually she *was* a bit offended. Maybe it was the early start making her over-sensitive, she thought as she attempted the same stretch that Roo was doing, but Roo seemed to be in an especially tetchy mood today. Why couldn't she just be happy that Dee had had a better time with Andy than she'd expected to?

Stretching her other leg, Roo glanced across the empty mat to Dee's left, which they'd brought in for Minnie. 'Where is she? Honestly, this was her idea and she's twenty minutes late – the class is about to start . . .'

The yoga teacher, who'd been working her way around the room, appeared in front of them with a trio of spray bottles on a little bamboo tray.

'Can I offer you two an essential oil spritz before we begin?' she asked in a cashmere-soft voice. 'There's soothing camomile, energising peppermint and relaxing lavender.'

'Definitely not the last one,' Roo said firmly. Dee looked at her. 'What? I find relaxation stressful. Energising, please.'

'Soothing for me,' Dee said quickly. 'And can I have double? Thanks.'

After she'd sprayed them the teacher glided to the front of the studio and clapped her hands gently to get everyone's attention.

'We're going to start today's practice now,' she said with a smile. 'This is hatha yoga, so we'll be moving our bodies very *slowly* and *deliberately* while focusing on relaxing and being mindful. We're all coming to this with different experiences, so if at any point you'd like some foam blocks to make the poses easier please just raise your hand. OK, when you're ready I'd like you to move to your table position, then arch your back in cat pose and let it hollow out as you become a cow . . .'

Just then the studio door flew open and Minnie breezed in. She was carrying a TK Maxx bag and was dressed like Rizzo from *Grease* in shimmery black leggings and a pink denim jacket over a white vest.

'Sorry! Sorry!' she stage-whispered as she picked her way around the matts. 'I forgot to pack my sports bra so I stopped off in Covent Garden to pick one up, but I slipped and fell into a rail of *ridiculously* cheap Agent Provocateur . . .'

'I don't know if you've noticed, Minnie,' Roo whispered urgently, 'but the class has started . . .'

'Hello to you too, Roo! I know, I know, I'm the absolute worst.' Minnie dumped her things down on the floor, shrugged her jacket off and settled herself on her hands and knees on the free mat. 'Hiya, Dee! Ooh, I know what I was going to tell you, I was reading this article about platonic co-parenting on the tube – apparently when it comes to conception most straight co-parents opt for the old-fashioned approach . . .'

She gave Dee a *Carry On* nudge and a wink. Roo made a noise like a car backfiring. Dee, her face on fire, caught the yoga teacher's eye – even she was looking pretty un-serene now.

'Sooo, when you're ready we're going to move from cat pose into a downward facing dog,' the teacher said with exaggerated calm; Dee could have kissed her. 'Try to hold it for at least five breaths, and keep your weight evenly distributed – lengthen your tailbone and lift your sit bones.'

Dee got herself into position; almost immediately her shoulders started screaming at her. Next to her Roo, who had applied herself to studying yoga with her usual dedication, was frowning with concentration (although she might just have been frowning at Minnie). As far as Dee knew, Minnie had never done yoga before in her life, but all the dance lessons she'd done as a teenager meant she was a natural.

'I'm so excited for you and Andy, Dee!' she went on, with no reduction in volume from being upside down. She turned her head in Roo's direction, her tied-up curls bobbing in the air. 'Don't you think it's exciting? I know I kept calling him Grumpy Andy but he's nice really, I think. One of those gruff Northerners with a heart of gold.'

'I'm sure he is,' Roo said in the voice of someone trying to explain to a child why they couldn't just eat ice cream for every meal. 'But even putting everything else aside, Andy's life doesn't sound very settled or stable to me. Is he really in a position to think about becoming a parent?'

Dee could feel the un-asked follow-up question hanging in the air between them.

Are you, Dee?

'Excuse me, he has a job,' she protested, 'and a car . . .'

'So did Ted Bundy, to be fair . . .' Minnie inhaled with ease, then exhaled. 'But anyway, if you *do* have a baby this'll make such a great story to tell your grandkids, won't it? I mean, ideally the cafe you met at would be in rural France, and you'd have just moved there to heal your broken heart – oh, and Andy would be French, of course . . .'

Although she was businesslike when it came to her own love life, Minnie was an avid consumer of Netflix seasonal romances – she had the *Christmas Prince* trilogy on repeat throughout December, and had once watched *A Castle For Christmas* six times in a week.

'Ideally Dee wouldn't be making any rash decisions,' Roo said with as much finality as someone with their bottom in their air could. 'And whatever it is that they're doing, Dee and Andy aren't dating – she's been very clear about that.' She turned her head to Dee. 'Have you heard from the fertility counsellor yet? If you haven't by Monday, I really think you should phone her. Or I can.'

Dee's arms were shaking with the effort of holding the pose. Relax, she told herself. *Relax, relax, relax.*

The yoga teacher tiptoed up to her silently and deposited two foam blocks at the top of her mat.

The studio's showers were the luxurious waterfall kind. Dee stood under hers for about twice as long as she needed to, relishing not having to worry about accidentally knocking the shower out of its holder with the top of her head and drenching the room like she did at Hiro's. She squeezed more Aesop body wash into her palm (her blood type was going to be Geranium Leaf if she carried on at this rate) and lathered it up. This was the second time today that she'd felt average-sized, and she was enjoying it. Also, she wasn't in a hurry to get stuck in the middle of Roo and Minnie again.

When she eventually stepped out into the changing room she saw that Minnie, who still hadn't showered, was talking animatedly to the yoga teacher by the sinks in her towel, waving her arms to bring the story she was telling to life. As she watched them laughing together like they'd known each other their entire lives, Dee wondered if she'd ever effortlessly charmed anyone. No, she decided – she might have managed *effortful* charm a few times, but nothing like this. It was easy to see why Minnie was so brilliant at her job: people hired her to sprinkle stardust over their parties, and she did so without fail. As Minnie herself said only half-jokingly, she was an event herself.

Roo, who was already fully dressed (she was meeting her in-laws for a holiday-planning dinner at six), came over from the lockers, vigorously towelling her hair.

'I wish I could do that,' she said, looking at Minnie. 'Hey ho, at least most of my patients are unconscious – no charm required.'

Dee wondered, not for the first time, if Roo had actually read her mind; after the way that their conversation before the class had gone, it was a reassuring feeling. They both watched Minnie skip into a shower, tossing her towel over the door behind her with a burlesque flourish.

'I got my period this morning,' Roo said suddenly, in such a normal voice that for a second Dee didn't realise what she was saying. 'It was two days late. I'm never late, and I really thought I might be . . . You know. Anyway, I'm not. So, there you go.'

She dropped her own towel into the laundry basket next to them.

'I'd already added a Bugaboo to my Amazon basket,' she went on as she replaced the lid, not looking at Dee. 'Can you believe that?'

'Oh, Roo . . .'

Dee's throat felt tight. She imagined Roo allowing herself to hope as she scrolled through Amazon listings and felt like someone was squeezing her heart in a vice. As she put an arm around her best friend she wanted to tell her that she knew what it was like to want more than you had, and to worry you would never get it. That nothing made you feel more lonely. That she understood, or was trying to. But the words all felt embarrassingly hollow, and she was overwhelmed by guilt. And before she could say anything, Roo had detached herself from the hug.

'I'd better get going,' she said, and Dee's heart sank: she knew that whatever Roo had needed in that moment, she hadn't been able to give it to her. 'Will you say goodbye to Minnie from me? I know she'll be ages.'

'Cambridge's medical school has twice as many students as Oxford's – hmm, I'm not sure if that's a good thing or a bad . . .'

Fourteen-year-old Roo, who was spending her Saturday

going through a sheaf of university prospectuses with a high-lighter, tailed off.

'You're being very quiet,' she said to Dee, flicking her plait over her shoulder. 'What's wrong?'

Dee was sitting next to Roo on Roo's neatly made bed, holding a university prospectus of her own. It was for Sheffield (she was going through a Pulp phase), but it could have been anywhere really: the words had been dancing meaninglessly in front of her eyes ever since she'd opened it.

'Mum and North Face Richard broke up last night,' she said, folding the corner of a page down, then back on itself. 'He was the one who ended it.'

'That's good, isn't it? Now you don't have to go on any more long rainy walks on Sundays.' Roo got her can of Fanta from the bedside table and raised it in a toast. 'Good riddance to him and his fleeces, that's what I say. What a silly man, though, he'll never do better than your mum – she's gorgeous and he has Monty Python sketches where his personality should be. Also his trousers were always far too short.'

'He wasn't the worst boyfriend she's ever had,' Dee shrugged; her shoulders felt like they had rocks on them. 'He wasn't actively bad like Colin the Dickhead. He was just sort of . . . inert.'

'Like argon,' Roo nodded in agreement (she was angling to take her Chemistry GCSE a year early). 'How's your mum taking it?'

Dee grimaced. 'Badly. She called in sick from work, she can't stop crying. They've already had a go at her for taking too much time off this month. I just . . .'

She didn't need to finish the sentence. She'd told Roo everything the first time Roo had stayed over, sleeping top to toe with her in the wobbly bed that had been there when she and her mum had moved into the flat – she'd felt she owed Roo an explanation for how different their home lives were. Roo had listened very attentively, then hugged her and never mentioned it again.

Now, Roo put the Fanta down again, and put a hand on Dee's arm.

'Dee, it isn't going to happen again,' she said quietly. 'Honestly.'

Which bit? Dee thought as she fought back tears. *My mum losing her job or my mum trying to kill herself?* She looked around Roo's bedroom, the only bedroom Roo had ever had: the Gills had bought their house before Roo was born. Downstairs Mr Gill was in the kitchen making up a snack tray for them with peanuts and Mini Cheddars ('Brain food!' he'd always announce when he brought it up to them) while Mrs Gill talked to her sister, one of Roo's four aunties, on the phone in the living room.

'I wish I lived here with you, Roo,' Dee said in a monotone, then instantly felt sick with guilt at having abandoned Alice, even only for a second in her imagination.

'Trust me, you really don't,' Roo said emphatically. 'My mum still times me brushing my teeth and having a dad who's a coroner is a nightmare. Remember when we went to Splash Pad for my birthday and he kept going on about how you can drown in three inches of water? The manager had to ask him to wait outside in the end, people were complaining.'

Dee tried to force herself to smile at the memory, but she

couldn't. Mrs Gill's laughter drifted up the stairs towards them, and she pictured Roo's auntie laughing on the other end of the line – and all her other aunties, and her cousins, and the grandparents she'd gone to India to see over the Easter holidays, surrounding her in a protective circle. Safety in numbers, she thought. That was what Roo had.

'Mum's all I've got, Roo,' she said in a voice that was barely a whisper.

Roo looked shocked.

'That is *not* true, Dee,' she said fiercely, squeezing Dee's arm. 'You'll always have me – and I will *always* look out for you.'

Dee tried to listen to a podcast on the way back to Hiro's but she couldn't concentrate: she was worrying too much about Roo. She thought about all the knowledge she'd amassed about her over nearly a quarter of a century – the way the tip of Roo's tongue poked out when she was reading, the crush she'd had on Tony Robinson in *Time Team*, the fact she washed her back with Head and Shoulders once a week because she was convinced it stopped it getting spotty. But did any of that really mean anything if they couldn't say the right things to each other now? Even now, sitting on the tube with her phone in her hand and her chat with Roo open, she kept starting messages then second-guessing herself and deleting them. She didn't end up sending her anything.

Dee found Hiro and Poodle lying on the carpet in the living room with the record player and a small mountain of empty takeaway cartons between them.

'Dee! Hey! You're back!' Hiro raised himself on his elbows

unsteadily, and nearly fell over as he swept an arm across the floor. 'I got you some crispy chilli beef, I know it's your favourite . . .'

'We got day-drunk and now we're going to be night-hungover.' Poodle giggled; she was dressed in a purple velvet catsuit with stirrups for feet. Hiro rolled on to his front and stifled a burp.

'Are you all right to crash on the sofa again tonight, Dee?' he asked. 'Sorry . . .'

That explained the beef. There weren't any curtains in the living room and Dee had really been hoping to have a lie-in.

'Of course,' she said quickly, turning towards the bedroom. 'I'll just go and get my stuff.'

Hiro waved a hand in the air. 'No rush, we're going out for drinks – take your time.'

He got to his feet and wobbled off towards the hall. Poodle sat up and did a cat-like yawn.

'I'm so sorry about your guy, sweetie. Hiro told me,' she said, putting a manicured hand on Dee's foot. 'But honestly, I was single for a long time and I'm really glad things panned out that way – it gave me so much time to work out what really made me happy. Maybe that'll be your story too.'

Dee tried to imagine herself as someone like Poodle, who lived glamorously at the top of a mansion block in Maida Vale with a Maine Coon named Elizabeth Taylor. It was a stretch.

Hiro reappeared with their coats. 'Come on, wife-to-be,' he said unsteadily, helping Poodle into her leopard-print bomber jacket. 'You head downstairs, I just need to talk to Dee for a sec.'

Something about the way he was avoiding her eye made Dee's stomach drop.

'Is everything all right?' she asked as Poodle shut the door behind her, trying to keep her voice steady.

'Yeah, yeah – totally!' Hiro still couldn't look at her. 'I just, er, thought I should let you know that Poodle and I have decided to move in together before the wedding, get some practice at the whole married life thing.'

'Wow, that's great!' Dee's voice was at least an octave too high. The beef, she realised with creeping dread, had been nothing to do with sleeping on the sofa. Something much worse was heading her way.

'Yeah, it is. But obviously she's got loads of stuff, and I've got loads of stuff too . . .' Hiro waved awkwardly at the groaning clothes rail in the corner of the living room. 'So we're looking at renting a bigger place together. Which means . . .'

He didn't need to finish the sentence. Dee felt a horrible, anxious fizzing starting up at the base of her spine. This was the closest thing she'd had to a home for years, and she was going to lose it.

'It's really early days, we haven't even had this place valued for letting yet,' Hiro said quickly, the words all tumbling out on top of each other; he looked exactly like Kirsty the GP had when she'd broken the news to Dee. 'I just wanted you to be the first to know. So you can, you know – start thinking. About where you're going to go when I have to start properly renting it out at the full market rate.'

After Hiro and Poodle had gone, Dee moved her duvet and pillows through to the living room then crawled into her makeshift bed, trying to squash down the panic that was gripping her. It would be months before the new tenants arrived, she told herself. But months wouldn't change the fact that the rent she was paying him would barely cover a room in a shared house – and seeing as Jonas had only just moved in there wasn't much chance of a room coming up at Minnie's any time soon. So she'd be living with strangers probably, just like she had when she was twenty-five.

She got her phone out, desperately wanting to bury her head in the digital sand. Both Minnie and Roo had messaged their group chat.

Minnie:
Is Mercury in retrograde?

Roo:
I have no idea what you're
talking about

Minnie:
I'm just really bloated this
week. Sometimes planetary
alignments can do that

Roo:
Minnie, I'm sorry, but that's
nonsense. Hormones and
salt cause water retention. It
has nothing to do with the
planets

Minnie:
That's such a Capricorn thing
to say 🌚

She had another notification, she saw. Andy had messaged, just like he'd said he would.

Andy:
Guess how many edible
flowers got eaten today?
I'll give you a hint, it was
none
I hope your day's been more
successful

Dee:
It was until about five
minutes ago . . .

He replied straight away. Dee blinked, surprised; being with Nat had meant seriously adjusting her expectations of response times. A twenty-four-hour wait barely registered now.

Andy:
Anything I can help with?

Dee:
It's OK, thanks Andy

145

I don't really want to talk
about it

Andy:
Understood
Well, the offer's there
Anyway, these questions you
were saying your friend Roo
sent you
You know, the ones about
platonic co-parenting

Dee:
What about them 😶

Andy:
Should we . . . go through
them?

Dee:
What, now?

Andy:
Well, not all of them. We
could make a start though.
Do one every time we see
each other, maybe

146

It's Complicated

Dee:
OK . . . sure! Why not? I'll
screenshot her email, hang on
Here you go

Andy:
Blimey, straight in at the
deep end . . .
Let me just put the kettle on

Dee:
Isn't it a bit late for tea,
Andrew?

Andy:
No it bloody isn't, D . . .
Is Dee short for anything?

Dee:
Diana
I was named after
the Princess of Wales
My mum was a big fan

Andy:
Really??!?

Dee:
I don't know why you're
laughing

I too am tall and extremely
stylish

Andy:
And I'm sure you're very
involved in charitable causes
All right, where shall we
start?

Dee:
Hmm
Maybe question two?
'What are your career
plans?'
Well, personally I'd like to
not be paid in burritos
Which is a thing that has
actually happened to me

Andy:
Wow. That's . . . bleak
Princess Diana never had to
put up with that shit

Dee:
Indeed she didn't
How about you?
Three Michelin stars?
A spot on *Masterchef: The
Professionals?*

Andy:
God, no, none of that
I'm not even sure I want to
stick with cooking
But like I said, it's all I've ever
done
I got my first kitchen job
when I was fourteen

Dee:
That's young
What made you decide to
stick with it?

Andy:
I ask myself that question a lot
It wasn't that long after my
dad died, I suppose
I liked being out of the
house, being busy
You don't get any time to
stop and think
And because you're always
working with the same
people you feel like . . .

Dee:
. . . a family?

Andy:
Yeah
That's it, exactly
You actually call the meal
you all have before service
'family dinner'

Well, I think that's the first
question done
Wasn't so bad was it?

Dee:
It wasn't! Well done us

Chapter Ten

Minnie popped her head up over the top of Hiro's monitor.

'Are you done yet, Dee?' she asked, yawning. 'Jonas's classes are super popular – it's five now, we need to get going if we want to bag a locker . . .'

It was Tuesday afternoon, ten days after yoga. Minnie had turned up at Dee's office uninvited shortly before three o'clock – she and Dee were meant to be going to one of Jonas's spin classes at Boombox after work, which Jonas had given them free passes for, before having pizza at Minnie's. Minnie had spent the next two hours wandering around the office fiddling with things and generally driving everyone mad, leaving a trail of lidless biros and discarded magazines in her wake. Now, she did a slow spin on Hiro's chair – he'd said he was going out to get a snack, but Dee strongly suspected that he was hiding in the bathroom until Hurricane Minnie had blown through.

Dee tried to focus on the email from Roo that had just appeared in her inbox. Like a bailiff, she'd sent it to Dee's work account so Dee couldn't pretend not to have seen it.

Good news: I spoke to my friend at the Whittington, and she's got you a last-minute appointment with the fertility

counsellor – somebody cancelled so a spot opened up.
Anyway, it's at 10 a.m. on Monday 22nd.

Monday 22nd was Dee's birthday. Maybe this was
Roo's idea of a present, Dee thought as she clicked out of
the message, a now-familiar lump starting to harden in her
throat. They'd been messaging each other with their usual
frequency, sharing the same sorts of links to articles and
tweets that they normally did. But it felt to Dee like a draw-
bridge had been pulled up – Roo hadn't mentioned the fact
she'd thought she might be pregnant again, and Dee knew
in her bones that she'd failed her in her hour of need. And
talking to Roo about her own life right now felt like a no-win
situation: if she brought up Andy, Roo would probably give
her another lecture and things between them would get even
weirder, and if she didn't then that would be one more thing
she wasn't telling her.

The email underneath Roo's was from Morag. It contained
a PDF of the brochure copy Dee had sent over, marked up
with Morag's corrections. They were textbook Morag: lots
about *omnichannel brand amplification* and *customer journeys*.
*Sorry to only just be reverting to you on this one, I needed to bring
in all the key stakeholders*, she'd written at the bottom of the
document. *The feeling around the table is that it's time to back-
source this, because we're losing control of the messaging. We want
to revamp and reboot the format – and to do that we need to estab-
lish a base set of Lego pieces that we can then fine-tune as we grow
horizontal solutions. This is no time to bite the bullet!*

'Roo's off to Craggy Island next week, isn't she?' Minnie
went on, opening one of Hiro's drawers and peering into it.

'It's going to be so shit for her having no reception, I'd literally die. And sorry to say it, but that house they're staying in definitely looks haunted.' She pulled out a stack of pastel Post-its and flicked through them impatiently. 'Dee, come *on*, it's five past five now . . .'

Dee sighed. 'I'll just let the agency's only client know I can't look at their feedback on the fifty-per-cent-off flyer right now because I'm going to the gym with you, shall I?'

'I tell you who's going to have *considerably* more than fifty per cent off tonight,' Minnie announced. 'Jonas teaches shirtless sometimes, apparently he "runs hot".' She did another chair-twirl that sent her skidding chest-first into the lamp Hiro had clipped to the corner of his desk. 'Ow. That hurt.'

On the screen Morag's words danced even more meaninglessly than usual in front of Dee's eyes.

'OK, fine,' she said, closing the email in defeat. 'Let's go.'

Minnie clapped her hands in delight and jumped off the chair, then skipped round to Dee's desk to plonk a kiss on her cheek.

As they walked down the stairs Dee checked her phone to see if Andy had messaged. He had: in the week and a bit since they'd last seen each other at the market they had abandoned Roo's list of questions and moved on to one of their own. Right now they were talking about their favourite foods.

> Dee:
> OK, if you could only eat
> one carbohydrate for the
> rest of your life, what would
> it be?

Andy:
You want me to say 'oven
chips', don't you?
Well, I'm not playing your
game, Jensen

Dee:
Curses, foiled again . . .

Andy:
I'm going to go against type
here and say pasta

Dee:
Same! When you come
round to mine I'll do you the
house special

Andy:
Which is?

Dee:
Philadelphia carbonara. Pasta
bows, half a tub of cream
cheese, slices of ham

Andy:
I don't know what to say,
Dee. Pasta bows?!?! Slices
of ham?!?!?!

> Dee:
> I grate cheddar over the top,
> too

Andy:
This changes things

> Dee:
> Don't knock it until you've
> tried it . . .

'Oooooh, you're talking to *Andy*,' Minnie said, slowing down to snoop at Dee's screen as they left the office. 'God, you two message loads, don't you? You never message me this much.'

Boombox's reception area was a sea of swishy ponytails and Lululemon co-ordinated sets.

'I didn't realise this place was a female-only gym,' Dee said in wonder to Minnie as they went to pick up their shoes from the front desk.

'Oh, it isn't – this is just what happens when Jonas is teaching,' Minnie replied brightly. She stepped up to the desk and beamed at the ponytailed man who was checking members in. 'Hiya! There's two of us for the six o'clock spin class, Minnie Marks and Dee Jensen. I'm a size five and Dee here's a nine.'

The man looked pained. 'We don't actually go that big in the women's shoes, I'm afraid . . .' he said apologetically to Dee. 'Is an eight OK? Or you can have a male pair?'

Dee knew from bitter experience that an eight definitely wouldn't be fine. But the thought of having to take a pair of men's shoes was too humiliating.

'I'll manage with the smaller size!' she said, and he passed a pair over the counter. She tucked them reluctantly under her arm and followed Minnie to the changing room, getting her phone out to reply to Andy's last message.

Andy:
I don't think I will be trying it

Dee:
If I make it for you, you'll
have to

'Andy again, is it?' Minnie said, craning her neck. 'How many times a day do you message each other, would you say?'

'I don't know, a normal amount?' Dee said, more firmly than she'd meant to. She started getting changed, hoping that would be the end of the discussion; after spending all day trying to decipher Morag's impenetrable screeds she had a headache, and she really wasn't in the mood.

The spin studio was down a flight of industrial-looking stairs in the basement. Dee and Minnie, who'd changed into a heather-purple cropped top and leggings set, joined the end of the long line that had formed outside it. The two women in front of them were talking about Jonas.

'He was in my dream last night,' the one on the left was saying to her friend, who was wearing the same outfit as

Minnie but in grey. 'So we were on an oil rig in a storm, and . . .'

Dee shuffled back in her too-small shoes, kicking herself for not having just taken the men's ones.

Minnie was fanning herself. 'God, it's hot down here, isn't it?' She whipped off her top to reveal a matching sports bra. As its hem bumped against her chest she winced.

'Ow,' she said loudly. '*Ow*. God, my tits have been incredibly sore for ages. It's like having two rocks strapped to my front . . .'

Minnie's outfit twin turned around and gave Minnie a kind smile. 'Something that really helped me with breast tenderness when I was expecting was ginger tea,' she said. 'You just have a cup first thing – the Holland and Barrett own-brand stuff is great.'

Minnie burst out laughing. 'Hahaha, oh my God, no, not like that! I'm not pregnant – this is one hundred per cent Maryland chocolate chip cookies.' She patted her stomach and gave the woman a good-natured grin. 'Thanks, though!'

A ripple of excitement went through the line. Dee turned and saw Jonas coming down the stairs, wearing a white singlet and red shorts like he'd just stepped off the set of *Baywatch* and a microphone headset. Minnie jumped up and down and waved manically at him; when Jonas spotted her his face lit up.

'You are here!' he beamed when he got to them. His hair was still damp from the shower and he smelled like a steelworks in a pine forest. 'I saved you two bikes on the second row, twenty-three and twenty-four – I already adjusted them so they are the right height.' He looked at Dee. 'I remembered you are very tall, so yours I set up as I would for a man,' he said, completely without malice. 'Haha!'

'Ha,' Dee replied weakly. Her left foot had started to go numb.

The spin studio was nightclub-dark and reverberating with pounding techno music. As they clattered in, Jonas was leaning casually against the instructor's bike on the podium, taking what appeared to be a series of very pressing spin-related questions from female attendees. Dee and Minnie found their bikes; hers, Dee was dismayed to see, was indeed the perfect height for her.

As they clipped themselves in and started pedalling to warm up, Dee couldn't help noticing that Minnie wasn't speaking. The last time they'd gone to a gym class together (a free barre taster session) she'd talked so much during the pliés that they'd been asked to leave. The silence was unsettling.

'Wow, she's *putting on perfume*,' Dee whispered to get the conversation going again, nodding at a woman on the front row who'd produced a tiny bottle from the back pocket of her leggings and was now enthusiastically applying its contents to her pulse points. 'I wonder if Jonas just thinks the world smells of Chanel, like the Queen does with fresh paint.'

Minnie gave the woman a cursory glance. 'That's funny!' she said with about a quarter of her usual enthusiasm. She pedalled half-heartedly for a bit, then turned to Dee. 'I defin-itely can't be pregnant,' she muttered under her breath, and when her eyes met Dee's they were full of something Dee couldn't remember ever having seen in them before: doubt. 'Can I?'

'Well, you haven't slept with anyone recently, so ...'
Minnie, Dee noticed as she slowed her legs down, was chewing her lip. '*Have* you slept with anyone recently?'

Minnie looked away again. 'No,' she said, staring at the ceiling. A beat. 'I mean, not really.'

Dee stopped. 'What does "not really" mean?' she whispered, swivelling in her saddle to face Minnie. 'And who?'

Jonas leapt on to his podium bike. 'Hello, Boombox!' he shouted into the microphone as the opening beat of Primal Scream's 'Rocks' started blasting out of the speakers. 'Are you ready to have a party?' Everyone whooped and cheered. 'It sounds to me as though you are! OK, please to add three full turns to your dials ...'

Minnie looked back at Dee. She was chewing her lip.

Dee's eyes widened. 'Wait ... what? *Jonas?* Minnie, are you being serious?'

Minnie suddenly unclipped her shoes from the pedals. 'Let's go,' she whispered hoarsely, grabbing Dee's hand. 'I'll say I felt ill or something.'

Dee hobbled out of the studio after her, hopping from foot to foot to get her shoes off.

The changing room was empty. Minnie went and sat on the bench furthest from the door, balling her top up in her hands. Dee followed her. She could feel the music coming through the floor.

'Why didn't you say, Minnie?' she asked as she sat down. 'When was this?'

'After we got back from the first run we did together.' Minnie sighed dramatically. 'He pinged his quad so I offered to give him a massage. We got a bit carried away

159

and we ended up . . . fooling around, and then I guess we technically had a *bit* of sex, but he didn't . . .' She pulled a face. 'You know. Nothing actually *happened*. It was literally only for, like, ten seconds. Then we both decided it was a bad idea, what with us living together.' She looked at the floor. 'Sorry, Dee. I should have told you and Roo, but I thought you'd tell me off – well, I thought Roo would, anyway . . .'

Dee had a guilty flashback to her and Roo's conversation at the Wetland Centre.

The two of them sat in silence for a moment. Minnie gave her chest a poke.

'They really do hurt,' she said, frowning. 'And my last period was ages ago. I don't feel sick, though, which is a good sign – right?'

'I'm probably not the best person to ask . . .' Dee nudged a knee gently against Minnie's. 'But I mean, if you're worried, you could do a pregnancy test? We could stop at a chemist on the way back to yours.'

'Oh, I'm not really worried,' Minnie said, unconvincingly. 'Like I said, nothing actually *happened*.' She went quiet again and put her head on one side. 'I could just do one anyway though, couldn't I? Might as well.'

Half an hour later Dee stood outside the pharmacy on Haggerston Road, waiting for Minnie to emerge. It was six thirty – normally Roo would be on her train home, Dee thought as she got her phone out and went into their chat.

I've just narrowly escaped going to Jonas's spin class. How's your day been? x

Dee could see Minnie through the window, laughing and chatting to an assistant as she paid. She knew that if Roo was here she'd remind them of the time that Minnie had gone to A & E with what she thought was a brain tumour but which had turned out to be a migraine caused by eating an entire Aero Easter egg.

Oh, you know, same old. I'm starting packing for the holiday tonight, the weather forecast looks biblical. Say hi to Minnie from me x

Just then Minnie trotted out of the pharmacy, carrying two cellophane-wrapped oblongs with 'Clearblue' printed on them. Dee quickly stuffed her phone back into her bag, as though Roo might somehow be able to see what was going on through WhatsApp.

'They were BOGOF so I got two,' Minnie said, fanning herself with the tests, before pulling out a bright red lip gloss and swiping it on. 'And this was half price because the lid's got a scratch on it! Good, eh?' She replaced the lip, stuffed it into the pocket of her shirt and held the test aloft. 'To Casa del Marks!'

They walked along the edge of Stonebridge Gardens towards Kingsland Road.

'What if Jonas comes home while I'm doing the pregnancy test?' Minnie said, carefully folding a strip of her favourite strawberry-flavoured gum into her mouth to avoid the lip gloss. 'I'm not sure what I'd say to him if he asked me why I was weeing on a stick. I suppose I'd have to say it was a lateral flow test and pretend that's how I thought you were meant to do them.'

'Or you could just . . . shut the bathroom door?' Dee suggested; it didn't matter how much time she spent on it, Planet Minnie – a place where you apparently peed in front of your very attractive male flatmates – still felt entirely alien to her.

Minnie didn't seem to have heard. 'Maybe we could stop at Andy's and do it there,' she mused. 'He lives round here, I think. I'm sure he wouldn't mind if we stopped by, we'd be really quick. Ooh, now I know we said we were getting pizza at mine for dinner, but maybe he'd make us something! Maybe we could stop at the Turkish grocer and pick up some of that bread I really like . . .'

As she struggled to parse this latest abstract poem of a thought-chain, Dee realised that she'd nearly missed something important. 'Hang on, how do you know where Andy lives?'

'He told me when I went to the cafe last weekend,' Minnie replied blithely, unwrapping a second piece of gum. 'He still won't make me pancakes, the bastard, but we had a nice natter. Pretty shit about his mum moving to New Zealand and them basically never seeing each other now, isn't it? She literally got on a plane with a one-way ticket the day after he turned eighteen – bye bye, Andy, see you in five years maybe, if you're lucky.' She shook her head. 'Although to be honest with you, I reckon Rabbi Debbie would be thrilled if I was on the other side of the world, I'm very bad for business . . .'

Dee waved away Minnie's offer of the gum packet. 'I didn't know that about Andy's mum,' she said quietly. 'Wow, that must have been really hard for him with his dad not being around either.'

Minnie looked shocked. 'Seriously? Have you guys not talked about this stuff? You're the one who's meant to be having a baby with him, Dee, not me . . .'

'Excuse me, we are just *exploring* the *possibility* . . .'

Minnie was right though, Dee thought as she tailed off – they'd been dutifully asking each other questions, but when it came to the big stuff there was still so much they didn't know about each other. He was an open book, he'd already proved that. But she was scared of showing too much of herself, of asking too much of him. She'd always been like this, and she didn't want to be any more.

Minnie blew a gum bubble, popped it, then looped an arm through Dee's. 'Anyhoo, how are you feeling about yours and Andy's little project, if I'm allowed to call it that?'

Dee resisted for a second, then decided to let herself be swept off on the tide of Minnie's enthusiasm. 'I think . . . OK?' she ventured. 'I mean, we're obviously just talking, it's incredibly early days. But I thought even that would be really stressful, and actually it's not at all. He's just really . . . straightforward.'

'Straightforward is good! Unstressful is good!' Minnie beamed, squeezing Dee's arm. 'I think the whole point of life is to have the least stressful time that you possibly can. I'm not sure Roo would agree with me about that, though – there are two kinds of people in this world, the ones who take the lift and the ones who take the stairs, and Roo is *definitely* a stairs person.'

'Hah. You're not wrong there.' As soon as she'd said it Dee felt awful – she'd violated one of the unspoken principles she'd set herself for their three-way friendship, that it was

OK for her to talk about Minnie to Roo, but not to talk about Roo to Minnie.

'She just worries about you,' Minnie shrugged, drawing her closer. 'I do too, obviously. Just differently.'

Minnie was being kind, Dee told herself. And Roo was too. But she was starting to get a bit fed up of feeling like a Rubik's cube that her two best friends seemed so determined to rearrange.

Back at Minnie's empty flat Dee ordered the food – her usual margarita with extra cheese and no basil, and a spicy sausage calzone with garlic dipping sauce for Minnie, which was the sort of pizza that only an extremely attractive person could get away with eating in company. While she was ordering Minnie sat at the kitchen table and unwrapped the Clearblue box like it was a Christmas present.

'Right, it says you get the result in sixty seconds,' she announced, peeling the plastic off. 'Two lines means you're pregnant, one line means you're not. No lines means you peed on the wrong bit, I guess.' She jumped up and padded into the bathroom with it. Thirty seconds later Dee heard a flush, the soft whoosh of the sink tap, then the creak of the toilet lid's hinges: Minnie, as usual, had left the door open.

There was a nearly full string bag of oranges in the fruit bowl on the worktop: wrinkled leftovers from Minnie's short-lived, Jonas-inspired health kick. Dee decided to juice them while they were waiting for the food to arrive; even she couldn't mess that up, she thought as she opened the cupboard labelled with Minnie's name in glitter pen and rummaged around in the chaos until she found a hubcap-shaped Pyrex juicer. There was a bag of pasta bows next to it. She took them both out, took a picture of the bows and sent it to Andy. He came online straight away and started typing.

Andy:
Sorry but that sort of photo
needs a trigger warning

Dee:
It's for your own good . . .

Andy:
I'll be the judge of that
How's your day been?

Dee:
Oh, fine
Work was . . . worky
Minnie took me to a spin
class and Roo's booked
me an appointment with a
fertility counsellor

Andy:
A what now?

Dee:
A counsellor that you talk to
if you have fertility issues

165

> The appointment's next
> Monday, pray for me

Andy:
Well, you're meant to be
sorting our next meeting
And the cafe's closed on
Mondays
Do you want some
company?

Dee's finger hovered. Her first instinct was to say no, like she always did when she got this kind of offer – she hated the idea of anyone's life being made more difficult on her account. But something stopped her. She *did* want some company, she realised – she was dreading this appointment, and having someone to sit with in the waiting room would make it a bit easier. Roo would be working and ten o'clock in the morning was far too early for Minnie, who normally got dressed around midday.

'Minnie, you'll never guess . . .' she called out, before something made her stop. It had been well over a minute since Minnie had gone into the bathroom. And for the second time that day, Minnie wasn't saying anything at all.

She turned around. Minnie was standing completely still in the doorway, her face pale, holding up the test. In its window were two pink lines.

'We can't ever tell Roo about this, OK?' she said hoarsely. '*Ever.*'

*

166

From: Minnie Marks
To: Dee Jensen
Subject: You know
Wednesday, 17 October, 10:40

Hi Dee! Putting all this is an email so I don't accidentally send it to the group chat instead of just to you 🤢 I'm on the British Pregnancy Advisory Service website and their calculator says I'm seven weeks pregnant, which seems like a LOT of weeks, but apparently they work it out from the date of your last period rather than when you . . . ANYWAY, I can have a 'medical abortion', which means having a phone consultation then taking two pills basically. They give you one at the clinic, then you take the second one at home. That sounds OK, doesn't it???

From: Minnie Marks
To: Dee Jensen
Subject: Update
Wednesday, 17 October, 12:03

OK, I called them for the consultation and they were really nice, they can see me first thing on Friday of next week! So only ten days to wait.

From: Minnie Marks
To: Dee Jensen
Subject: One more thing
Wednesday, 17 October, 12:07

Hmm, someone has to come with me to the clinic in case I die. Can I put your name down on this form they've sent me?

From: Minnie Marks
To: Dee Jensen
Subject: Just FYI!
Wednesday, 17 October, 12:11

I've put your name down.

Thanks, Dee!!!!

From: Dee Jensen
To: Minnie Marks
Subject: RE: Just FYI!
Wednesday, 17 October, 12:19

Sorry Minnie, I was in a meeting . . . That's great they were nice and they can see you so soon. Of course I'll come with you. Hang on in there xxx

From: Minnie Marks
To: Dee Jensen
Subject: RE: Just FYI!
Wednesday, 17 October, 12:25

Thanks, Dee! Don't know what I'd do without you 🖤🖤🖤🖤 Do you have an egg cup at work by the way?

From: Dee Jensen
To: Minnie Marks
Subject: RE: Just FYI!
Wednesday, 17 October, 12:27

???????

From: Minnie Marks
To: Dee Jensen
Subject: RE: Just FYI!
Wednesday, 17 October, 12:31

Apparently there's three egg cups of blood involved – just realised I have no idea how big an egg cup actually is 😄 Don't worry!

Chapter Eleven

Thirty-five, Dee thought grimly as she squeezed herself on to the tube early the following Monday, wasn't getting off to anything like as relaxing a start as thirty-four had. Last year her birthday had fallen on a Sunday, and she, Roo and Minnie had gone to Margate: they'd been on some rides at the Dreamland amusement park, eaten fish and chips on the Harbour Arm, screamed as they dipped their feet in the tidal pool and drunk cocktails next to the sea as the sun went down. It had been a perfect day. This year she was sweating on the Central line in the rush-hour crush while trying to work out how she was going to get to her appointment with the fertility counsellor later that morning, and fielding a stream of texts from Minnie.

Minnie:
Urgh, Dee, I feel SO SICK
I'm not even *being* sick
Just doing these weird
heaves
Thank God this is all going
to be over soon
THIS IS HORRIBLE DEE
HORRIBLE

H
O
R
R
I
B
L
E

Dee:
I'll call you ASAP, OK?
Stay strong, Minnie xxx

She was wearing the badge that had been on the front of her joint birthday card from Roo and Minnie, a sheep-shaped one that said *Happy Baa-Day To Ewe* but might as well have had *TRAITOR* written on it. She kept waking up in the night from a thin, anxious sleep and remembering: Minnie was pregnant but didn't want to be (and wouldn't be for much longer), Roo wasn't but did, and it was up to her, Dee, to make sure that those two worlds never collided. The idea of lying to Roo about this, not just now but for the rest of her life, was unfathomable – but what else could she do? Roo finding out that Minnie, who had never wanted children and didn't even think she *could* have them, had ended up pregnant would crush her – along with their friendship. The thought made her feel cold with panic. She put her phone away and tried hard to focus on the one part of today she was actually looking forward to: the breakfast with Ines that she was on her way to.

Until Ines had come along Dee had done her best to ignore her birthday. The few that she could remember when her parents were together had been dominated by them arguing, and after they split up Alice's expensive, over-the-top attempts to make the day feel special just made her sad and worried. Her dad had also forgotten more than once. Noticing how reluctant Dee was to make plans for her sixteenth, Ines had suggested that the two of them do something fun in the morning, just the two of them. They'd gone to a famous Italian cafe near Ines's old flat in Bethnal Green, where everything came with chips and the owner sent you home with a foil swan full of leftovers. When he found out why they were there he climbed on to the counter and banged on a jug to get everyone's attention, then led the room in singing 'Happy Birthday' (before, for no clear reason, playing 'Je T'Aime Moi Non Plus' over the tinny speakers; this was part of the tradition, Ines explained). It was easily the nicest birthday that Dee had ever had.

For nearly two decades they'd been meeting at the same cafe in exactly the same way. They'd order what they always did, 'Happy Birthday' would be sung and Serge Gainsbourg would be blasted out of the stereo to the general bemusement of everyone present. The details of the ritual were very important to Dee. One year Ines had toyed with the idea of ordering something different – Dee had looked so startled by the change, she'd said with a laugh as she told the story, that she'd switched back to her usual omelette. At the end of the meal, as the cafe's door dinged behind them on the way out, Dee was always comforted by the fact that whatever else might happen over the next twelve months, breakfast with Ines would be waiting for her at the end of it.

As she walked down Bethnal Green Road from the station she saw Andy had messaged her. All week she'd been expecting him to cry off coming to the hospital with her, and she was sure that was what he'd be doing now. Who in their right mind would want to spend one of their days off like that?

Andy:
Just checking – your
appointment's at 10, right?
I'll get there just before
Nice day for it

Dee:
That's right, it's 10!
OK, see you then
Thanks, Andy

She put her phone back in her pocket, rebuking herself for assuming the worst. She was learning that whatever Andy's other faults, he didn't say things unless he meant them.

Ines was at their usual table, which had two presents wrapped up in spotty paper on it, at the back of the cafe, drinking an espresso and reading a book. She put it away when she spotted Dee, her eyes twinkling.

'For you,' she said, pushing the parcels across the table towards Dee. 'The squashy one's from Al, the other one's from me. Happy birthday, Dee-Dee.'

Dee hugged her stepmum, then sat down and opened her presents. She started with Ines's, which turned out to be a beautiful aluminium coffee pot – a twin of the one Ines had brought round all those years ago.

'I just thought it was about time you had one of your own,' Ines smiled. 'I know your landlord's got one of those machines but they're not the same. Now, Al says to tell you that if you don't like hers you can take it back to the shop, she's kept the receipt . . .'

Every year, for no clear reason, Alice gave Dee some kind of scarf or shawl. This year's was an extremely long knitted one that wouldn't have looked out of place on Doctor Who.

'I'll add it to the collection,' Dee said with a grin, folding the scarf into her bag. 'Thanks, Ines – and thank you for coming all this way.'

'Of course.' Ines's smile turned into a yawn. 'Sorry,' she said, covering her mouth. 'I'm not sleeping very well at the moment.'

'Is it Ronnie? When Roo stayed over with me he was snoring so loudly it woke me up, he's definitely getting worse . . .'

Ines shook her head. 'For once, no. I wanted to wait until I saw you to let you know this – my brother phoned when we were at the Wetland Centre to tell me that my father has cancer. It's everywhere, apparently – he doesn't have long to live. He's an awful man and I never expected to see him again, but it's still . . .'

Dee's mouth had gone dry. Ines never spoke about her family; Dee barely knew any more about them today than she had after the conversation they'd had at the zoo twenty years earlier. The details of her stepmum's life before she'd moved to England were still locked away, and only Ines had the key. Dee had always justified knowing so little to herself on the basis that Ines was a private sort of person; she never really talked about her work either. But that was a cop-out. She thought back to how shaken Ines had looked when she'd come off the phone that morning. She could – *should* – have asked a lot more questions. But she'd always been reluctant to rock the boat where her stepmum was concerned.

'God, I'm so sorry, Ines. Do you . . . want to talk about it?' she asked tentatively.

'That's very sweet of you.' Ines gave Dee's hand a pat. 'But no, I'm fine. Or I will be. And work's been keeping me very busy since I found out, which is good, I think – although sometimes it can feel a bit like banging your head against the same brick wall over and over again. Tolstoy didn't know what he was talking about: unhappy couples are all very much alike.'

It was actually a relief that Ines seemed so determined to change the subject; it made Dee feel less guilty for not having raised it before. She'd just been respecting Ines's wishes, she tried to convince herself.

'I honestly don't know how you do your job,' she said, putting her new coffee pot down on the floor next to her bag. 'I can barely deal with my own love life, let alone anyone else's.'

Ines drained her coffee. 'We never got on to what happened with Nat, did we? Do you want to?'

She actually didn't, Dee realised. What she really wanted to talk to Ines about was the situation with Roo and Minnie. But as she tried to find the right words she ran into the same reluctance she'd felt whenever she'd considered asking Ines for advice about Nat. It wasn't that Ines would say the wrong thing – it was that Dee wasn't at all sure the right thing was something she wanted to hear.

'Ines, did you . . .' she began, before losing her nerve. Her stepmum gave her a searching look; she was going to have to finish the sentence somehow. 'Did you ever want children?'

Ines looked amused. 'Hah! That's what I'd call a two-coffee question . . . hello, yes, could I get another one of these? And she'll have a latte. Thank you.'

She turned back to Dee and rested her chin on her hands.

'Well – where I grew up you had to be married to a man if you wanted to have a child. And I always knew that wasn't on the cards, so I never really thought about it. Then when I lived in Brighton there were a few women I knew who'd come to arrangements with male friends or people they'd found through adverts, but that wasn't for me either. I don't think being pregnant would have suited me at all, do you? Anyway, I'd have had to give up smoking, and my most serious relationships at that point in my life were with Ms Benson and Ms Hedges.'

Dee laughed. 'You gave up eventually, though.'

'I did – for you and Al.' Ines tilted her head. 'Anyway, why do you ask? Is having children something you're thinking about?'

Dee could feel everything she'd been stuffing down weighing dangerously on her, just under the surface. This stuff was like asbestos, she thought – it wasn't an immediate problem as long as you didn't disturb it. And she wasn't going to start pulling up the floorboards on her birthday.

'No reason,' she said quickly. 'Shall we order the food? I know you've got to get off to work.'

'Good idea.' Ines glanced across at the menu on the wall. 'I was thinking I might branch out and get the full English, actually . . .' She caught Dee's eye and burst out laughing. 'Or maybe not.'

Roo:
When you get to the
Whittington, go to the
Dartmouth Park Hill entrance
Obstetrics and Gynaecology
is in the Kenwood Wing
Don't be late!

The Whittington looked like a hospital that someone had built while they were drunk-playing the Sims: glass blocks were stacked randomly on top of brick ones. As she approached the giant revolving door Dee scanned the stream of messages that Roo had sent her while she'd been having breakfast with Ines. She was wearing her spotty Zara dress; she'd already left the house when she'd realised it was the same one she'd worn at her first appointment with Kirsty the GP.

She was actually going round in the door when Roo video called her.

'Roo? Everything OK?' Dee tried to step out but she'd left it too late; there was a really bleak metaphor somewhere in there, she thought as she started going round for a second time.

'Yes, fine – I just wanted to check you hadn't got lost,' Roo said. 'You didn't reply, I was worried.' She was in the canteen at St Thomas's, dressed in her well-ironed blue surgical scrubs. 'Happy birthday, by the way.'

'Thanks.' The door spat Dee out into an overheated reception area. There was Andy with his coat over his arm, in jeans and a rainbow-striped jumper that was objectively a bit Gap Kids but which she actually didn't hate on him. 'Look, Roo, I've got to go, Andy's here . . .'

'Wait, what?' Roo was looking at her like she'd just announced she was going bungee jumping. 'You invited Andy along to your appointment?'

'Well, you're working today and Minnie . . .' Dee braced herself for the first of a lifetime's worth of half-truths. 'Minnie's ill. And I wasn't feeling great about going by myself.'

Andy spotted her and waved. HI, she mouthed over the top of her screen as she closed the gap between them. SORRY.

'Can I talk to Andy, please?' Roo's voice was the loudest sound on Earth; Andy stopped, frowning. 'Why not? Minnie's met him – I'd like to as well.'

Dee looked at Andy. Andy looked at Dee. He shrugged amiably.

'Um, OK then . . .' She turned her phone around and held it up for Andy, her heart thumping. 'Andy, this is Roo – Roo, this is Andy.'

Andy leaned into the screen. 'Hiya!' he said to Roo in a cheerier voice than Dee had ever heard him use before.

Roo was regarding him coolly. 'Hi, Andy,' she said, folding her arms.

As Dee chewed the inside of her cheek waiting for Roo to say something else, a thought struck her. She had spent two thirds of her life deferring to Roo's judgement. Had Roo ever actually asked herself what Dee might think about something, and changed course because of it? The second the thought had formed in her brain she felt sick with guilt. She was the one in the wrong here, she reminded herself – and she was always going to be the one in the wrong with Roo from now on, thanks to Minnie.

'Dee was saying you're an anaesthetist, Roo,' Andy offered eventually. 'That must be tough – difficult to switch off at the end of the day, I'd imagine.'

'It is, actually,' Roo said crisply. 'You find yourself looking at people and wondering how easy they'd be to intubate. Anyway, I can't stay, I need to go and explain to my next patient that anaesthetics aren't actually a government mind-control tool. It was good to virtually meet you, Andy. I hope we get to see each other properly soon.'

'I hope so too,' Andy said, actually sounding like he meant it. He handed the phone back to Dee, who went to say goodbye to Roo – but Roo had already rung off.

'Sorry about that,' she said with a grimace; the words felt entirely inadequate. 'She isn't normally quite that terrifying, she's just having a bad week.'

'Why are you apologising? She's great,' Andy smiled, and Dee let herself start breathing again. 'She obviously really cares about you. Remind me never to get an anaesthetic at St Thomas's, though. Waiting room's this way.'

The waiting room, which was off to their left, was no-frills – there was a noticeboard, a row of bolted-together blue plastic chairs and a rack of a magazine called *Gurgle* with a chubby baby on the front. 'PLEASE TAKE ONE', the sign on top said, in a way that felt more like an order than a suggestion. Andy sat down at the end of the row nearest the rack. The chairs really were close together, Dee thought as she tried to work out where to sit. Uncomfortably close. She put her bag on the chair to his left and lowered herself into the next one along.

Andy had taken a copy of *Gurgle*.

'You know, I'm sure there's a worse baby-related word they could have gone with as a title for this particular publication, but I'm struggling to think of one right now. Can you?'

'Leak? Splat?' It wasn't that she didn't want to sit that near Andy, Dee thought, trying not to stare at a lurid poster about antibiotic-resistant gonorrhoea. It was more that she didn't want *him* to think she wanted to sit that near him, which was ridiculous really. For a while she'd really felt like she was managing not to overthink all their interactions, but that period had clearly come to an end.

Andy was frowning at her badge.

'Hang on, is it your birthday today? Why didn't you say?'

Before Dee could answer she heard her name being called.

'Dee Jensen?' A woman with short grey hair and turquoise-rimmed glasses stood holding a clipboard in the doorway to the department, smiling beatifically. 'I'm Mary! Come this way, both of you!'

If you did an image search for 'fertility counsellor', Dee thought as she stood up, Mary would be the first result. She was wearing Birkenstocks and a loose sea-green linen smock dress with sparkly tights underneath. There was a second pair of glasses hanging on a chain around her neck, along with a pendant that looked suspiciously like something from an anatomy textbook. Her musings on Mary ground to a screeching halt when she realised that Andy was standing up too.

'Wait, are you . . .' When she'd accepted Andy's offer she'd thought he'd be waiting out here for her, but now she actually thought about it that made even less sense than him coming in to her appointment. Andy had stopped halfway out of his seat.

'Sorry, I thought you wanted . . .'

'No! No. I mean, not no – yes, but only if you want to, you don't . . .'

'Do *you* want me to?'

'I don't . . . I don't *not* want you to . . .'

'We haven't got all day, you two!' Mary trilled. Dee and Andy looked at each other, and another seemingly endless second stretched between them before Dee felt herself giving him a nod. It was settled, then: Andy was coming to see the fertility counsellor with her.

Dee and Andy followed Mary all the way down the corridor in total silence until they got to an open door. They were both trying very hard not to look at each other, Dee felt; both of them knew they had crossed a Rubicon. This was a significant step beyond *just talking* – it was doing.

If Mary had noticed the atmosphere it didn't seem to bother her in the slightest.

'Sorry about how the place looks!' she said cheerfully as she ushered them into a rather drab and dingy room. There was a bin bag taped over one of the windows, huffing like bellows. 'It broke in that storm we had last winter but getting anything fixed around here is impossible . . . Anyway! Make yourselves comfortable.'

There was a desk at the back of the room with a wheely chair behind it which Mary took, and two plastic chairs on the other side that were identical to the ones in the waiting room, though thankfully more spaced out. Dee and Andy sat on those.

Mary was looking pointedly at Andy. 'Hmm, you're very young,' she said to him. 'Are you sure about this?'

Dee and Andy exchanged a look of mutual bafflement. 'I'm actually the one with the, um . . . problem,' Dee said, her face glowing.

Mary frowned. 'Really? Normally women are very enthusiastic about the whole thing. It won't affect your sex life and complications are very rare. It isn't even an irreversible decision, to be honest with you – boy bits are much less tricky to reconnect than girl ones . . .'

Andy's ears looked like they were about to catch fire. 'Look, really sorry to interrupt,' he said, 'but what are we actually talking about here?'

'You're here for pre-vasectomy counselling, aren't you?' Mary glanced down at the clipboard, frowning. '*Oh*. Goodness, I'm so sorry, I mixed you up with the couple I'm seeing after this!' She ran a finger along her list and squinted. 'So you're Dee . . . Ah! Got you: premature ovarian failure. Deary me, what a phrase that is.' She looked up again with a smile. 'Before we get going, can I just say how nice it is to see a couple together in this situation? You wouldn't believe how many women come in for counselling without their partners. It's sad, really.'

'Oh, we're actually not—' Dee began. Then she stopped – Andy looked like he was on the verge of correcting Mary too, and she was more than happy for him to be the one who did it. But then Mary was talking again, and suddenly it was too late: the music had stopped and on top of everything else that had happened in the past five minutes, here they were, sitting in chairs marked Boyfriend and Girlfriend.

'How about we start with some introductions? That will help me figure out how I can support you both while you look at all your options.' Mary leaned back in her chair, which creaked ominously. 'Why don't you tell me a little bit about yourselves, your jobs and your families?'

Mary stared at Andy in a way that said, *You first*. Dee realised that she herself was wearing exactly the same poker face that she'd adopted as a teenager whenever she'd found herself sitting through a love scene on television with her mum and Ines. It was meant to convey that she had zero thoughts connected to love and sex, that she didn't even *know* what either of those things were . . .

Andy cleared his throat.

'OK, well – my name's Andy Jones, I'm forty, and I'm from Lytham in Lancashire originally,' he said. 'I'm working as a chef at the moment but before that I was a restaurant consultant. Family-wise . . . um, my dad died when I was thirteen, and my mum emigrated to New Zealand. I don't have any brothers or sisters; it's just me.'

'Mm-hmm.' Mary had been nodding along. 'And when did you last see your mum, Andy?'

'Five, maybe six years ago?' Andy shrugged. 'The flights are so expensive . . . plus she's got her own life out there now:

she's really busy with her book group and her hiking club and all kinds of stuff.' He paused. 'To be honest with you, I think she just wanted to get away from it all. My dad was sick for a long time before he died, so there were really painful memories around every corner for her at home. I can't blame her for not wanting to be reminded of them.'

He stopped and looked at Dee. Mary was sitting with her hands in her lap, also apparently waiting for Dee to speak.

'Um, hi! I'm Dee Jensen,' Dee began, feeling uncomfortably like she was on *Blind Date*. 'I'm thirty-five . . . well, today, actually, and I've always lived in London. I'm a copywriter. My parents split up when I was seven. I don't see my dad much; he lives in Denmark. My mum and my stepmum got together when I was a teenager. And it's just me too – I'm an only child as well.'

Mary tilted her head thoughtfully. 'So you're both only children, and you've both experienced the loss of parents, in different ways,' she said. 'That's very interesting.'

Dee and Andy glanced at each other again. Andy never exactly looked comfortable when he was sitting down, Dee had noticed – the curse of being six-three in a five-ten world – but right now he looked really, *really* uncomfortable.

'What do you mean?' Dee asked apprehensively.

Mary smiled. 'Oh, just that it will obviously have shaped how you think about families, probably in ways that you don't even realise right now. I know everyone always says opposites attract, but in my experience those sorts of similarities can be very helpful if you're looking to . . . oh, bugger! Sorry, excuse my French . . .'

A sudden gust had blown the bin bag away from the

window, and it was now flapping around like a bat. Mary leapt up and started patting it down, her spare glasses and necklace clacking against each other.

Dee risked a glance at Andy. He was staring straight ahead. What was he thinking? What did she *want* him to be thinking? Nothing, she decided. She wished both of their minds could be as flat and featureless as fields freshly covered in snow.

Mary finished retaping the bin bag to the window frame and then sat back down.

'I *really* must talk to Facilities about getting that fixed . . .' she said, smoothing her smock down as she resettled herself in her chair. 'What was I saying? Ah yes, common ground. It's so important if you're going to embark on a journey like this together, you really do need to be able to speak each other's languages. You need to be a *team*.' Speech delivered, she leaned back in her chair and smiled with satisfaction, then opened one of her desk drawers. 'Now, I've got some things for you to read . . .'

Twenty minutes later Dee and Andy emerged into the corridor. Dee was clutching a sheaf of leaflets that Mary had talked her through in excruciating detail while Andy did a decent impression of someone who'd been turned to stone. She couldn't look at him – she couldn't imagine ever being able to look at him again.

'Well, that was . . . an experience, wasn't it?' she said to the floor once they were out of earshot. 'Sorry, I was going to tell her that we're not a couple but . . .'

'Yeah, I was about to as well,' Andy said quickly. 'But then the moment just sort of . . . passed, didn't it? And I thought it would have been really awkward to say anything. Even more awkward, I mean.'

'It really would have.' At least they were both as mortified as each other, Dee told herself. That was something. They were comrades. Not for the first time she found herself thinking about how far she'd come recently. In just over a month she'd gone from being too embarrassed to eat a piece of cheese in front of Nat to spending half an hour sitting next to a man she'd drunkenly propositioned while they listened to a lecture on fallopian tubes. If that wasn't personal growth, she didn't know what was.

'Really sorry to hear about your mum, Andy,' she said quietly. 'That must have been hard.' Andy acknowledged this with a nod. They passed another gonorrhea poster. 'Do you think Mary's necklace was actually . . .'

Andy shook his head. 'I decided to do an Indiana Jones and not look directly at it; safest way. And thanks.' They were back in the waiting room now. 'Anyway, much as it pains me to change the subject, how come you didn't say anything about today being your birthday?'

Dee hesitated. Personal growth or not, she still felt like there'd been quite enough heavy conversation for one day.

'I'm just not really a big birthday person,' she shrugged unconvincingly.

'Thirty-five's a pretty big birthday, Dee . . .' Andy raised an eyebrow. He glanced down at the leaflets she was holding. 'I feel a bit left out not getting any of those. Maybe I should have told Mary about the forum I joined. Well, the Reddit group – it's for people who are considering platonic co-parenting. It's really interesting, actually; you should have a look.'

Dee felt a flush creeping up the back of her neck and across her face. In the three weeks since their Tesco Express agreement neither of them had actually said *platonic co-parenting* out loud – deliberately, Dee guessed, to avoid making the situation feel even odder. It was just a phrase, but in spite of that and all the embarrassment they'd just been through together, she still felt self-conscious about hearing it. 'You're such a nerd, honestly,' she said, trying to diffuse the tension she was feeling.

'Less of that, thank you,' Andy said, stepping into the gap in the big revolving door. 'I've only got two A-levels and one of them's General Studies. Not all of us grew up in west London and went to Hogwarts.'

'Excuse me!' Dee pretended to be outraged as she followed him in. 'Me and Mum were completely broke until she met Ines. And St Jude's is a state school, I'll have you know.'

'A *fancy London* state school. Not a proper one like mine. You wouldn't have lasted five minutes.'

'Oh God, here we go,' Dee pretended to roll her eyes. 'I suppose you had to walk twenty miles each way to get there across the hills in the snow, didn't you?'

'Without shoes.' Andy put on a solemn face as they stepped out on to the street. 'And the canteen only served coal.'

'Don't tell me, you had to play your ukulele if you wanted seconds . . .' Dee got her phone out to check the time and saw she had a message from Roo. *How did it go? Andy seems nice.* She smiled again.

'You made a good impression,' she said, turning her phone around so Andy could see. 'Look, she's called off the hit.'

'First impressions aren't my strong point, as you might remember . . .' Even so, Andy looked pleased. 'I'm sure she's just being polite.'

Dee snorted. 'Trust me, she's not; Roo doesn't do politeness. You should have seen what she was like with my . . .'

She was about to say *my ex*, but calling Nat that suddenly struck her as a bit overblown given they'd never officially been boyfriend and girlfriend. Objects appear smaller in the rear-view mirror, she thought.

'The last person I was seeing,' she finished. 'She couldn't stand him.'

'What happened there?' Andy shrugged his coat on. 'I don't think you've ever told me.'

Dee thought about deflecting the question, but she decided that would be stupid. Andy had always been open with her about his life, she owed him the same.

'We met when we were in sixth form – we did English together and we were quite close for a while but nothing ever happened, he actually got together with someone else. I was really into him, I always sort of . . . thought he was my one that got away. Anyway, we met up again this summer and we started seeing each other, but I think we were just on different pages. He ended it over the phone when he was in Romania for work.'

Andy had been listening with a strange, almost disapproving look on his face.

'I think you're well out of that one, to be honest, Dee,' he said abruptly. 'Doesn't sound much fun to me at all.'

That wasn't very comradely. Dee felt her hackles rise. It wasn't Nat she wanted to defend – it was herself. She didn't want Andy thinking she was some kind of romantic disaster zone, even though that was exactly what she always had been.

'No, there were fun bits, actually,' she said with something close to indignance. 'It was just a bit . . . complicated.'

'If you ask me, any situation that takes you more than a sentence to explain is bad news,' Andy said with Roo-like briskness, getting his phone out. 'Sorry, I've got to dash – I'll message you later, OK?'

There was a bench just ahead surrounded by a corona of cigarette butts. After Andy had gone, Dee went and sat on it, trying to settle the feeling of disquiet that had taken hold of her in the last few minutes and get her bearings back. She got her phone out and saw she had another update from Minnie. *Dee, I had to go back to bed and now I feel so sick I can't even get out of it to get a Coke!!!* She was trying desperately to think how to reply to both Minnie and Roo when a message from her dad came through.

Hey there kiddo, have you looked at the photo yet?

Nothing about her birthday. He'd probably forgotten it again, Dee thought as a familiar combination of emotions swirled itself into the mix. She felt angry and disappointed, and angry with herself for feeling disappointed. She shook her head and went back into her chat with Roo, but before she could start typing another message came through. This one was from Andy.

So I was thinking . . . How would you feel about me cooking you dinner this week? My place is a bit lacking in the furniture department but I could come to yours? This definitely wouldn't be a birthday thing, by the way. Just a thing that happens to be quite soon after your birthday . . .

Chapter Twelve

'You might still be able to stack them up?' Roo suggested from inside Dee's phone.

They were on a video call: Roo was sitting cross-legged on the carpet in her bedroom at home, packing for her holiday with Sam's family, and Dee was in her kitchen. In front of her on the hob was a tray of what were meant to be profiteroles but looked more like pancakes. It was Thursday, and Andy was meant to be coming round to cook dinner. He'd offered to do the whole meal, but Dee had insisted that she would make dessert – an insistence she was now regretting even more than the random assortment of items she'd panic-bought from the corner shop just in case there wasn't enough food (four bottles of Grolsch in a blue plastic bag, barbecue-flavour lentil crisps, a Toblerone).

Dee gave one of the profiteroles a poke. It let out a sad little sigh.

'No, I definitely won't. And that was the last of the flour too. Fuck, fuck, fuck. Why did I even decide to make profiteroles, Roo? What year is it, 1997?'

'Turn your phone back a second so I can see them properly,' Roo instructed. She peered at her screen – she was an accomplished baker who appreciated the fact that as long as you followed the instructions to the letter, you got results. In baking, she always said, there were no unknowns.

'Ah, you put all the egg in at once, didn't you?' she said ruefully. 'You have to add it a little at a time or the profiteroles get too wet and they won't rise. Have you made the sauce already? I'd bin them and just turn it into hot chocolate, to be honest. Or you could . . .'

Before she could finish the sentence, Dee had opened the pedal bin with her foot and tipped the profiteroles into it with a whoosh. She was shamefully grateful for the excuse this gave her to break eye contact with Roo – it didn't matter how many times she told herself that people kept secrets from each other all the time, and that she and Minnie (whose abortion was booked for the following morning) were doing this to protect Roo, she still felt wretched.

'You've got a backup, right?' Roo's voice broke into her thoughts.

'I think there's half a Viennetta in the freezer . . .' Dee tried her hardest to look and sound normal.

'Which flavour?'

'Mint, obviously. The best one.'

'That'll do.' Roo picked up a jumper off her bedroom floor and started rolling it into a space-saving sausage. 'I still don't understand why Andy's coming over to yours to cook, why can't you go round to his? Have you even been there yet?'

In an instant Dee swung from feeling guilty to prickly and annoyed, then back to guilty. How had talking to her oldest, closest friend suddenly turned into a game of 3D emotional chess?

'I think it's nice that he's offered to come and cook for us here,' she said defensively. 'And I'm sure there'll be plenty of opportunities for us to spend time at his as we get to know each other.'

Roo stopped rolling the jumper.

'You're actually serious about this, aren't you?' she said. 'You're actually thinking about going down this road with him.'

Dee hesitated. The truth was, she still had no idea what she was going to do. Whenever she tried to think that far ahead she felt like she was staring into thick fog. But what she did know was that for the first time in her life she was doing something because *she* wanted to do it. And the more Roo interrogated her, the more she wanted to dig her heels in, in a very out-of-character way.

'If I was, would that be so terrible? People start families all the time in all sorts of ways and nobody bats an eyelid. *You* don't bat an eyelid. Anyway, you said Andy was nice.'

Roo looked startled by the change in her tone, and Dee felt miserable all over again. She knew she needed to turn the conversation around quickly, or by the time Roo got back from her holiday it would have set between them like a broken bone healing badly. But she couldn't see a way to.

The buzzer went. Dee jumped.

'He's here, I'd better go,' she said, relief and dismay churning inside her. 'Hope the rest of the packing goes all right, good luck with your early start tomorrow. Let me know when you get to the island?'

'I will. Dee, I . . .' Roo hesitated, then stopped herself from saying whatever it was she'd been about to say. 'OK. Love you.'

Lying to Roo like this was bad enough, Dee thought – how was she going to do it the next time they were actually in the same room? And every time after that? For the rest of their lives?

'I love you too, Roo,' she said quietly. 'I really do.'

Once Roo had rung off she put her phone down on the counter and checked her reflection in the window above the sink. She'd taken half a day off and had planned looking on SpareRoom at places she might be able to afford to move into once Hiro had let the flat, but the results were so depressing that she'd given up.

To fill the time before Andy arrived she'd washed and dried her hair and put on what for her counted as quite a lot of make-up: mascara and eyeliner, blush from a pot and a lip tint in the same shade of dusty pink that Minnie had cajoled her into buying on one of their shopping trips. She was wearing a loose, flowery jumpsuit that Minnie had also twisted her arm into getting on the grounds that it was 'very Kate Bush', but which she suspected made her look like an eighties *Blue Peter* presenter. It had dawned on her while she was getting dressed that she didn't actually like any of her clothes.

The air outside the kitchen window was heavy and wet; it had rained every day this week, downpours alternating with drizzle. Dee smoothed her flyaway hair down one final time, checked the time – it was seven o'clock on the dot – and went to answer the buzzer.

'Hi, Andy?' Her voice came out all squeaky when she lifted the receiver off its cradle; she cleared her throat and veered into a raspy impression of Kathleen Turner. 'Come on up.'

Why are you being like this? she thought as she unlocked

the door, tapping her foot on the carpet. She heard footsteps coming up the stairs, and then he was there in an overcoat, holding a paper grocery bag from the Italian food shop on Brecknock Road in his arms. He was dressed more smartly than she'd seen him before in a blue and white checked shirt buttoned all the way up, darker jeans and proper lace-up shoes. There was something else that was new about him too.

'Wait, you wear glasses? I thought . . .' She stopped herself, realising how ridiculous what she'd been about to say would sound. 'I just thought you couldn't wear glasses if you worked in a restaurant, that's all.'

'I think you might have confused being a chef with being in the RAF, Dee . . .' Andy took his coat off and hung it up on the rack by the door, in between Poodle's leopard-print cape and Hiro's fluorescent green puffa. 'I don't wear them that much, just when my eyes are knackered. Anyway, hello.'

'Hello! Hi! Sorry, come in!' The glasses in question were faintly vintage-looking, with a thicker bit at the top. They suited him, Dee thought as she went to close the front door. Stepping around him to do it felt awkward – the hallway really wasn't big enough for two people.

Andy followed her into the kitchen.

'Love the balcony,' he said, putting the bag on the counter and starting to unpack it. The first thing he pulled out was a bottle of vodka. Dee burst out laughing.

'No wonder your eyes are tired . . .'

'It's not for drinking, don't worry.' Andy followed it with a bag of rigatoni pasta, garlic, a shallot, a bunch of basil leaves, some tomato paste in a tube covered in Italian script and a carton of double cream. 'The vodka goes in the sauce for the pasta. Something smells good, by the way, have you been baking?'

'Unfortunately it looked very un-good and it's now in the bin.' Dee was extremely glad she'd got rid of the evidence. 'I hope you like Viennetta.'

'Food of the gods.' Andy rolled up his sleeves. 'Right then, where would I find pans?'

Dee opened the bottom drawer with her foot, then picked up the packet of pasta that Andy had just put down: it was thick and pleasantly rough to the touch, like expensive gift-wrap. It was the brand that Alice had sometimes splurged on when she was in a really good mood – the same one, in fact, she'd come home with the day she'd first mentioned Ines to Dee.

'I can't remember the last time someone who wasn't Minnie cooked for me,' she said, putting it back on the work-top as Andy held Hiro's biggest pan under the tap.

'Well, I just hope I can still remember how to make this . . .' Andy finished filling the pan and turned around with it in one hand. He must actually be pretty strong, Dee caught herself thinking – it was funny what you noticed about people when you saw them doing something new. 'I've been so off cooking for myself since I started this job, most of the time I just come home and stick something in the oven – as you'll recall from our Tesco encounter.'

'Because you're spending so much time doing it during the day now?'

'Partly that.' He set it down on the hob and started peeling the shallot. 'But I think it's mostly because I've never really cooked for just me before. It feels a bit sad.' He picked the knife up and did something clever with it for ten seconds, leaving the shallot in neat cubes. 'For a long time I was with someone I met in college. Then me and my . . . my most recent ex met when I was twenty-nine and she was thirty-six. So a decade, near enough.'

Dee found she had a very uncharacteristic urge to dig for details. 'What happened there?'

'Why did it end, you mean?' Andy shrugged. 'Nothing dramatic, it just ran its course. Neither of us was the same person at the end of it as we were at the start. And the people we were at the end just wanted different things, ultimately.'

Dee thought back to their conversation on the bench, and the one in Tesco. Opening up to each other about this stuff had felt almost inconsequential when they were strangers. It didn't feel like that now, with him in her kitchen and the flipped coin of their maybe-arrangement spinning in the air. Because they'd never earmarked a point where they'd sit down and actually decide if they were going to do it or not, every conversation felt like it had the potential to be the one where the coin landed.

'Like . . . children?' she ventured.

'I only realised that after we'd split up, but on some level, yes. Ultimately I just wanted to do my own thing. She – my ex – had a really big family all living nearby, loads of siblings and cousins, so I got absorbed into that. Which was lovely, don't get me wrong, and losing it definitely left a hole. I actually think that was one of the things that made me see how much I wanted a family of my own.'

Dee cracked and pulled one of the Grolsches out of the carrier bag.

'I expect you did a *lot* of your own thing while you were travelling,' she said as she opened it, immediately regretting the clumsy, sub-Minnie innuendo.

'Hah – no, not that much.' Luckily Andy seemed unbothered by it. 'Almost none, in fact. It had been a decade since I'd tried to flirt with anyone new, I was seriously rusty. And I got sunburned every time I went outside in Australia, which didn't help. The one date I went on in Melbourne, the woman literally got a spray-bottle of Factor 50 out of her bag in the bar and gave it to me. Anyway, I think having some time to myself did me good – suppose you could say I'm a serial monogamist. This past year has been been the longest I've ever been single for.'

Whenever Dee met a serial monogamist she felt how she imagined medieval peasants had as they stared up at the ceiling of a cathedral: full of awe and very, very small. What must it be like to find it so easy to love and be loved?

'I'm the opposite,' she said, not quite looking at him. 'My longest relationship didn't last much more than six months. It's something I've always really wanted, but . . .' She hesitated, but there was no going back now. 'Let's just say you're not the only one who didn't get much traction on Tinder.'

'Really?' Andy sounded surprised. 'I just mean there are loads more straight men on apps than women, aren't there? And you've got all your own teeth and hair, so . . .' His eyes flicked to the rail of clothes on the other side of the room. 'Have I just breathed in a bit too much vodka or is that a Sesame Street costume?'

'Oh – er, yes, actually, it is.' Dee, smarting from the fact that the nicest thing Andy could think of to say about her was that she wasn't a priority candidate for *Extreme Makeover UK*, followed his gaze: Poodle's Oscar the Grouch suit had just come back from the dry cleaner. 'They're my landlord's fiancee's, actually, she's a burlesque performer. There isn't much space at hers so she keeps most of her costumes here. He's letting the place out properly soon so I'll have to find somewhere else to live – we work together so I'm paying him less.'

Andy's face fell. 'Really sorry to hear that, Dee,' he said with a genuineness that took her straight back to their first conversation on the bench by the canal. 'Where will you go?'

A feeling almost like vertigo swept over Dee as she thought about the adverts she'd looked through on SpareRoom earlier. Unless something miraculous happened at Minnie's in a couple of months' time, she was going to be living with strangers and eating all her meals in her room.

'I'm sure it'll work itself out somehow,' she said unconvincingly, having another swig of her beer. 'What about you, then?'

Andy put a frying pan on the heat and glugged some olive oil into it. 'What about me?'

'What's your place like? Minnie was saying you're living near Haggerston.'

'Living is a strong word . . .' He nudged the shallot into the pan with the knife and reached for a wooden spoon. 'But that's right, I'm not far from the cafe. I'm just looking after the flat – it's pretty empty and my stuff's mostly in storage still from when I was travelling so it doesn't feel at all like home. Honestly, it's depressing, but I'm looking for somewhere more permanent. Getting to viewings around work is basically impossible, though. Mind if I use some of your chilli flakes?'

'Of course.' Dee prised the battered packet out of the spice rack and passed it to Andy, then popped the cap off another

Grolsch and slid it along the counter to him. He intercepted it, and the little relay they'd just performed made her smile, in spite of her on-edgeness. Hiro and Poodle filled this place with sequins and music and takeaways, but although they always made a point of trying to include Dee in whatever they were doing, she couldn't help feeling like a ghost loitering on the fringes of their shared life. Just then, just for a moment, the flat had felt like home – her home.

Andy gave the pan a final stir, switched the gas right down and turned to face her.

'Happy not-birthday, then,' he said, raising his bottle in a toast.

As they clinked the bottles together, their knuckles brushed. They'd never touched before, Dee suddenly realised. Of course, you had this kind of moment with everyone you met and eventually ended up touching. She'd just never noticed it actually happening before. Her eyes strayed to the clock on the oven. It wasn't even quarter past seven, and pasta didn't take very long to cook. At this rate the evening would be over by eight thirty.

'I know what we could do!' she said with all the naturalness of the speaking clock. 'Why don't we sit down and go back to Roo's questions before we have dinner? We sort of abandoned them halfway through, didn't we?'

Andy shrugged good-naturedly. 'Sure, if you like,' he said, turning the gas off. 'These can sit for a bit.'

Dee followed him across the room at an Amish distance – after all her terrible jokes and the knuckle-brush, she was suddenly feeling like she couldn't trust herself to act normally – and sat down on the sofa as far from him as she could without actually falling off it. Andy put the bottles on the coffee table and got his phone out of his pocket, then found Dee's screenshot of Roo's email.

'OK, looks like we skipped question one. "What are your beliefs?" I guess that means religious ones, doesn't it?' He looked up at Dee. 'Well, I don't have any personally. My mum's Catholic though, and I don't think that ever fully leaves you. She used to go to church every Sunday, but my dad didn't believe in any of that so he'd make lunch while she was out. As soon as I was old enough to be useful I started staying behind to help him with the roast – that's how I got into cooking, to be honest.' He put his head on one side. 'How about you? Where do you stand on all of that?'

Dee stretched her arm out to take the beer; she was actually so far away from Andy that she nearly lost her balance doing it.

'I'm not religious either. I used to sort of want to be when I was younger, I think I liked the idea of someone upstairs keeping an eye on things . . .' She lifted the bottle to her lips and swigged, hoping it would help her relax. 'My mum and I nearly became Jehovah's Witnesses once – we got doorstepped by this couple from the Brent Congregation and Mum invited them to stay for lunch. They were still in the living room at midnight – they were nice, actually. But it turned out you had to get to the Kingdom Hall for eight on a Sunday and neither of us fancied that. It was just after—'

She stopped. Her instinct was to skate over what had happened like she usually did. But Andy had always been honest with her – she owed him honesty in return. That was the whole point of this. She leaned down to put the bottle on the floor.

'My mum had a sort of . . . breakdown, actually,' she went on, sitting up slowly so she wouldn't have to look at Andy until the last possible moment. 'After my dad left. She swallowed a bottle of sleeping pills. I don't know if she really wanted to die but she would have if she hadn't gone to hospital. She was diagnosed with something called cyclothymia; it's where you have really erratic mood swings with big highs and lows. She jokes about being a failed manic depressive.'

The only clear memory she still had of those confusing and frightening few weeks after Alice had been discharged was of the neighbour who'd taken her to hospital kneeling to button her duffel coat in the hall of their flat. *You look after your mum, you hear?* she'd whispered, and Dee had thought she was angry with her.

Andy was looking at her. She'd made a big mistake, she thought, feeling her heart start to race. She shouldn't have told him, it was obviously too much to expect him to be able to handle.

'She's so much better now,' she went on quickly, trying to smooth things over. 'She's on a few different medications that really help lift her mood – to be honest they can lift it a bit too much sometimes, although that's obviously loads better than the alternative. And Ines is there to look after her, thank God. When it was just me, I felt . . .'

'Like you had to be the adult?' Andy suggested. He put his bottle on the floor too. 'When my dad's cancer came back, my uncle took me to the pub and told me I was going to have to be the man of the house once he was gone. Then he bought me a pint and made me drink it. I was only twelve. I threw up on the way home. It's—'

The sound of the door buzzer cut him off. Andy blinked.

'Did you secretly order a takeaway or something?' he asked, raising his eyebrows. He stood up and walked to the front door, then picked up the intercom.

'Um, hi?' he said into it. There was a pause, and Dee watched as his expression changed from confused to mildly alarmed. 'Hiya, Minnie – what are you . . . Uh, OK. Sure.'

Dee stood up, went and got her phone and saw she had fourteen missed calls – all within the past half hour, and all of them from Minnie. She also had several dozen WhatsApps. But before she could read them there was a machine-gun burst of knocking on the door. Andy opened it – Minnie was standing on the mat carrying what looked like a very full overnight bag.

'I told Jonas,' she announced dramatically, looking at Dee. 'I need to come and stay with you. Just for tonight – I've sorted somewhere else out for afterwards. I'll drive us there. Please?' She turned to Andy, as though she'd only just remembered he was there. 'Sorry to just turn up like this, Andy. I'm having an abortion tomorrow because I got pregnant after not really having sex. It's all very unfortunate.'

'Oh. Right.' Andy was doing a truly incredible job of controlling his face. 'That sounds quite . . . stressful?'

'Are you OK?' Dee crossed the room and touched Minnie's arm. 'Did Jonas take it badly?'

'No!' Minnie dropped her overnight bag on the floor and kicked the door shut behind her. 'The opposite. He said he'll support me whatever I want to do, and now he won't stop fussing over me. He's being so *nice*, that's the whole problem. Every time he asks me if I want a peppermint tea or a sodding foot rub I feel so embarrassed. I think I might have to move out properly, but I'll worry about that once I've got tomorrow out of the way. Have you got any crisps, Dee?'

Dee caught Andy's eye. They looked at each other, and he raised his eyebrows in a way she read as meaning *It's fine*.

'There are some lentil ones over there,' she said, pointing to the ones she'd bought earlier. Minnie tore them open.

'Perfect, ta. Ooh, barbecue flavour . . . Crisps are the only thing that stop me wanting to barf. It's better in the evenings but I still feel like I'm stuck in a tumble dryer. Urgh!' She tore the packet open and started attacking its contents, then spotted the pans. 'Oh! You two haven't eaten yet! God, sorry – I can go and sit in the car until you've finished dinner?'

Dee and Andy looked at each other again. This time Dee was the one doing the eyebrow code.

'Don't be silly, Minnie,' Andy said. 'There's plenty to go round. Do you like pasta?'

'You're wasted in the cafe, Andy,' Minnie said as she dropped her fork into her bowl. 'I'm serious: you're an incredible cook! Pasta is normally just pasta, but that was PASTA. Capital p, capital ass, capital ta. Would you ever go back to working in restaurants?'

The three of them were squashed around Hiro's fold-out table, which was barely big enough for two. Minnie, who considered herself something of an expert on vibes, had insisted they turn the harsh ceiling lights off and light candles instead – after rummaging in the bathroom cupboard

Dee had found some tea lights, which were now flickering atmospherically in the glass ramekins that seemed to multiply every time Hiro got a supermarket meal deal. Minnie had also plugged her phone into the speakers so she could put on her Spotify ('No offence, Dee, but yours is just a load of Boring Man Music you bought to impress a load of boring men'); right now Madeleine Peyroux's gentle cover of 'You're Gonna Make Me Lonesome When You Go' was playing.

'No way.' Andy shook his head vehemently. 'Absolutely not. I'm too old to be cooking somebody else's food and getting the night bus home from work. This is a temporary stop-gap until I . . . until I figure out what I'm going to do next.'

Over dinner it had struck Dee how little time she'd spent actually *looking* at Andy. She wasn't really one of life's lookers. But right now, in semi-darkness and with Minnie as the centre of attention, she felt able to be a bit bolder than normal. His cheekbones were more noticeable in this light, and his eyes had crinkles at the corners. There was a bump on the bridge of his nose that looked like it might have a story behind it, and he had a scar on his jawline that definitely did. All in all, it was a good sort of face, she thought – a face you would always know where you were with. And the glasses definitely suited him.

'What about opening your own place, then?' Minnie pressed on. 'Then it would all be on your terms. Really, you wouldn't? Why not?'

'Money, for starters.' Andy got to his feet and started stacking up their bowls. 'But even if I did have enough cash, I wouldn't do it. My priorities are different now – I want a different sort of life.'

He caught Dee's eye and smiled, and the feeling that she might have something to do with *my priorities* made her fingertips fizz. Or maybe that was just the beer, she thought, opening a second.

'Well, I'll tell you something for nothing,' Minnie said cheerily, turning around to grab the defrosting Viennetta off the counter behind them. 'Dee might be impervious to your charms, but I'd jump you in a heartbeat if you made me this for dinner. If I wasn't pregnant, I mean. And if Dee wasn't here. Both of those things might make it a bit weird.'

Dee lost her grip on her drink, spilling half of it as she fumbled to get hold of it again. Flirting was just Minnie's way of breaking the ice, like shaking hands or talking about the traffic. There was rarely any intent behind it, and Dee knew for a fact that there wasn't any with Andy: if Minnie had wanted to seduce him, she'd have done it the first time they'd met. This was just Minnie being her usual unfiltered self, something Dee had thought she was immune to being embarrassed by. Clearly not, if the heat she could feel spreading up her neck as she mopped alcohol off the table with her napkin was anything to go by.

'Well, thanks for that, Minnie, that's good to know,' Andy said, turning away from them quickly and looking like he was about to drop the bowls he was carrying. 'I'll get some spoons for dessert then, shall I, Dee?'

Minnie blew him a kiss and tore the Viennetta open. 'You angel!'

Minnie made a half-hearted offer to help with the washing up, but she didn't argue when Dee and Andy told her that they'd sort it out, and took herself off to the sofa. They loaded the dishwasher in uncomfortable silence – Andy seemed pre-occupied, like he hadn't recovered from Minnie's declaration. Dee, who was still cringing, felt it was incumbent on her to get the evening back on track.

'You're safe, don't worry,' she whispered in what she hoped was a lighthearted way. 'She doesn't mean anything by it.'

Andy looked up; he was frowning. 'Sorry, what?'

'Minnie. What she said to you just now – she's honestly like that with everyone. Last week she told her dentist he had lovely eyes.'

'Oh, right – that.' Andy blinked and his expression cleared slightly. 'Hah! Don't worry, I've had worse.' He slotted a tablet into the dishwasher's drawer, then looked back over his shoulder at Minnie, who was now absorbed in a days-old copy of the *Evening Standard* she'd found in the recycling bin. 'I'm just glad we were in when she arrived.'

The *we* felt nice – Dee pocketed it, trying to shake off her lingering unease. Just then a loud sniffle came from behind them. They both spun around, stepping away from each other: Minnie was lying on the sofa with her head in her hands, the newspaper abandoned.

'Minnie!' Dee rushed over and squeezed in next to her. 'What's wrong?'

'I just . . .' Minnie looked up: her pink cheeks were streaked with tears. She held her phone out at arm's length. 'Jonas messaged me saying he'll come tomorrow if I want him to.'

'Well, that doesn't sound so terrible . . .' Dee rubbed her back. '*Do* you want him to?'

'No! I'm a total idiot, I don't want any witnesses to that.' Minnie wiped a hand across her eyes, leaving a smudge of mascara on her knuckles. She looked at Dee, then down at the sofa, almost in embarrassment. 'I mean, a tiny part of me does want him to come.' She sniffed again, more quietly this time. 'But I just told him not to, so it doesn't matter. And he doesn't even know where it's happening – actually *I* don't even know where it's happening, I really need to look at that leaflet they sent me . . .'

Andy went and sat down on her other side, a little way away from her.

'If you change your mind tomorrow and want him with you, I'm sure he'll be there,' he said gently. 'And you're not an idiot, Minnie. Far from it.'

Minnie looked at him, hiccuped, then shuffled herself upright.

'Thanks, Andy,' she sniffed. 'You're the best. Mind if I watch some TV, Dee?'

Before Dee could reply she'd grabbed the remote, flicked the television on and started channel-hopping.

'Hmm, definitely not the news, don't want those bad vibes, not massively in the mood for a documentary about bears . . . oh hell no, absolutely not *Dragon Quest* – I know Pound Shop Tom Hiddleston's not in it yet but still . . .'

'Sorry, who's Pound Shop Tom Hiddleston?' Andy asked. 'Is he a character in the show?'

'No, Nat Flynn, Dee's arsehole ex,' Minnie said breezily as she continued to flick through channels. 'You know, the *actooorrrrr*. Ooh, look – Ina Garten's on Food Network! Ah, it's the one where she throws a surprise birthday party for Jeffrey, I *love* this one.'

Andy had got his phone out and was typing something.

'Is that him?' he said, turning it around so Dee could see. She instantly recognised the grid of photos; she was intimately acquainted with the first dozen pages of Nat's Google image results. She nodded reluctantly, feeling overheated.

'Wow, handsome guy,' Andy said, without enthusiasm. He put his phone down on the coffee table and stood up. 'Right, I'm going to get another drink – anyone want one?'

As he walked away Dee saw that his phone, which he'd left facing up, had lit up with a new message. She didn't quite manage to stop her eyes straying to it. It was from someone saved in his address book as 'C New Number'.

Let's talk more tomorrow. Good night, you x

Chapter Thirteen

When Dee was woken up by the jangle of her radio alarm the next morning, the other side of her bed was empty. Minnie wasn't normally an early riser. But then, Dee thought as she rolled over, today wasn't a normal day.

She stuck an arm out, grabbed her phone and switched it off airplane mode. She saw she had a message from Andy and smiled to herself. *Good luck to Minnie today*, it said. *Hope you're having Viennetta for breakfast*. Then she remembered the text she'd seen on his screen the night before, and the same odd, unmoored feeling she'd had then washed over her. 'C New Number' could be absolutely anyone, she told herself – although the chummy use of 'you' and the x at the end probably narrowed things down a bit. At the back of her mind was the last question on Roo's list. *What will happen if one of you meets someone?* Obviously she was going to have to think about that eventually – she just hadn't expected it to be quite so soon. Anyway, her imagination was probably just running away with her. And she definitely had more important things to be worrying about today.

She replied to Andy's message – *Thank you!!! Good luck at the cafe!!!* – then swung her legs out of bed, grabbed a jumper off the floor and pulled it on over her pyjamas. As she stood up she felt something stick to the underside of her foot. It was the information leaflet the clinic had sent Minnie, which they'd gone through together before going to sleep. Dee wondered if she ought to take it through to Minnie, then decided that might be insensitive. She peeled it off her foot and nudged it under the bed, out of sight.

The bay window in the living room was open. Minnie was leaning over the tiny balcony in her pants and the *Flintstones* T-shirt Dee had lent her, staring out on to Camden Road. There was an open bag of chocolate chip brioche rolls dangling from one of her hands, and a packet of Silk Cut in the other.

'The only time I don't feel sick is when I'm eating . . .' she said when she heard Dee's footsteps. 'I found these in the fridge. Hope that's OK.'

Dee nodded and perched on the arm of the sofa. She remembered how Andy had sat with Minnie the night before and tried to sit exactly how he had.

'I got a reminder text from the clinic just now,' Minnie went on, slotting a cigarette into her mouth. 'You know, like the ones you get from the hairdresser. *Don't forget your abortion!* Do you reckon they'll send me another one afterwards asking me to rate the service I received out of five?'

She lit the cigarette and took a drag. A second later her expression changed and she spat it out.

'Argh, for God's sakes!' She ground the butt into the floor of the balcony with her bare foot, then stared down accusingly at her stomach. 'It's the size of a speck of dust but I still feel *responsible* for it . . .'

She opened the bag and pulled out a brioche. Her hands, Dee noticed, were trembling slightly.

'Minnie, look . . .' Dee got off the sofa and took a couple

of tentative steps towards her. 'Are you . . . I mean, if you need a bit more time to think about this then we can just call the clinic – I'm sure they'll understand.' She put a hand on her arm. 'Or if you've, you know, changed your mind . . .?'

Minnie shook her head emphatically.

'I'd have to stop work and move back home,' she said, biting into the brioche. 'I couldn't spend all weekend in bed watching people doing their make-up on TikTok or stay out late or bleach my hair or have sex. And yes, OK, fine . . .' She chewed. 'Those don't sound like the most meaningful experiences in the world, but you know what? They're meaningful to *me*.' She swallowed defiantly, then pushed the rest into her mouth. 'Literally everything I love about my life is incompatible with having a baby. I am very, very sure I don't want one, now or ever.'

Dee squeezed in next to her on the balcony and put her arm around Minnie. Minnie rested her head on Dee's shoulder.

'You don't have to convince me,' Dee said into the mass of blonde curls. 'It's your decision. I'm behind you one hundred per cent.'

'I know, I know. I just . . .' Minnie detached herself. 'It's not exactly a fun way to while away an hour or two, is it?' She shrugged. 'And I'm not very good with blood. Never have been.'

She dropped the bag of brioches into the window box hanging over the little balcony, then turned back to Dee. She was crying.

'It makes me so sad that I can't ever tell my mum about what happened,' she said with a sniff. 'I mean, she's Reform, so she's not against abortion, but she isn't exactly subtle about wanting to be a grandmother. This would be something she'd be disappointed about if she knew. And another thing.' She wiped streaks of last night's mascara away with the pad of her thumb. 'It must be pretty rubbish for her, to be honest – she only got one child, and she ended up with an embarrassing atheist who eats bacon rolls and never wants to have kids. The whole not getting to choose your offspring thing is pretty shit, isn't it?'

'Oh, Minnie . . .' Dee pulled Minnie into a hug and stroked her hair. 'You know, I think you'd have made a brilliant rabbi. You're very wise, and you're so kind to everyone. And you'd host the best Friday-night dinners. Half of Dalston would end up converting to Judaism just so they could get an invite.'

'Do you really think I'd be good at it?' Minnie's voice came from her chest. 'I mean, I *was* pretty handy with the Haggadah . . .'

They stayed like that for a while. Dee closed her eyes, hugging her tighter: the thought of Minnie taking anyone's disappointment to heart was awful, like watching the Piccadilly Circus lights go out. Then she heard a rustling noise – Minnie had retrieved the bag of brioches from the window box and was shaking it open behind her back. They both burst out laughing.

'It's a good thing I'm calling time on this whole shebang today, isn't it – can you imagine what eight more months of this would do to me?' Minnie said, getting a second roll out of the bag. 'I'd be like Henry the Eighth: they'd have to winch me out of bed in the mornings. Do you want a shower first or shall I go?'

*

'So, I've decided something,' Minnie announced as she pulled up opposite the abortion clinic behind Goodge Street an hour later, one hand on the steering wheel and the other in a fresh bag of salt and vinegar crisps. 'If there are protestors outside and any of them tell me that I'm going to hell I'm going to say, "Thank you for your concern, but I'm a Jew and we don't believe in any of that stuff."'

She switched the engine off and started meditatively transferring the contents of the bag to her mouth. Although they were technically in a parking space, at least a third of the Golf Ball was sticking out into the traffic – Dee was finding it hard to ignore the furious honks from other motorists. She also couldn't quite stop her eyes straying to the dashboard clock.

'Minnie, obviously take as much time as you need – but it's eight forty-five now and we were meant to be in there twenty minutes ago. So, you know. Not too much time.'

'All right, all right, give me a second,' Minnie said with her mouth full of crisps. She still had the *Flintstones* T-shirt on, which she'd knotted just above the waistband of her jeans. She saw Dee's face and shrugged. 'I'm not going to need them afterwards, am I? And I hate wasting food. Hang on a second . . .' Her phone, which was in the cupholder, had lit up. 'Oh no, Roo's messaged the group. God, I feel like such a heel keeping all this from her, Dee, I really do.'

'How do you think I feel?' Dee got her phone out, wishing hers was the kind of nausea that crisps could help.

At the airport, flight delayed, we're hiking up to something called the Old Man of Storr tomorrow apparently, Roo had written. *Already missing London and you both x*

Minnie had put her own phone away. 'I guess it's OK to

lie if you're just doing it to protect someone else from pain,' she said, not sounding entirely convinced. 'But . . .' She chewed her lip, then crumpled up the empty crisp packet and dropped it into the footwell. 'OK, ready – let's go.'

They got out of the car, bought a ticket and waited for a break in the traffic to cross the road. There was a woman with a tight perm in an anorak hovering just ahead of the clinic – as they got closer she stuck an arm out like she was trying to hail a taxi and flagged them down.

'Excuse me, do you know . . .' she began in a strident voice, reaching into the pocket of her coat for something. Dee put her arm around Minnie.

'Um, no thank you,' she said quickly, steering Minnie away from the woman. 'We don't want to talk to you about any of that. And she's Jewish, actually, so it's all irrelevant.'

The woman looked confused. 'I was just wondering if you knew where the Senate House is,' she said, pulling out a tourist map. 'My daughter is at UCL and she's asked me to meet her there.'

'Why don't you fancy Andy?' Minnie asked suddenly. 'I was thinking about it when I woke up this morning and couldn't get back to sleep. Does he give you the ick? I was seeing a guy once who gave me the ick just by wearing aviator sunglasses.'

'Minnie . . .' Dee felt her blood pressure shoot up; even by Minnie's standards this was an intrusive line of questioning. But Minnie had a lot on her mind right now and she was about to go through a medical procedure, she needed to make allowances for that. 'No, he doesn't give me the ick.'

'So what is it, then? I'm not saying you *should* fancy him

just because he's a bloke – but you get on really well, he makes you laugh, you're single, he's single, you're cute, he's cute . . . I mean, *do* you think he's cute?'

As she thought about this – or tried to – Dee felt like she was running into a wall in her head. Its bricks were snatches of her and Andy's conversation in Tesco Express. *This would be as friends, just to be clear*, he'd said. *I'm absolutely not asking you out or anything like that. Romance isn't on my agenda.*

'I just don't think about him like that,' she said, hoping she sounded more self-assured than she felt. 'And Andy doesn't think about me like that either. The whole point of what we're doing is that it's platonic.'

'Fair enough,' Minnie shrugged. 'I think you're missing a trick, but it's your life. Also, I know I can't really throw stones in the decision-making glasshouse right now.'

The clinic had whooshing electric doors that led into a small, overheated waiting room. It was empty apart from a man and a woman in suits who both looked like they were on their way to work. The chairs they were in were the same blue plastic ones that she and Andy had sat on at the Whittington, Dee noticed with a little jolt.

Minnie gave her name to the receptionist, who typed it into her computer, then leaned across the desk.

'Are you OK to go straight in, Minnie?' she said in a soft, quiet voice. 'I don't want to hurry you, but the doctor's waiting.'

Dee turned to her. Minnie was twisting the knot in the *Flintstones* T-shirt. She suddenly looked very pale.

'Minnie, are you OK?' she whispered. 'Do you want me to come in with you?'

Minnie paused; then she shook her head firmly. *I don't want any witnesses*, Dee remembered her telling them the night before. 'Just wishing I'd brought more crisps in my bag,' she said, giving Dee a wink. 'See you in a bit, OK? Don't do anything I wouldn't.'

Dee waited until the receptionist had shown Minnie into a side room, then sat down a couple of seats away from the suited man and woman. She picked up a copy of *Take a Break* from the table and tried to read it, but the words danced around in front of her.

'What are the odds?' she heard the suited woman saying. 'I book a babysitter at vast expense so I can go on my first date in two and a half years, he's actually better looking than his photos, we have sex, the condom breaks, I think to myself, oh well, I'm forty-three and it took me eighteen months of trying before my son turned up, no need to bother with the morning-after pill. Then, boom – pregnant. Seriously, what are the odds of that sequence of events playing out in the way it has? One in a million? Less?'

'An egg must have just been sitting there, waiting for its moment to strike,' the man replied with a wink. 'I guess your body throws everything at it once you get to your age. Like how the dinosaurs went on a killing spree right before they went extinct.'

'Less of that, thank you very much.' She pretended to hit him with a rolled-up copy of *That's Life!*. 'I actually went to my GP before I called this place. You know what he said when I told him I wanted to have an abortion? He looked at me down his glasses and went – I swear I'm not making this up: "But you've already got one child, haven't you?"'

Like adding a whole extra human to my life would be no big deal.'

'Speaking of dinosaurs . . .' The man rolled his eyes. 'Did you tell him you're a single parent who gets no help at all from her eight-year-old's father?'

'He'd probably have given me a bell to hang around my neck.'

The two of them burst out laughing, then stopped abruptly when the receptionist glared over her monitor at them.

'If you think about it,' the woman went on in a whisper, picking up the conversation again once the receptionist had gone back to her computer, 'there's this expectation of inequality that's just *baked in* from the start at a language level, even before you get to maternity leave, childcare costs, all the rest of it. When we talk about someone "fathering a child" we just mean them getting somebody pregnant, right? But linguistically, mothering a child is an ongoing thing. It's forever.'

Dee flipped distractedly through *Take a Break*. 'MY WEDDING DRESS WENT UP IN FLAMES . . . AND SO DID OUR LOVE', proclaimed the headline she landed on. She took a picture to send to Andy. They'd shared so many photos over the past few weeks that it had become second nature to do it whenever she came across something funny or strange, or just . . . well, anything, really. But it felt riskier today, somehow.

You think you've got problems . . . she typed nonsensically into the caption, before sending it. And then, suddenly struck by self-consciousness, *hahahaha!*

Andy came online. Dee imagined him sitting on the steps

at the side of the cafe's kitchen taking a break before break-fast. Two blue ticks appeared. He started typing. He stopped. He started again. He stopped again. Finally, there was a reply.

Hah!

He wasn't typing anything else. And now he'd gone off-line. Dee felt deflated. There was nothing wrong with his reply. She'd sent him something she thought was funny, and he'd responded with a laugh. So why had the whole exchange left her feeling so exposed? And why was she now imagining him showing the picture to someone whose name began with a C?

The clinic doors whooshed open. Standing on the thresh-old, dressed in the tightest, whitest T-shirt imaginable, jeans that hung off his hipbones and a Boombox-branded back-pack, was Jonas.

The suited woman let out a gasp. 'Christ, if I wasn't already pregnant I would be now . . .' she whispered to her friend.

'Dee!' Jonas strode dramatically across the waiting room. 'I am here to support Minnie,' he announced, dropping into the chair next to her and shrugging the backpack off his shoul-ders. 'She should not have to go through this alone.'

'Sorry, hi – is Minnie your girlfriend?' the woman in the suit asked, leaning across Dee.

'*Do* you have a girlfriend?' her friend chipped in.

'Minnie's just' – Dee attempted to turn herself into a human shield for Jonas – 'seeing the doctor now. I don't think she'll be too much longer.'

Jonas nodded. 'I bought these for her,' he said, unzipping the backpack and pulling out a bunch of red grapes. 'Seed-less. Minnie hates the pips.'

218

He was trying unsuccessfully to balance them on his lap when the door of the room Minnie had gone into opened. Dee caught a glimpse of a young female doctor sitting behind a desk, then Minnie appeared with an empty white plastic cup in her hand.

'DONE,' she mouthed at Dee, dropping it into the recycling. Then she spotted Jonas and her face lit up. 'You came! I didn't know if you'd get my message in time!'

Jonas jumped to his feet, shaking the whole row of seats. The grapes rolled on to the floor.

'Minnie . . .' he said in a voice choked with emotion. For a second Dee wondered if he was going to rush over there and sweep her into his arms (the looks on the suited duo's faces suggested that they were thinking along the same lines), but he just knelt down to pick up the grapes. 'These are for you,' he said to her rather shyly, standing up and holding them out. 'They are seedless.'

Minnie grinned. 'Well, aren't you a sweetheart?' she said as she took them from him, tucking her arm through his and beckoning to Dee. 'Come on, let's get out of here. Sorry about the squeaking when I walk, they gave me the world's biggest sanitary towel to wear. It's *audible*.'

Outside the clinic Jonas took it upon himself to halt the traffic for them, standing in the middle of the road with his palms raised. All he was missing was a whistle and a hat.

'Was it OK?' Dee whispered to Minnie as they crossed over to the Golf Ball. 'What did they say?'

'Oh, fine.' The colour was coming back into Minnie's cheeks. She patted her pocket. 'I've got the other pill in here: I'm meant to take it tonight. The doctor said nothing really happens until you take the second one; I might just feel sick. And that's nothing new, is it?' She opened the driver's door and dropped into the seat, swinging her legs round like a film star getting into a Rolls-Royce. 'Sorry, Dee, just remind me – what's your mum's postcode again? W Seven . . .'

'One LG.' Dee watched her typing the address into her satnav. 'Wait, why are you . . .'

Minnie looked round. 'Didn't I tell you? I thought I'd said last night. Argh, sorry, sieve brain . . . Me and her were just messaging the other day like we do sometimes, and I asked her if I could come and stay with her and Ines for a bit while I get my head together. I didn't say exactly why but they've been so lovely about it.' She clipped her seatbelt in, then shut the door and fired up the engine.

Dee and Jonas watched the Golf Ball kangaroo-hopping down the road with the grapes on the dashboard, both lost in their own thoughts.

'Do you think Minnie would like to go on a date with me?' Jonas suddenly asked.

'I mean, probably not right now this second . . .' Dee raised her eyebrows. Jonas looked crushed. 'That was a joke. Look, why don't you ask her in a few days' time?'

'Yes, I will.' Jonas nodded. 'That is a good idea, thank you.' He looked down at Dee. 'What will you do now?'

The Golf Ball turned the corner on to Goodge Street and disappeared. Minnie, at least, knew exactly where she was going.

'Honestly, Jonas,' Dee said heavily. 'I have absolutely no idea.'

*

When Dee got to the office, Jay was waiting for her by her desk, wearing a silver suit that made him look like an oven-ready turkey and her least favourite of his ties (a wide one with an ironic Bugs Bunny motif). He had Persephone with him. She was dressed in the uniform of the international school she attended at vast cost – a red jumper over a dark blue kilt, with white knee-socks and T-bar shoes, all topped off with a little navy beret. She looked like a furious mime artist.

'Dee!' There was a note of desperation in Jay's voice. 'Surprise! Yeah, so, funny story – Seffy's school had to close for the day because the boiler broke, and Biz is flat out helping ladies of a certain age realign their chakras. So yours truly's doing daddy daycare! Mind just keeping an eye on this one while I call Richard Root back? He said it was urgent.'

Before Dee could say anything Jay had high-tailed it into his glass-walled office, leaving her with Persephone.

Persephone fixed Dee with an interrogator's stare. The grudging acceptance that Dee had earned when she'd babysat a month ago seemed to have evaporated: apparently it was necessary to prove yourself afresh to Persephone every time you met her.

Dee cleared her throat. 'How's your day been so far, Persephone?' she asked.

'Boring.' Persephone surveyed the Anvil office with disdain. 'That plant looks dead,' she said, pointing at the knackered fern on the shelf above the printer.

'Yes, it probably is.' Dee racked her brain for another conversation starter. 'Are you doing anything nice for half-term?'

'Just going to Soho Farmhouse,' Persephone replied,

sounding existentially bored by the prospect of having milkshakes brought to her child-sized sunlounger. 'But my best friend Otty's going on holiday to the Seychelles. Do you have a best friend?'

'I've got two, actually,' Dee said, getting her phone out. Persephone looked dubious. 'No, really, I'll show you a photo of them – one's called Roo, and the other one's called Minnie. I met Roo at school, like you and Otty. And I met Minnie . . .' She decided not to get into their origin story; you couldn't really explain the Gordon's toilets to a six-year-old. 'When I was a grown-up. Roo's a doctor in a hospital and Minnie helps people who want to have a really fun party. Here, this is them.'

She showed Persephone the photo of them taken in Margate the previous summer. She'd made it her phone's background because it always made her smile. Or it had done until recently. Persephone ran her finger over each of their faces in turn, as though she was checking they were real. Then she nodded, satisfied. She seemed to appreciate being provided with this level of detail.

'Do they have husbands?' she asked in a slightly less accusatory tone. 'Daddy is Mummy's first husband but Daddy was someone else's husband before he met Mummy.'

'Oh, was he?' Dee blinked, taken aback. It seemed astonishing that Jay had found not just one but two actual human women who were prepared to pledge themselves to him, but there was no accounting for taste. Then she felt bad for thinking that; he was Persephone's dad at the end of the day, and she probably thought he was the bee's knees. Or – she looked down at Persephone's cross little face – maybe not.

'Roo has a husband. Minnie doesn't; I don't think she wants to have one.' She decided to pre-empt Persephone's inevitable follow-up question. 'And I don't have a husband either.'

Persephone thought about this for longer than she'd thought about anything else Dee had said. A whole series of expressions passed across her face; you could practically hear the cogs turning.

'That's OK,' she said eventually, putting a hand on Dee's arm with the solemnity of Mother Theresa blessing a leper. On the other side of their desk divider Hiro burst out laughing.

Just then Jay emerged, chomping away on his Nicorette. Judging by the whiff of Marlboro Red that accompanied him, he'd taken the opportunity to double up by having a quick smoke out of his office window.

'Cheers for that, Dee,' he said, as though she'd just posted a parcel for him. 'Morag's left Root and Branch. I know, shocker! It's effective immediately so I'm guessing it wasn't a fond goodbye. The new marketing manager starts on Monday. He's raring to get stuck into the Black Friday sale mailouts, apparently . . .' He gave her the thumbs-up. 'Come on, Seffy, let's stick the iPad on, eh?'

As Dee watched oven-ready Jay rustling back towards his office with his daughter, Hiro stuck his head over the divider.

'It's interesting that he waited for the only female member of the team to get here before palming his daughter off on to her, isn't it?' he said archly. 'Almost like he thinks looking after children is a woman's job. I was here ages before you and I'm a perfectly responsible adult. Well, more responsible than you, anyway.'

'Cheers for that.' Dee sat down; her chair creaked ominously. 'Hiro, were you at Anvil when Jay and Bizzy got together? Persephone just told me he was married before.'

Hiro nodded. 'Mm-hmm, he was indeed. He was with someone else when they met, then they got together and decided they wanted to have a baby, but it ended up taking forever . . . Jay told me the whole story when we were at the Content Marketing Awards the year before you joined. Drama all round.'

'Wait – you mean they had fertility issues?'

'Yup, very much so. Four rounds of IVF, every drug under the sun, no coffee or alcohol or processed food, the works. Tens of thousands of pounds. Honestly, seeing it all play out put me off the whole thing, it looked absolutely horrific. Then I met Poodle, and she's never wanted kids, and I want to be with her, so . . .' He shrugged. 'We're getting a second cat when we move into our new place, did I tell you? Another Maine Coon – we've found a breeder in Epping who's got a litter due in six weeks.'

Dee flinched at the mention of Hiro's new home: another ticking clock. She turned to look into Jay's office: he was at his desk, typing laboriously with two fingers in classic boomer style, while Persephone scowled at an iPad in his Eames chair. It was depressing knowing that Jay and Bizzy, whose domestic troubles she'd assumed only extended to choosing which shade of Farrow & Ball greige to paint their living room, had been through so much to make their dream of a family come true.

'Well, I'm glad they got their happy ending, I guess,' she said, turning back to Hiro.

'Ageing man gets together with much younger woman, both of them incredibly annoying – truly the stuff of fairy tales.' Hiro snorted. 'Semi-relatedly, have you heard from you-know-who?'

Dee looked at him blankly. 'Who?'

Hiro gave her an incredulous look. 'Er, Nat?'

'Oh.' Dee switched her brain on to that track – it felt strange, like putting her shoes on the wrong feet. 'No, I haven't, actually. I don't even know if he's back in the country.'

'Wow . . .' Hiro whistled slowly, shaking his head. 'Well, I've been boycotting *Midsomer Murders* ever since those photos came out, just so you know. And I'll continue to do so until you get an apology from him.'

Somewhere between the conversation she'd had with Nat on Minnie's step and now, Dee had stopped combing through Lulu Hartley's Instagram Stories for glimpses of him. Some time after that he'd stopped being the last thing she thought about at night, and she was now at the stage where she could look at a Twix without feeling anything much at all. She still thought about Nat every day, but that felt mostly like force of habit: the emotional equivalent of triple-checking you'd switched the cooker off before going out. The speed with which she'd recovered was genuinely shocking to her: after spending the best part of two decades keeping the torch she'd carried for him alight, it had been snuffed out in less than a month.

'You might be waiting a while for that . . .' she said, turning her computer on. 'And you can watch it if you want to. I honestly don't mind.'

*

Lunchtime came and went, and Dee still wasn't hungry. At three she dragged herself to the sandwich shop at the bottom of Poland Street and bought a giant white-chocolate-coated flapjack, which she found herself walking listlessly in the direction of Soho Square with. The bench she usually sat on was already occupied so she took the one next to it, shooing the circling pigeons away with her foot as she sat down. Her stomach hurt. Normally she'd have messaged Roo jokily asking her if she was dying, and Roo would have sent her a link to a Wikipedia article about a horrible illness, but she was too terrified of letting anything about Minnie slip to do that today.

Andy hadn't sent her anything all morning; his last WhatsApp – *Hah!* – was still there at the bottom of their chat. It wasn't the sort of message that needed a reply, but Dee decided to send one anyway: *Thanks, by the way.*

Andy came online straight away.

Andy:
What for?

Dee:
Persuading Minnie to
message Jonas. Him being
there today meant a lot
to her

Andy:
Ah, I'm glad. Really hope
she's OK.

I'd better run, packing up
early today. Talk soon x

Did Andy have evening plans? He'd normally say if he did. Her mind raced ahead: the fact he hadn't this time made her think whoever he was seeing was someone he didn't want her to know about. Like C, whoever she – it was definitely a she – was. An icy feeling spread down Dee's spine.

Minnie was messaging her.

So yeah, the bleeding's started. This is not the most fun I've ever had in a bathroom. Feel quite shivery and gross. Two to three egg cups of blood doesn't sound like a lot, does it? It is a *lot*. I wish you were here Dee 😟

Dee was about to phone her when another WhatsApp notification appeared. It was from her dad: *Kiddo! Have you had a look at it yet? The photo I sent you.*

Dee dug her nails into the bench's frame. *Not yet Dad, sorry. I've had a lot on my plate this week.* Karl, she saw with dismay, was recording her a voice note.

'Ah, come on, Dee, is it really that bad?' His carefree, hail-fellow-well-met voice was like nails down a blackboard. 'When I was your age we didn't take life too seriously. Lighten up!'

When you were my age you had a child, Dee thought, feeling her blood pressure rise. *Who you never saw.*

A typed follow-up appeared underneath the voice note: *Want to tell your old man what's been going on in your life?*

That was the last straw. Dee held the microphone button down and started recording a voice note of her own.

'You really want to know, Dad? OK, well, at the start of the summer I started seeing this guy I'd spent literally half my life thinking was the answer to all my problems. Then that guy turned up in the *Daily Mail* holding hands with a famously beautiful woman and I found out that my fertility is going down the pan. Then I got drunk and ended up suggesting to a man I barely know that we start a family together; no idea if that's actually going to happen or not. My job is a joke and I'm paying six hundred pounds a month to basically house-sit for one of my colleagues, who's about to evict me because he needs to rent out his flat. Oh, and it was my thirty-fifth birthday last week – I guess you forgot about that.' She stopped and drew a breath. 'So. There you go. That's what's going on in my life.'

She took her finger off the screen and watched her note uploading. Two ticks – grey, then blue. Another crystal-clear memory popped into her head, of waiting by the old landline in the hallway for Karl to call her on Sundays, coiling the cable anxiously around her finger as she watched the minute hand on the clock move. He was meant to phone her every week, but more often than not something came up, or there was a problem with the connection, or he forgot about the time difference and rang in the middle of the night instead. It had ruined almost every weekend. She started recording again.

'And another thing,' she added. 'You can't just expect to be able to walk back into my life like nothing ever happened in the past. A lot happened, and it doesn't work like that. OK?'

She released the message into the ether. Two ticks. Grey, then blue.

Typing . . . Karl's status said. *Online. Typing* . . . Then he was just *online* again. And then he was gone.

Chapter Fourteen

Ealing always had its fireworks display on the first Saturday in November. As Dee sat on the steps of the Town Hall waiting for Roo to phone her, she could smell the tang of burned-out sparklers in the air. The signal on the Isle of Skye was so bad that arranging this call had become a precision operation timed to coincide with Roo's midday trip to the Spar up the hill where you could get 4G. Unfortunately this was exactly when Dee was meant to be meeting Minnie (whose stay with Alice and Ines at Milton Road was going so well that she'd just extended it by another week) for brunch in Ealing. And she had no idea what she was going to say if Roo asked her why Minnie was there.

Just before twelve – Roo set her watch and her phone five minutes fast to make sure she was never late for anything – Dee's screen jumped into life. She pressed the green button with the now familiar combination of dread and guilt smothering her, and there was Roo scowling in her cagoule and a knitted bobble hat. The gorse bushes behind her were being blown nearly flat and a merciless wind whipped down the line.

'Can you hear me?' Dee cupped her hand around her phone. 'Wow, looks pretty blowy. How was the Spar?'

'I'm not . . .' Roo was having to shout. 'God, this sodding wind – Dee, let me just . . .' She crouched down so she was

230

out of the worst of the gusts and lowered her voice. 'I'm not at the Spar. I haven't been in yet.'

'Why not?'

'I . . .' Roo looked over her shoulder like she was checking there was nobody listening. She closed her eyes for a second, grimaced, then opened them again. 'I don't even understand how this happened, there's barely anyone female here – literally every other person I've met has been a retired trawlerman called Willie . . . but anyway, I saw a pregnant woman walking in just as I was about to. And I felt completely ridiculous, Dee, but I just couldn't do it. Everyone chats to each other in there and it's so small, I just couldn't face trying not to listen while she talked about her due date and names and all that stuff. I've been out here for twenty minutes waiting for her to leave.'

Another blast of wind roared overhead. Roo looked so small crouching on the scrubby verge, and so alone. Dee wished more than anything that she could reach through the screen and gather her up in her arms. She felt ill.

'I hate this, Dee,' Roo said, so quietly that Dee had to strain to hear her. 'I hate having to take my temperature every morning at exactly the same time and not being able to get out of bed in the night because if I do the reading won't be accurate and I won't *know* if I'm ovulating. I hate the fact that me and Sam don't even really want to touch each other right now but we still force ourselves to have sex. I hate how I won't read books with "Girl" or "Wife" in the title because they annoy me so much but I'm a member of three different pink forums with "Mum" in their names. I hate that my career is going really well but I barely even think about it because my head is full of peeing on sticks and taking a million different supplements and literally having to run away when I see a pregnant woman. I hate, hate, *hate* that this is me, and this is my life. And there is *nothing* I can do about it.'

'I am so, so sorry, Roo . . .'

As the words left Dee's mouth the pain she'd been feeling turned into cold, hard fear. If Roo had been this upset by seeing a pregnant stranger going into a shop, how many thousands of times worse would she feel if she found out about Minnie? Minnie was right: they could never, ever let that happen.

'I just . . . I wish I could take it all away,' she finished lamely.

Roo shook her head. 'I don't know why you're sorry, you haven't done anything.' She sighed. 'I'm the one who should be apologising, I've been such a miseryguts recently. I'm going to make it up to you and Minnie when I'm back from holiday, I promise. Anyway, thanks for letting me get that off my chest.' The clock at the top of the tower struck midday, scattering the pigeons. 'Wait, are you in Ealing? I recognise those bongs. And those steps you're sitting on.'

'Yup, I'm outside the Town Hall.' Dee swallowed hard, trying to think of something – anything – to say next. 'Remember when we did our Safe Cycling exam around the back of it in Year 7? You got full marks and I got told never to go on the A4020 again.'

'I still have the certificate.' Roo managed a smile. 'Look, I'd better go and see if the coast's clear in the Spar; Sam's family will be wondering where I've got to with the shopping. Say hi to your mum and Ines from me.'

'I will.' Dee nodded, pathetically grateful that Roo's assumption about why she was in Ealing had spared her having to tell an outright lie.

Roo rang off, and her phonebook photo came back on to Dee's screen. It was one of her and Sam's wedding photos. Dee, who'd been Roo's only bridesmaid, was in it too, standing behind them on the steps of the Surrey country house hotel they'd got married in. When the photographer had suggested she step out of the shot, Sam had insisted she stayed and Dee had actually cried. She'd been so worried Sam would come between her and Roo, and he never had.

'So . . . how are things?' Dee prompted Minnie, who was sitting opposite her, absorbed in a plate of tortilla.

Minnie looked up; she was wearing hummingbird-blue eyeshadow that faded out to an electric pink, and her curls were freshly bleached.

'Pretty good!' She tapped the tortilla's lid with her fork. 'A little more cooked in the middle than I'd like, but . . . oh, wait, you mean how am *I* doing after the abortion, sorry.' She put her fork down and shrugged. 'Relieved, mostly. Still a bit crampy, but the bleeding's stopped. They tell you to take another pregnancy test afterwards to make sure it's worked, so I did that last night . . . all clear.' She raised her eyebrows and dug in her bag for her phone. 'Lucky that first test I bought was buy one get one free, eh?'

Dee smiled weakly. They were sitting under a heater outside Reineta, the Spanish deli in Ealing's new Dickens Yard development, so that Minnie could smoke. Meeting here had been Minnie's suggestion: she already seemed to know more about the neighbourhood than Dee ever had when she'd lived here. That wasn't the only way she'd made herself at home: today Minnie was wearing a mohair jumper that looked like a melted My Little Pony and a pair of very long tracksuit bottoms, both of which Dee strongly suspected had once belonged to her.

Minnie was frowning at her screen; it had a new crack across it. 'Argh, I've just seen the photo Roo sent us yesterday of them all on some jetty,' she said, looking up and biting her lip. 'She's back on Wednesday, isn't she?'

Dee nodded. 'She called me when I was on my way here. I don't think she's been having the best time.'

'Shit, really? Poor Roo.' Minnie looked genuinely distressed. Then she looked back down at her phone and her face lit up. 'Ah, Jonas has messaged! He's been checking up on me every day, bless him – he keeps trying to send fruit baskets to Milton Road. Sorry, let me just send him a quick reply, he worries otherwise.'

While Minnie was typing Dee sent the photo she'd just taken to Andy with the caption *Greetings from the Costa del Ealing!* A single grey tick appeared; his phone was off. He worked on Sundays – he'd probably just left his phone at home, she told herself. Or he'd got someone to cover for him and he was having a lie-in. It was absolutely none of her business what he did with his weekends, she reminded herself – they had no claim on each other's time. She had no claim on anything about him.

She felt Minnie's eyes wandering in the direction of her screen.

'Whatever you're about to say, don't . . .' she said, turning her phone over. Minnie huffed, before something in the distance caught her eye.

'Ah, there's your mum!' she cried, waving across Dee and jumping to her feet. 'I invited her to join us, hope that's OK? We had a little impromptu get-together last night for the fireworks and we're both in need of some carbs . . .'

Still trying to process this information, Dee turned in her seat: Alice was coming towards them from the main road, wearing a teal polo neck and cream capri pants with black-and-white saddle shoes, all topped off with a tartan coat. Dee watched her and Minnie signalling to each other in their own private semaphore – Minnie was a natural with Alice, she thought sadly. And she never had been.

'Hello, you two!' Alice called out to them across Dickens Yard. 'I don't know about you, Minnie, but I feel like . . . oh, what's that line from *Withnail & I*?'

'Like a pig shat in your head?' Minnie giggled, jumping up and enveloping her in a hug. 'What can I get you to eat? I'll go in and order for you.'

'Oh, whatever you fancy, I'm not fussy.' Alice patted her back, then looked down at Dee. 'Ronnie adores this one; the two of them are as thick as thieves. He's even started sleeping on her bed instead of ours! I just wish you could stay forever, Minnie.'

'I do too!' Minnie blew her a kiss and disappeared into the cafe. Alice sat down in the now-empty seat next to Dee and pecked her on the cheek.

'We missed you last night!' she said, as though Dee had turned down an invitation. 'After we'd finished dinner I thought it might be fun to make s'mores – you know, those chocolatey American campfire things – so I went out to the Co-op to get some marshmallows and bumped into Frank, and he and some of his friends from college ended up coming over. The next thing I knew it was half past two and Minnie was having to Deliveroo us some emergency crisps!'

'What, Frank from number forty-eight? As in the one who grows weed in his mum's attic?'

'I think that's just a sideline, he's hoping to become an architect,' Alice said mildly. 'But yes, him. He showed us how to roll a giant joint with a whole packet of papers!'

Her mum's eyes were slightly bloodshot, Dee noticed, feeling the back of her neck start to prickle with anxiety. 'Did you smoke it?'

'Yes, of course we did. Don't look at me like that, darling, it's no biggie. I never dabbled in that sort of thing when I was Frank's age, my hands were far too full – so I'm just having some harmless fun now, that's all.' Alice gave her a nudge. 'You ought to pop round to number forty-eight and see if he's got anything going spare, it might stop you being such a worrywart.'

'Is it harmless? Are you sure it doesn't interact with . . . you know, medication?' Dee knew she was sounding like a real prig but she couldn't stop herself. Old alarm bells had started to ring.

Alice waved a hand in the air. 'I'm sure it's *fine*. Anyway, now I've got you here, I keep meaning to tell you, I got a message from your dad on Facebook the other day. Is everything OK with you two?'

Alice had never subscribed to the theory that you shouldn't criticise your child's other parent in front of them: throughout Dee's childhood the only person higher on her

villain list than Karl had been Margaret Thatcher. But over
the past few years Dee had noticed a definite thawing of
relations between the two of them. They followed each
other on Facebook, and Alice had commented approvingly
on several of his posts about the B & B. Even though she'd
spent years wishing that her parents could just get along
civilly, Dee couldn't help feeling slightly irked by this development. It was easy for them to be Facebook friends now
when the stakes were so low. Why couldn't they have co-
operated effectively when it actually would have made a
difference?

'He's been sending me all these voice notes about his
potato crop and photos I haven't even opened. I don't know
why he's bothering, to be honest. And he forgot my birthday again.'

'I imagine he's trying to impress you,' Alice said with surprising equanimity, ignoring the last bit. 'I know he's your
father but he's still a man at the end of the day, and men
can't stand women thinking badly of them. And I think he's
extremely aware that you don't have the highest opinion
of him – with good reason, I might add.' She laced her fingers together. 'I think he'd love it if you went to Denmark
to visit. You could stay in one of those nice little cabins him
and Sofia rent out – that could be how you celebrate your
birthday next year, couldn't it? Oh, also, I was going to call
you later but now I don't have to. Guess who I bumped into
at Ealing Adult Education this week?' She grinned trium-
phantly. 'Cheryl Flynn! She was on her way into Genealogy
for Beginners as I was coming out of the collaging class I
teach. You *know* – Cheryl Flynn? Nat's mum? She's still in the

area. Exactly the same house, in fact. Must be worth a small fortune by now, with Crossrail.'

There had been a time not so long ago, Dee thought, when she'd have had not only Nat's mum's name but the names of his entire family at her fingertips. And now she genuinely hadn't had a clue who Alice was talking about.

'Um, OK – wow. Right. How did that go?'

'*Well*, I was all set to challenge her to a duel, but actually she was lovely! Nat's been staying with her and apparently he's been moping around ever since he got back from Romania.' Alice gave Dee a wink. 'Maybe you should give him a call.'

Dee scrunched up her toes as hard as she could. 'How's Ines doing, Mum?' she asked in a strained voice. 'Is she working today?'

'No, she's in charge of the clean-up operation at home,' Alice said blithely. 'You know how hopeless I am at tidying, I just make things worse. Anyway, stop changing the subject. Will you think about what I said? About Nat?' She took Dee's hands and held them. 'I just want you to be OK, darling. That's all. It isn't good to be alone.'

Dee left Minnie and her mum sharing a chocolate brownie and making plans to go to the cinema. Her own Sunday stretched ahead of her. She checked her phone, saw that Andy still hadn't seen her message, and decided to walk to Hanwell to see Ines – partly so she'd feel less like she'd lied to Roo, and partly because time with her stepmum always pulled her out of a slump when she was feeling low.

When she got to Milton Road she could hear the hoover

going. It stopped when she rang the bell – a couple of seconds later Ines opened the door with her sleeves rolled up, holding a can of Febreeze.

'Welcome to Woodstock,' she said dryly. 'I do hope you've brought some flowers for your hair.'

Inside there was a lingering sticky-sweet scent in the air. Dee stepped over the hoover's cord and followed Ines into the kitchen, slowing down to glance into the living room. The familiarity was instantly comforting: Ines's metal coffee table was still heaped with Alice's books and magazines and catalogues, and her armchair still had its usual sparkly throw (also Alice's) flung over it. There were photos on every surface, in frames studded with shells or pieces of mirror that Alice picked up on holiday. A big one on the mantelpiece showed her, Ines and Dee in Cornwall, each of them holding an ice cream. Ronnie was lying across the back of the sofa, snoring his head off.

'Are you still hungry?' Ines went to open the fridge. 'There's some leftover dip in here, and we're crisp millionaires right now as you can see: Minnie organised a midnight delivery.'

Dee was about to drop gratefully into one of the chairs around the kitchen table when something stopped her. There was an ashtray by the fruit bowl, and an open packet of Benson and Hedges next to it.

'Um, are those yours?'

Ines nodded. 'One of Frank's friends brought his guitar and I needed something a little stronger than Walkers to get me through "The Times They Are A-Changing" . . .' She closed the fridge and turned around. 'Anyway, how was brunch?'

What did it matter if Ines had started smoking again? Minnie smoked like a chimney and that had never been a problem, Dee told herself as she sat down, trying to force herself to relax. This felt like one, though – and she really didn't know why.

'Oh, fine,' she said quickly, hoping that her face hadn't given her away. 'Mum told me she bumped into Nat's mum – apparently he's sad about things ending between us, which is a bit hard to take given he was the one who ended it . . .' She actually wasn't that upset by what Alice had told her, but it felt good to let out some of the frustration she'd been feeling all morning. She threw her hands up. 'Why are men so complicated? Honestly, I think Mum did the right thing deciding to get off that roller coaster.'

Ines raised her eyebrows. 'I don't think your mum *decided* anything, Dee-Dee,' she said as she crossed the kitchen. 'We fell in love, there was no decision-making involved – and I like to think I've got a bit more to me than whatever the opposite of a roller coaster is. Also, having relationships with women definitely isn't the easy option, take it from me. People are extremely complicated, full stop.'

'You're right. Sorry.' Dee, stung into self-awareness, realised that she hadn't even asked Ines how she was yet – she was a terrible stepdaughter. 'Have you . . . had any news about your dad?'

Ines pulled a chair out and sat down opposite her. She suddenly looked very tired.

'Apparently his doctors have said there's nothing more they can do in terms of treatment – it might be a week, it might be months. It's a horrible way to die: when you get to my age you develop an encyclopaedic knowledge of cancers, barely a month goes by without someone you know being diagnosed. I wouldn't wish this one on anyone, not even a violent bully like him.'

She looked away, out of the kitchen window. Dee put a hand on Ines's rolled-up sleeve and squeezed. As soon as things had settled down a bit she was going to take Ines out and talk to her about everything they'd never talked about before, she decided – really talk to her. Maybe she could even take her on holiday, if she ever managed to get a better job and sort her living situation out.

'I'm really glad you got away from him,' she said.

Ines nodded. 'Yes, so am I. Although maybe I didn't, you know?' She put her hand over Dee's and turned back to her. 'Anyway, on a happier note, look what I found when I was sorting the living room out.'

She took a Polaroid out of the pocket of her trousers and turned it around so Dee could see: it showed a very young-looking version of her sitting on the peeling steps of a Regency townhouse. She was wearing overalls and squinting into the sun with her hand shading her face.

'This was in Brighton in 1982,' Ines said, passing it to Dee. 'I got a job as a hospital porter at the Royal Sussex when I first moved to the UK. It was sort of how I ended up doing what I do now – nobody wanted to be around the psychiatric ward, but I didn't mind it at all. I lived in that building in Kemptown, which was the gay village in those days. It's an Airbnb now, run by some company called Rainbow Holiday Rentals; I looked it up just before you got here.'

A scrabbling noise came from behind them – Ronnie had ambled over to his litter tray by the back door and was now digging in it furiously, sending pellets flying across the kitchen.

'Your timing is impeccable, Ronnie,' Ines sighed, getting to her feet. 'I literally just finished hoovering.' She picked up the packet of cigarettes. 'I'm going to have another one of these to fortify myself before I sort that out. You don't mind, do you?'

I'm scared of you changing, Dee caught herself thinking, *because I'm scared of what you changing means.*

'Of course not,' she said quickly.

Later, as Dee stepped outside on to Milton Road again, a flock of wild parakeets exploded over the rooftops, brilliant green and orange. Dee remembered repeatedly asking her mum about where the birds came from when she was growing up, and how Alice had given her a different answer every time: they'd escaped from Hanwell Zoo; Jimi Hendrix had released them into the wild on Carnaby Street; the 1987 hurricane had blown a hole in the roof of an aviary. Not long after Karl left for America she'd suggested they try to feed the parakeets. Dee had stood for hours in the scrubby garden of the flat they were renting with an outstretched palm full of food, trying not to move in case she scared the birds away. Every time there was a rustle in the trees her heart leapt, and every time it turned out to just be the wind she had to blink away tears.

The parakeets scattered. Dee got her phone out. Andy had read her WhatsApp now but he hadn't responded. Unease started fizzing in the pit of her stomach. She clicked out of their chat, then went into another one and sent a short message, which she was shocked to receive a near-instant reply to.

As she started walking towards Brent Lodge Park she felt

like she was brushing shoulders with all her younger selves. There she was aged eleven, eating a Twister with Roo and fretting she was doing it wrong, at fifteen enduring her first kiss with Max from her Biology class (he was five foot four, and she'd felt like Gandalf to his Bilbo Baggins), and at eighteen writing her personal statement and struggling to think of a single reason why a university would choose her over anyone else. All of the Dees had been consumed with worry, and all of them had hoped that one day they wouldn't be. But she was starting to realise that was never going to happen. Life was only going to get more complicated and more serious; she was reaching the age where every decision had the potential to stop the music, leaving her sitting in whichever chair she'd managed to grab.

She sat on the bench near the adventure playground and waited.

'Dee?'

She turned: there was Nat, in jeans and a darker denim jacket with a sheepskin collar and a new pair of Chelsea boots, holding a Tesco bag in each hand. The scene felt completely unreal, like she was watching herself watching him.

'I was literally round the corner when I got your message. Can I?' he asked, nodding at the bench.

He was wearing Comme Des Garçons, the one she'd sprayed herself with in Liberty to feel closer to him. Smelling it was like hearing a song you used to dance to on the radio and feeling your feet start to move of their own accord.

Taking her silence as an invitation, Nat sat down next to her, wedging the bags between his feet. He only left a couple of inches of space. The last time they'd been this near each other they'd just had sex, Dee realised with a blink. She remembered lying back awkwardly on her pillows, concentrating furiously on holding her stomach in and making what she hoped he would think were the right kinds of sounds.

'My mum said she saw yours at Ealing Adult Education the other day,' Nat said in an unusually subdued voice. 'I got back from travelling last week – I thought about calling you, but I didn't think you'd want to hear from me.' A beat. 'It's good to see you. I've really missed you, Dee.'

He'd never said that to her before. She'd got very good at not minding him not saying it, at shrinking her hope that he'd miss her right down until it was so small that nobody would even know it was there. What a sad thing to be good at, she thought now.

'Nat?' He turned to face her almost eagerly. 'Do you remember that time we sat on your mum's front step after school listening to Massive Attack? We were watching that family play frisbee, and you said maybe that would be us one day.'

A whole series of expressions passed across Nat's face.

'I . . . don't remember, no,' he said eventually. 'But I did used to do that. I'd come here to the park and watch parents having a really nice time with their kids and just wish I'd had what they did. And I always got the feeling you were doing the same. That was one of the things I liked about you.'

She didn't doubt that Nat was telling the truth. But he wasn't saying any of this stuff to her because he had serious plans for them, or because he wanted to know her inside out – he just liked how weaving this temporary intimacy between them made him feel. She was an audience.

Her expression must have changed, because Nat looked pained.

'Dee, about Lulu . . .' he began; he obviously thought that was what was bothering her. 'Nothing physical ever happened, I swear. But I get why you were upset by those photos. And I'm sorry that I ended things over the phone like that, it was a really shitty way to behave. I've started seeing a therapist – just over Zoom, but she's really good. She thinks I unconsciously sabotage all my relationships because I'm scared of things going wrong like they did for my parents. For what it's worth, I think she's right.' He met her eye. 'I didn't get the part – not the one I auditioned for, anyway. I got another one but they don't need me until December, so I'll be around until then. Do you think we could . . .'

'Hang out?'

It was so strange, Dee thought as she looked at him looking at her. At the start of all this, whenever she'd seen Andy, all she'd been able to see was not-Nat. Now, with Nat, all she could see was not-Andy.

'Good luck with everything, Nat,' she said, standing up. 'I really mean that.'

As soon as she got the train back to London from Hanwell she got her phone out. It didn't take her long to find the subreddit that Andy had mentioned when they'd been at the hospital: there was one called r/PlatonicCoParents. But trying to find a poster who might be him proved much less straightforward. She was starting to wonder if he'd even posted anything when she spotted it – something by a user called @AJ_Fleetwood. Her finger twitched as she tapped.

Hi everyone! Long-time listener – well, since last week – first-time caller, be gentle with me. I (M, 40) recently started discussing the possibility of co-parenting platonically with a friend (F, 34). Very early days and obviously a lot for us both to think about. I'm not the biggest reader but I was thinking it might be good to get some books on the subject. Does anyone have any recommendations? Thanks in advance, A

Dee had opened Reddit feeling vaguely unnerved by the idea of what Andy might have said about her. Now, as she put her phone away, she saw that she needn't have worried. He hadn't said anything about her at all.

Chapter Fifteen

Dee had always prided herself on her ability to compartmentalise. When it came to sweeping things under the carpet and carrying on, she was Olympic-level. But today – the following Friday after her visit to Ealing – she was finding it almost impossible to focus on work.

There were several reasons for this, and the first was Bizzy. Jay's wife had wafted into the office on a cloud of Le Labo's Santal 33 an hour ago – she had a gap between client meetings in Soho, she'd explained, so she was going to 'catch up on a teensy bit of admin' at Anvil. Since then she'd been perched at the empty desk next to Dee's applying cuticle oil and having loud phone conversations.

'I just want to know how it was allowed to happen,' she was saying now with her iPhone clamped to her ear; Dee had deduced that she was talking to another parent from Persephone's school. 'I don't think that's unreasonable, do you? Anyway, I'll let you know how I get on when I speak to the headmistress. OK. OK. Byeeeee.' She hung up.

'Everything all right?' Dee asked, more out of ingrained politeness than a genuine desire to know what was going on at the Lycée Français in South Kensington.

Bizzy sighed dramatically.

'Persephone put a piece of pasta up her nose yesterday.

They don't seem to realise that it could easily have been a medical emergency – a piece of macaroni can go a *long* way. And Seffy isn't even supposed to eat pasta! I made it very clear to them when she joined that she's wheat intolerant . .'

'When I was six I put a sequin in my eye after watching an advert for contact lenses,' Hiro interrupted from the other side of the desk divider. 'I nearly went blind.'

Bizzy shuddered in her cashmere, before her gaze drifted to Dee's still uneaten breakfast of a cinnamon Danish.

'You know, foods with a high glycaemic index produce free radicals, which can be very toxic,' she said seriously, before giving Dee what was clearly intended to be a reassuring smile. 'But it's not the end of the world if you're having them in moderation, obviously!'

Hiro stood up. 'Just off to poison myself at Subway,' he said pointedly, pulling his coat on. 'Do you want anything, Dee?'

'I'll go out in a bit – thanks though, Hiro.' Dee tried to focus on the email that Cleet Guster, Root and Branch's new head of marketing, had just sent her about the Black Friday promotional materials (*Excited to make your acquaintanceship!* he'd written; it seemed entirely possible that Cleet was not a human at all, but some kind of bot built by Richard Root from old emails). But she found her cursor straying towards her other browser window, which she'd shrunk right down so nobody would see it if they wandered past her desk. It contained the second reason she'd been finding it hard to concentrate: her latest unsuccessful attempt to track down the restaurant consultancy that Andy had worked at with his ex. It didn't help that he had such a common surname – Andy

Jones almost sounded like a made-up name, she'd thought earlier.

There had been a definite change in the tone of their WhatsApp conversations since he'd come round to cook dinner. The shared confidences and in-jokes were gone: in their place were banal observations about the weather and their days. She'd been sending him messages like *Why do envelopes come in packs of ten but stamps in twelves?* and he'd been replying with things like *Bit chilly out today!* There was so little of his personality in this week's messages that she'd taken to scouring the internet for scraps about him to fill the gaps. Like he'd told her, he wasn't on social media: he didn't have a personal Instagram account and he wasn't on Twitter or Facebook. A Google image search yielded a couple of photos of him in kitchens, but nothing that would reassure her about the here and now. Although Dee couldn't exactly say which of them this new awkwardness had begun with, she was certain it had something to do with the message she'd seen on Andy's phone, the one with the x at the end.

She'd been trying to calm herself down by confronting the worst-case scenario head on. If Andy *had*, as she suspected, met someone he was interested in, any possibility of him and Dee becoming platonic co-parents would be dead in the water. But if that happened she wouldn't be any worse off than she'd been a month ago, would she? If anything, she'd be in a much stronger position to make decisions after all the talking they'd done. But it didn't feel that way to her at all.

Her phone lit up, and her heart duly sank. There was the third reason her brain felt like scrunched-up tinfoil: her group chat with Minnie and Roo. It had had tumbleweed blowing through it for the past few weeks – she and Minnie had both been too scared of letting something slip to be active in it, and Roo had barely had internet access. But Roo had just messaged now, she saw. *Right, I've finally finished the last of my holiday laundry*, she'd written. *When are we doing something? I've missed you both x*

Dee turned her phone over. Whenever they met, it would be the first time she'd seen Roo in person since everything had gone from bad to worse. She had absolutely no idea how she was going to face her, especially after the video call they'd had on Sunday when Roo had been so upset about seeing the pregnant woman.

'Bizzy?' Bizzy looked up from the Net-a-Porter sale. 'Can I ask you something?'

'Shoot!' Bizzy beamed, and Dee felt despair at being so lost in her own life that she was going to someone who probably put crystals in unmentionable places for help.

'You . . . know about fertility stuff, right?' she began, not sure how much of what Hiro had told her was common knowledge.

'Oh my goodness, yes, professionally and personally,' Bizzy nodded earnestly. 'Lots of my clients are having trouble conceiving, and I had issues on that front too. How can I help?'

'Well, um, my best friend's been trying for a baby for eighteen months and she's finding it really hard. This is the first thing she's ever tried to do that hasn't worked out the way she hoped, and I . . . I don't know how to help her. So I was just wondering if you had any advice, really.'

'Oh, you're a *lovely* friend!' Bizzy exclaimed, and Dee felt like something she'd scrape off her own shoe. 'Well, I think you just have to listen and be there, really. That's all you can do. But what *I* would say to your friend if she was my client is that it's really important not to lose sight of the bigger picture. When you're dealing with fertility issues you think that starting a family is going to be your happy ending. But of course, it's just the beginning – and honestly, Dee, trying to get pregnant is the easy bit compared to what happens afterwards. I never used to worry about anything before I had Seffy, and now I worry about everything all the time!'

Bizzy's phone lit up – she swooshed her hair over her shoulder and answered it.

'Hello? Oh, *bonjour* Madame Blanchet! Thank you so much for calling me back. Yes, it's about what happened to Seffy yesterday lunchtime . . .'

Dee looked at the clock in the corner of her computer screen: it was nearly two. Her appetite was non-existent right now, but she should try to eat something. As she pushed her chair back and took her pink coat off the back of it her thoughts swirled around what Bizzy had said. She'd always hoped that having a family of her own would lift a weight from her shoulders – and maybe it would. But it could just as easily do the opposite. Of course, she'd known that was true; you'd have to be stupid not to in her position. But knowing something and *really* knowing it were two very different things.

When she got to the bottom of the building's stairs Dee saw that there was a woman in a trench coat with a holdall just inside the front door. She was tiny but had a huge mane of coppery ringlets that reached halfway down her back, and her high cheekbones made her look like an imperious lioness. When she saw Dee she put her head on one side.

'Dee?' she said in a strong Glaswegian accent. 'I'm Morag – Morag Craggs. We need to talk.'

'Three years,' Morag growled as they sat at the bar in the Mexican restaurant on Poland Street, which did two-for-one margaritas every afternoon. 'Three years waiting for him to leave his wife, and what happens when he does? He fucks off with Annie from Logistics, that's what. It turned out they'd been going to see this Boney M cover band together secretly for months.' She swivelled on her stool to face Dee, her green eyes flashing. 'Never get mixed up with a man whose favourite song is "Rivers Of Babylon", Dee – promise me that, OK?'

'I promise,' Dee agreed, although she still couldn't see the connection. Or square this Morag with the one who'd sent her all the po-faced emails about lawnmowers. She felt like she was on drugs.

It turned out that Morag – who was less than a year older than Dee, Glaswegian and swore like a sailor (each of these things was more of a shock than the last) – and Root and Branch's owner, Richard Root, had been having an affair on the understanding that Richard would one day make things official with Morag. When it became clear that wasn't going to happen, Morag had quit her job on the spot, left Hitchin and got straight on a train to London, where she'd accepted an offer from another company who'd tried to poach her. A new company that – and this was the most shocking thing of all – she wanted Dee to come and work for too.

'Prick,' Morag proclaimed. 'Online-only purveyors of fine cacti and succulents to people without much space. Don't let the name put you off, the founder's really sound and she's got some great investors behind her. The customers we're targeting may never have had a chance to learn how to grow things. We want them to feel like they're talking to a friend who's been there when they buy from us, not some patronising expert. I think you could really help us with that. It's a start-up, so salary-wise our hands are a bit tied right now . . .' Then she said an enormous number that nearly made Dee fall off her stool. 'But we'd review that at the six-month mark, and you'd get shares in the company too. And there'll be opportunities for travel, hopefully – you think about cacti very differently once you've seen them in the wild. Speaking of wild, can we get another round of these, pal? Cheers.'

Morag nudged their empty margarita glasses at the barman. She seemed unaffected by the use they had already made of the two-for-one deal. Dee, on the other hand, had the sensation that she was stuck in a washing machine.

'I honestly thought you hated my work, Morag,' she said, having to work quite hard to get the words out in the right order. 'You were always sending it back.'

'Oh, that was Richard, not me. All that jargon crap was me trying to impress him too – fat lot of good it did me.' Morag shook her head. 'I used to watch *Mrs Brown's Boys* with him, Dee. Can you believe it?'

'No, I can't,' Dee said truthfully. Richard Root was getting on for sixty and looked like he'd failed an audition to be a *Top Gear* presenter.

The barman put down two more margaritas in front of them. 'Er, should we maybe get some food . . .?'

Morag either didn't hear her or decided to ignore the suggestion.

'So, what about you?' she asked, nudging Dee's drink towards her. 'Your love life. What's the Dee Jensen story?'

Dee really wasn't sure if it was a good idea to be opening up to someone who might soon be her boss. But Morag, she was learning, was a hard person to say no to.

'Well, there was Nat . . .' she began cautiously. 'He ended things about a month ago . . .'

'Twat.' Morag gave a Roman emperor's thumbs-down. 'What does he do?'

'He's an actor.'

'Even worse. I want to see a pic – what's his name?'

'Nat Flynn.' Dee, hypnotised by the sheer force of Morag's personality, watched as Morag googled Nat.

'Yeah, he'd get it from me,' Morag said eventually, after forensically scrolling through several dozen images. 'I'd be straight out of there afterwards, though; I wouldn't fancy hearing about his *craft*. What made you stick around?'

Dee hesitated.

'I thought . . .' she began hesitantly; she felt like something was stuck in her throat, and she needed to get it out. 'I thought I could get him to love me. And that if I did, everything would be OK.'

Morag looked her dead in the eye.

'Dee, speaking as someone who threw away three years of her life on a married man,' she said with the near-religious certainty of someone four drinks down on a night out, 'I can tell you that is a very stupid way to spend your time. Don't waste another second trying to persuade anyone that you're worth loving – if they can't figure that out for themselves, *they* aren't worth it. Yes?'

Dee's phone, which she'd left on the bar just in case Jay called, suddenly lit up. Andy had messaged her.

Hey! Sorry I've not been in touch much this week. Are you around tonight? Feels like it's been ages since we talked properly, would be good to, I think.

When Dee looked up, Morag was watching her beadily.

'Who was that from?' she demanded. 'It was from *somebody*, I can tell. Come on, who is he? Or she?'

'He.' Dee turned her phone over; she suddenly felt very drunk. 'It's from . . . Andy. And he really is just a friend.'

'Andy! Good name, I like him already.' Morag tilted her head. 'Answer me this – if your friend Andy walked in here now and said, "Dee, how about it?", what would you say?'

The whole restaurant seemed to have gone absolutely silent. Dee thought of everything that she liked about Andy – his smile, his sense of humour, his honesty, his kindness. The way he was with her friends. The way he was with her. The way she was with him. She had been working very, very hard to stop two and two making four, she realised. And she just couldn't do it any more.

'I think I'd say yes,' she blurted out. Then she burst into tears.

'Whoa, hey now.' Morag yanked a paper napkin out of the dispenser in front of them and pressed it into Dee's hand. 'What's all this?'

'You don't understand, Morag, he'd never say that.' Dee blotted her cheeks. 'He doesn't feel that way about me, he's literally spelled that out several times.'

'Really?' Morag narrowed her eyes. 'Walk me through those conversations.'

Dee duly told her about what Andy had said in Tesco Express, and his comment at Hiro's about her having all her own teeth and hair.

'Hmm, well, maybe,' Morag said once she'd got to the end, in a way that didn't exactly inspire confidence. 'But regardless of all that, Dee, it sounds like the two of you need to have a conversation pronto. What else are you going to do, ignore the problem and hope it goes away?'

'Yes?'

Morag gave her a look that would have curdled milk.

'No, you're right, I know. I just . . . when I do he'll probably feel weird about it and won't want to see me any more. And I'm going to miss him so much.' She squeezed the napkin. 'I think I really do like him, Morag.'

Morag took Dee's hands in hers. 'Better to have loved and lost than to have been excited about spending the weekend with Richard Root at a Travelodge,' she said solemnly. Then she signalled to the barman again, nodding at their glasses. 'Can we get two more of these, pal?'

By the time they'd finished the margaritas and eaten a small mountain of tortilla chips, it was nearly half past four and the sun had set.

'What time did you say this place Andy works at closes,

five?' Morag said in the street as she typed her number into Dee's phone. 'OK, if you're quick you should be able to make it.' She grinned wickedly as she handed the phone back. 'Good luck – and give me a call about the job when you're ready. Right, which way's Charing Cross? I'm staying at my sister's in Orpington for a bit.'

As Dee tried to focus on Morag marching off towards Tottenham Court Road in the darkness, her fiery hair blazing behind her, she could feel all her borrowed courage draining away. The thought of presenting Andy with the mess of her feelings was completely horrifying. But Morag was right – she'd taken the lid off the box now, and there was no way of getting it back on. She got her phone out to check Citymapper for the quickest route to Haggerston and wondered if she ought to tell Roo and Minnie what she was about to do. No, she decided: she couldn't face another interrogation.

Dee got to Highbury and Islington in the middle of rush-hour and had to let two Overground trains go because they were so full. By the time she made it to the cafe it was well after five and properly dark. She hurried along the canal towpath, torn between praying Andy would still be there and hoping he wouldn't be.

He was still there – he was locking up, facing away from her – wearing a different coat to his usual one, a crombie with the collar turned up, and a knitted hat in the same colour. She stopped a couple of feet away, taking in every detail of his appearance like it was the last time she was going to see him.

'Andy?'

'Dee!' He spun around. 'Fucking hell – sorry, you scared me. Um, what are you doing here?'

'I got your message.' Dee took a deep breath; her chest felt like it was about to burst. 'Look, Andy, I think . . .'

Someone stepped out of the shadows: a woman. Her dark hair was up in a chignon, and she was wearing a short, black roll-necked jumper dress with black tights and black leather boots that ended above her knees.

'Hi!' she said in a husky voice, giving Dee a wave with a red-manicured hand that perfectly matched her lipstick. She looked and sounded like Sophia Loren.

Dee looked at Andy. Even in the darkness she could see that he'd gone pale.

'Carla, this is Dee,' he said extremely slowly. 'Dee, this is Carla.'

'His wife,' Carla added with a smile.

Missed call: Andy
Missed call: Andy
Missed call: Andy

Andy:
Dee, please can you call me
when you get this?
I tried to catch up with you
but you ran off too fast
I am so, so sorry you found
out about Carla like that

It's Complicated

Dee:
You're sorry I found out like
that or you're just sorry I
found out?
You've been married the
whole time, Andy
I literally can't believe it
Were you ever going to tell
me????

Andy:
I was going to
tonight, I swear
Everything I've told you
about my life is true, Dee

Dee:
You said you had an ex
Someone calling themselves
your wife doesn't sound like
an ex to me!!!

Andy:
Please can I call you?
It's too complicated for a
message

259

Dee:
Someone once told me that
any situation which takes
you more than a sentence to
explain is bad news
Please stop calling me, I
don't want to talk to you

Chapter Sixteen

'But why didn't you tell us, Dee?' Roo asked. 'That's what I don't understand.'

They were lying on Dee's bed an hour later – as soon as Dee had stumbled back to Hiro's and messaged the group to tell them what had happened, both Roo and Minnie had rushed round. Minnie was in the kitchen sorting food, even though Dee couldn't imagine ever wanting to eat again. Roo was lying on her side to Dee's right and Dee was staring up at the ceiling miserably.

'I honestly don't know what I'd have said.' Her voice was croaky, and she couldn't tell if the pounding headache she had was from the margaritas wearing off or from crying. 'I didn't really know how I felt until I talked to Morag today – or maybe I did but I just couldn't admit it to myself.' She tried to blink away what felt like another wave of tears. 'God, Roo, I've made such a mess of everything. Only I could get into a situation where the whole point is that you don't have feelings for each other, then develop feelings for the other person, and *then* find out he's been secretly married all along. Jesus Christ.' She winced as another steel band tightened itself around her skull. 'So much makes sense now. No wonder he's so good at cooking Italian food, he's got an Italian wife. And he probably never invited me round to his flat because it's full of her stuff. Maybe it was *their* flat. I bet that's why he's not on social media either. I'm such a mug.'

Next to her, Roo was frowning in the exact way she had when she'd been puzzling over a problem in Double Maths.

'Look, Dee, I'm absolutely not taking Andy's side here,' she said guardedly, 'but there's married and there's *married*. One of my colleagues is getting divorced at the moment and both of them are in new relationships now. Sometimes people's hearts work faster than the law does. I'm not saying that's ideal, but it happens. And it does sound like Andy was planning to tell you tonight, judging by that message he sent you this afternoon.'

Dee shook her head. 'Carla clearly had no idea who I was, and the message I saw from her on his phone was really flirty. Also they both looked really dressed up – like they were going out for dinner or something.'

A memory of Carla's perfectly applied red lipstick swam through her mind; she screwed her eyes shut. Roo reached for her hand and threaded her fingers between Dee's.

'As I see it, there are two issues here,' she said in a methodical voice. 'The first is that Andy wasn't totally honest with you about his relationship history, to a degree that's still to be determined. That might or might not be fixable depending on what he tells you when you next speak. The second is that your feelings for Andy are by definition going to make any form of platonic co-parenting impossible. And that isn't fixable.'

Roo found this sort of frank talk comforting, Dee reminded herself as she cringed inside. She was doing her best.

'Also he doesn't like me back. You forgot the most depressing bit of this whole saga.' The room had started to spin; she opened her eyes again and groaned. 'You were right about this whole thing, Roo.'

Roo's eyes were full of sadness. 'I really didn't want to be right, I just wanted you not to get hurt,' she said quietly. She hesitated, then let go of Dee's hand. 'Dee, do you remember that time when . . .'

Just then a white-patent-boot-wearing foot nudged the bedroom door open, and Minnie appeared with an extremely Minnie-looking tray of snacks: a jumbo bar of Dairy Milk, three Diet Cokes and a bag of truffle-flavoured crisps. She kicked the door shut behind her.

'Has he messaged you?'

'My phone's off.' Dee raised her head an inch; it felt like someone had poured concrete into it.

'Bastard.' Minnie sat on the edge of the bed, putting the tray down next to her and yanking off her boots. 'I can't believe he's pulled this Mr Rochester shit on us, honestly.' She kicked one boot across the room, then the other. 'He really didn't seem like a bastard though, did he? I like to think I've got a pretty good radar for bastardry and he didn't ding mine once.'

'Or mine,' Roo agreed. 'And I'm much less well disposed towards strangers than you, Minnie.'

'Is that a polite way of calling me a slut?' Minnie tore the bag of crisps open with a wink. 'Budge up, Dee.'

She climbed on to the bed and lay down on Dee's left, draping an arm over the top of the pillow so she could stroke Dee's hair. The bedside lamps cast a warm glow over the three of them. Dee felt pathetically grateful to be surrounded, with no choice but to stay where she was. It wasn't just Roo and Minnie's physical presences that were comforting – it was the way they were both so sure of everything. She regretted every moment that she'd spent being frustrated by them line-managing her: right now it felt like the only thing that was actually keeping her together.

After a while Roo sat up, crawled forward on the duvet and took the chocolate off the tray. 'Thanks for sorting all of this out, Minnie,' she said, snapping a row of squares off. 'I want to be in your bunker when the bomb goes off.'

'My pleasure.' Minnie took the chocolate from Roo and snapped some off for herself too. 'I mean, obviously it isn't, because this is all totally shit. But if there's one thing I know how to do it's cater for any occasion, happy *or* sad. Or bombs.' She waved the chocolate in front of Dee, who shook her head listlessly. 'Oh, Dee, you poor sausage, what a horrible shock. Thank God you've got your amazing new job to take your mind off everything. How are you feeling now?'

'I feel . . .' Dee stared at the ceiling again. 'Like I was drowning, and I grabbed something to stay afloat. But the thing I grabbed turned out to be a shark that bit my arm off. So now I'm still drowning, but I'm missing an arm.' She groaned. 'God, how totally desperate must I be to have latched on to a complete stranger like that?'

Roo, who'd been chewing methodically, swallowed her chocolate.

'Well, to be honest with you, Dee, I think desperation is a perfectly natural response to the social, political and economic situation we as women find ourselves in,' she said vehemently. 'The average man spends less than thirty per cent of his salary on rent, but for women in London it's over fifty per cent. I know, Minnie, it's absolutely shocking. So if you want to have a child in the current climate you need to have a really supportive family, be rich or in a couple – and if the first two were easy to do, everyone would be doing them. How many women do you know who've stayed in unsatisfying relationships because they literally have no other way of making adult life work? We're going back to the Middle Ages and the days of people having to make grim tactical alliances just to survive.'

Dee remembered standing in Hiro's kitchen watching Andy cook – how him being there had made it feel more like her home than anywhere else had in fifteen years. She covered her face with her hands.

'I just don't know how I can trust anyone again after this.'

'You just have to remember that even the nicest people do dickish things sometimes,' Minnie shrugged. 'You've either got to accept that and try not to worry too much about it or go and live in a cave.' She considered the little speech she'd just given. 'I think you were right, you know, Dee – I *would* have made a good rabbi.'

'And whatever happens, you've got us,' Roo said, giving Dee's shoulder a reassuring squeeze. 'Right, Minnie?'

'Damn right you do.' Minnie squeezed the other one. 'Friends are what matters. Romantic love's all just a big bloody con: your stupid hormones try to trick you into wanting to move to Kent with someone just because they're moderately good in bed.' She shook her fist at the ceiling. 'We can see what you're trying to do, Mother Nature! We're not falling for it!' She looked across Dee. 'Isn't that true, Roo? Scientifically, I mean.'

Roo tilted her head in grudging acknowledgement. 'Well, you could certainly argue that oxytocin constitutes a sort of artificial high that can alter human behaviour . . .'

'See! I was right!' Minnie beamed. 'I got that from one of Ines's books on the science of love – I was reading it in bed last night, it's *fascinating*.'

'Wait, what?' Roo narrowed her eyes. 'How did you get hold of Ines's book?'

Minnie, who'd just taken a gulp of her Diet Coke, started coughing dramatically. She stared at Dee as she spluttered, and Dee knew there was absolutely no way she was going to be able to make up a convincing explanation on the spot: with one obvious exception, Minnie was honest to a fault. The danger sign she'd taken her eye off momentarily loomed up at her again.

'Minnie's . . . moved out for a bit,' she said, shuffling herself into a sitting position and whacking Minnie on the back, probably a bit harder than she actually needed to. 'She's staying with my mum and Ines. There was . . . a bit of drama with Jonas last week. We didn't want to dump it on you while you were on holiday.'

Roo's eyes widened with concern. 'Are you OK, Minnie? Is it sorted now?'

Minnie cleared her throat. 'Yes, it's sorted,' she said unnaturally slowly, not looking at Roo. 'Very, very sorted.'

Her phone, which she'd dropped on to the duvet earlier, lit up; she grabbed it.

'Hah! It's The Admiral, he wants to know what I'm up to.

Probably hoping I'll say I'm in the bath or having a pillow fight with half a dozen of my closest girlfriends. Let me just send him a quick picture so he leaves us alone . . .'

Dee and Roo watched as she made her cheekbones pop and flashed the camera a winning smile, turning her face this way and that so it caught the light.

'Where did you learn to pose like that?' Roo asked as she snapped a photo, sounding genuinely impressed. 'I don't think I've ever taken a good selfie, I'm in awe of people who can.'

'This from the woman who takes people to the brink of death for a living then brings them back again.' Minnie grinned as she sent the photo. 'Don't you ever send Sam sexy shots?'

'Oh God, no – when you've been together for as long as we have that kind of thing goes out the window.' Roo blushed as she drank some of her Diet Coke. 'I suppose I did send him a slightly risqué one a few months ago while he was at that conference in Birmingham . . .'

'Show us, show us!' Minnie urged. 'Go *onnnnnn* . . .'

Dee expected Roo to demur, but instead she had another gulp from her can, then picked her phone up off the bedside table and passed it to Dee. The picture was of Roo in her bathroom at home, fully clothed with a mug of tea in her hand.

'I mean, it's a really lovely photo of you . . .' Dee began as Minnie leaned across her. 'I'm not sure I'd strictly call it risqué, though?'

'But I undid my jeans . . .' Roo protested, pointing at the screen. Minnie howled with laughter.

'Roo, you were wearing a *polo neck*,' she cried, thumping

the duvet. 'Come on, we'll take some hot ones now and you can send them to Sam – you know, set the mood for later. Dee, take my place, please.'

Before Dee could object, Minnie had hopped off the bed, scooped her tasselled handbag up off the floor and scampered round to to the opposite side. Dee moved into the space she'd just left, and Roo positioned herself in the middle of the bed, looking startled. Minnie perched on what had been Roo's edge of the bed.

'So if we just undo these . . .' she said to an increasingly alarmed Roo as she tackled her top button. 'Cute! Take my pulse, doc! So, make-up-wise I'm thinking a bold lip, like . . .' She rummaged in her bag and whipped out a burgundy gloss. 'This! Let's pop a bit on – say "Aaaaah" for me. That's perfect.'

Roo, who never normally wore make-up, flicked her eyes apprehensively at Dee across the bed. Dee gave her an encouraging nod, and Roo smiled bashfully back; she actually seemed to be enjoying her hijack by Minnie now. And Minnie was clearly having fun. Dee allowed herself to inhale and exhale as she watched Minnie fluffing up Roo's hair.

Minnie had hopped off the bed again and was now buzzing around to the side of Roo.

'So the golden rule of selfies is to always look up into the camera, never down or straight on,' she was saying. 'Ahh, you look so gorgeous! Now don't actually smile, just sort of *think* a smile with your eyes, if that makes sense? Chin up a little bit for me – bit less? Perfect!' She snapped away happily, then turned the phone around. 'Look at you, Roo! You're stunning! I'll put these on the group right now so you've got them. I hope Sam's sitting down when he gets these, let's put it that way.'

'Minnie!' Roo cried, making an outraged face but looking secretly delighted.

Minnie sent the photos, dropped her phone back into her bag and walked back around the bed to her original spot on Dee's left. She glanced back at Roo and grinned, chuffed with her handiwork.

'That lip gloss looks so much better on you than it does on me, Roo,' she said, retrieving it from the depths of her bag again. 'You can keep it if you like.'

She tossed it across Dee at Roo. Roo went to catch it but missed – it rolled off the duvet on to the floor.

'I've got it, don't worry.' Roo swung her legs off the bed and got into a crouch. 'My God, Dee, it's like a junk shop under here, have you ever thought about . . .'

She stopped. There was a long couple of seconds of silence, and then she stood up. She was holding Minnie's clinic leaflet – the one Dee had kicked under the bed on the morning of the abortion and then completely forgotten about.

'Dee?' Roo asked, and the way she said her name made her want to shrivel up and die. 'Why have you got this? Was someone playing a really horrible joke on you?'

Next to her on the bed, Dee could feel Minnie fidgeting in agitation. She looked from her to Roo and felt the crushing inevitability of what was coming. Minnie was a terrible liar who hated lying and Roo wasn't stupid.

'It's actually not Dee's,' Minnie said in a voice that was so quiet it was almost a whisper. 'It's mine.' Then she let out a short, slightly hysterical laugh and opened Dee's untouched can of Diet Coke with a hiss. 'I had an abortion two weeks ago.'

All the air seemed to have been sucked out of the room.

'But I thought that you couldn't get . . .' Roo shook her head like she was trying to wake herself up. 'So that's what the drama with Jonas was. Wow.' She turned back to Dee. 'Did you know about this? You did, didn't you? You must have done if it was under your bed.'

'We didn't want to hurt you!' Minnie pleaded, looking up at her. 'Roo, I'm so sorry – it's the stupidest, shittiest thing in the world that you're having a hard time getting pregnant when you'd be such an amazing mum, and I don't even want a baby and it just *happened* . . .'

Dee cringed. Minnie was genuinely trying to help, but she knew it would have the exact opposite effect. It was excruciating enough for Roo to feel she was failing at becoming a mother. It was a million times more humiliating to have someone else pointing that out to her. Especially if that someone was Minnie.

Roo stared at Minnie in appalled silence. Then she yanked a tissue out of a box on the bedside table and started attacking the lip gloss with it.

'It's all about you, isn't it?' she said with cold fury once she'd wiped it all off, scrunching the tissue into a ball and stuffing it into the pocket of her dress. 'Always. You turn up late for everything, all you ever talk about is yourself, you treat people like . . . like *Tamagotchis* that you can just play with when it suits you—'

Minnie gasped. 'Wow, it's all coming out now, isn't it?' She leaned back against the wall and folded her arms; Dee noticed her hands were shaking. 'Look, Roo, I really am sorry that we lied to you. But this has been shitty for me too. Nobody skips out of the door going, "Ooh, I'll treat myself to an abortion at lunch," do they?'

Without the lip gloss Roo's mouth looked almost bruised. She stared at Dee, waiting for her to say something. Dee tried to speak but she couldn't. She was stuck in an old nightmare and she couldn't wake up.

'You're unbelievable,' Roo said grimly. 'Both of you. And for the record, I don't need protecting, and I don't want your pity. I'm *fine*.'

Then she walked out of the bedroom, and out of the flat. The door slammed behind her with a bang.

By the time Dee had pulled some shoes and a coat on and caught up with her, Roo was already outside on Brecknock Road, jabbing at her phone to call an Uber.

'Roo!' Dee twisted her ankle on the pavement as she ran towards her. 'Please, just come back . . .'

Roo turned to Dee, and the look on her face was one that Dee had never seen before.

'What Andy did to you is exactly what you've done to me,' she said coldly. 'You realise that, don't you?'

Dee hobbled to a stop; her legs had started to shake, and her hands too. 'Tell me what I should have done instead,' she implored, her voice rising; she felt like she was being pulled apart inside. 'If I'd told you about Minnie you'd have been so upset and she'd never have forgiven me, and now you'll probably never forgive me for not telling you.'

Roo stared at her in silence. Then she cancelled her Uber and pushed her phone back into her bag.

'Don't call me, OK?' she said, turning away from Dee. 'I need some time.'

Back inside the flat Minnie was still on the bed, hunched over with her head in her hands. As Dee got closer she raised it, revealing puffy eyes and tear-streaked cheeks.

'Why did you let her say all that stuff to me?' she demanded. 'You just sat there!'

'Minnie, I . . .' Dee leaned down and wrapped her arms around her. For a couple of seconds Minnie stayed rigid. Then she shook her head and wriggled free. Her hair flower fell out on to the floor.

'I'm going to go too, all right?' She sniffed through her tears as she got off the bed and picked it up. 'I feel ill, Dee. Properly fucking ill. I'm really sorry but I just can't be here right now.'

Chapter Seventeen

After she'd cleared the food away Dee found herself hunched on the sofa, still in her coat with her chin on her knees. If someone were to peel away all her layers, she thought, this feeling – or the fear of it – would be what they ended up at. Even with her coat wrapped around her, she was cold to her bones. Although she'd spent so much of her life feeling lonely, she saw now that for the past five years she'd had absolutely no reason to: she'd been cocooned in the warmth of Roo and Minnie's friendship. But now they were gone. And she really was alone.

The buzzer went. Dee scrambled off the sofa and ran to the hallway to answer it.

'Roo? Minnie?' Her stomach was churning and her heart felt like it was about to explode out of her chest.

There was a pause.

'Dee, it's me,' a familiar voice said unsteadily. 'Can I come up?'

Hearing Andy speak was like brushing up against a radiator: instinctively comforting. But the feeling only lasted for a nanosecond before all the other ones rushed back to Dee. Regardless of what had just happened with Roo and Minnie she was still angry with him, and with good reason.

'No, you can't,' she said stiffly. 'I'll come down.'

She found him standing under the street lamp in the

concreted-over patch that served as the car park at the front of the building. He was still in his coat and hat, but he was also wearing the rucksack he'd brought to the market. Seeing it made Dee even angrier – it was a reminder of all the time they'd spent together when he'd been lying to her.

'Dee, hi.' He started quickly walking towards her, his face lined with worry. 'Look, I'm really sorry to turn up like this but I honestly didn't know what else to do – I know you said not to but I've been trying to call you.'

'Yes, my phone's been off.' Dee crossed her arms and bit the inside of her cheek to try to stop her bottom lip shaking. 'Just to be clear, I haven't been crying because of you. I was before, but Roo and Minnie came round and now they both hate me'

Andy stopped about six feet away from her. 'What happened? Are you OK?'

'Of course I'm not fucking OK!' Dee snapped; she was properly crying now but she didn't want to un-cross her arms to do anything about it. 'My whole life is falling apart! Everything is terrible! You've got a secret wife! And women in London have to spend twenty per cent more of their salary on rent than men do, did you know that?'

To his credit, she thought grudgingly, Andy didn't seem to have been thrown by this.

'I didn't actually know that, no,' he said after a second's hesitation. 'But it doesn't surprise me, women get a pretty raw deal.'

'Says the man who's been lying to at least two of them.' Dee reluctantly dragged the sleeve of her coat across her eyes to wipe the tears away.

274

Andy looked pained. 'Dee, please – can we go inside so I can explain properly? I've got something to show you.'

Dee shook her head. 'Anything you want to show me, you can show me out here,' she said, apparently now channelling Bette Davis.

'OK, OK. All right.' Andy shrugged his rucksack off, unzipped it between his feet and took out a bundle of papers. 'This is a copy of an application for something called a final order,' he said, holding it up. 'And it's what gets you divorced.'

'When Carla and I split up in 2021 you still had to wait two years if you wanted what's called a no-fault divorce: that's where neither of you has cheated on the other one or behaved unreasonably,' Andy explained. They were at opposite ends of the sofa with his folded-up coat between them. 'But earlier this year they changed the law to make things more straightforward – now you decide you want your marriage to end, then you have to wait a couple of months before you can request something called a conditional order. Then you wait another six weeks before requesting the final order. Carla and I had already separated, and we jointly applied for a divorce the week the law changed because we both just wanted to get it sorted. When you and I met we'd just got to the end of that six-week waiting period – so in theory it all could have been done and dusted within days. But her solicitor got ill, which slowed the whole process down, then mine got married and went on a three-week honeymoon, which I thought was pretty insensitive under the circumstances . . .' He saw Dee's expression and cleared his throat.

'Sorry, bad joke. Anyway, everyone's finally back at work now and we've made the final application. So as of next week I officially won't be married any more.'

Dee pulled her coat around her more tightly. She'd made a point of keeping it on even after he took his off – she didn't want it to look like she was letting her guard down again.

'But why didn't you tell me any of this before? Also, the flat you've been staying in, is it Carla's?'

'Mostly hers, but it's in both of our names – I got something when my dad died that I put towards the deposit. After we left London we were letting it out, but we're selling it now so I can get my money out and hopefully put it towards a place of my own. We've been dealing with that side of things together: Carla's got a boyfriend now who she seems really happy with and things between me and her are as good as they can be. We don't dislike each other, we just shouldn't be a couple. Anyway, we had some paperwork to go through from the estate agent, so we thought we might as well do it over a drink – her best friend's the general manager at this posh place near Liverpool Street and we were going there, that's why I'm in my Sunday best today.'

He pulled a self-critical face.

'And to answer your first question, I didn't tell you at the start because the first time we properly spoke I wasn't sure if I'd ever see you again. Also I didn't want to go on and on about my life when you were clearly in such a bad way about yours. Then we *did* see each other again, and I decided not to say anything then because I honestly thought the whole thing might be over and done with by the time we went to the market, and I could just give you the potted version then. Obviously it wasn't, though, and the longer I waited the worse it got. And honestly, Dee, I think I was just really embarrassed about the whole thing. I *am* really embarrassed. I never thought I'd be forty years old and getting divorced – my parents met when they were teenagers and they stayed together. Even though I know this is so much better than staying in an unhappy relationship, there's still a part of me that feels like a failure. That's why I'm not on social media.'

He got his phone out of his pocket and held it out to her.

'I promise I've told you absolutely everything now. If you want to look through my gallery or my messages for proof I'm completely happy for you to do that, I'm not hiding anything. I'll do whatever it takes to get your trust back. I'm just so sorry I've fucked this up so badly, Dee.'

He was clearly telling the truth. But that wasn't the only reason that Dee could feel her hostility ebbing away. It was that so many of the feelings he'd just described – the self-consciousness, the embarrassment, the muddled fear of the future – were ones she knew like the back of her hand. They were so much more alike than she'd ever realised. She took her coat off.

'OK, I believe you,' she said in a pinched voice, putting it over the back of the sofa. 'But I might just have a look at your Australian sunburn photos to cheer myself up.'

'Absolutely, be my guest.' Andy passed her the phone. 'The really hilarious ones are in the album called "The Melbourne Identity".'

As she scrolled through photos of Andy in sunglasses looking surprisingly tanned at various beach bars, the sense of relief Dee had been feeling started to fade. Yes, OK, he was single. But did that actually change anything for her? Not really, she thought despondently. Maybe there wasn't anybody else on the scene this time, but there would be eventually.

'All right, so what about you?' Andy asked. Dee looked up. 'You said something happened with Minnie and Roo earlier, do you want to talk about it?'

Dee's eyes started to swim again. She put Andy's phone down on the sofa. 'I've made such a mess of my life, I'm not even sure where to start.'

She told him everything. When she got to the part where Roo had stormed out she started to cry properly. Andy jumped up and grabbed the kitchen roll off the side.

'God, you've really been in the wars recently, haven't you?' he said, tearing a sheet off and passing it to her to use as a tissue as he sat down again. 'But look, they're your best friends, one argument isn't going to change that, even if it was a terrible one. If I were you I wouldn't try to do anything tonight – I'll head off in a second and let you get an early night, then you can message Roo and Minnie first thing in the morning. I think they're probably both more angry with themselves than they are with you. Once they've cooled down they'll see that.'

Then he reached across the sofa and gave her back a pat. It was something you'd do to an ageing relative, Dee thought as yet more tears spilled over.

'You . . . you don't have to go just yet if you don't want to,' she said, folding the damp piece of kitchen roll into smaller and smaller squares.

Andy considered this. 'OK then – well, in that case, how would you feel about trying my never-fail cure for a shitty day? All we're going to need is butter, flour and sugar.' Dee stared at him, and he stood up. 'Shortbread. Come on, up you get.'

He held a hand out for her. Dee hesitated, then took it. He had really good, capable hands, she thought as she let him pull her on to her feet.

She showed him which cupboard the dry ingredients were in, and they managed to find not just a block of butter but a bag of chocolate drops in the fridge. Hiro's apron – dark denim, tan strings, surprisingly nice given he only ever microwaved food – was hanging up by the fridge.

'Seeing as there's only one in the flat, I think you should have this,' Dee said, taking it off its hook and presenting it to Andy. 'You're the head chef. What would that make me?'

'Sous-chef.' Andy smiled as he pulled it over his head and tied the strings. 'But I'll demote you to kitchen porter if you eat the chocolate while my back's turned. OK, how about I weigh, then you mix everything together and I roll the dough out? Then we can both do the cutting.'

They set to work. Andy sliced a chunk off a pat of butter and cubed it, then sifted flour and sugar over it in a big bowl, which he passed to Dee along with the packet of chocolate. Dee did her best to concentrate on rubbing the ingredients together and kneading them into a ball, trying not to think beyond that.

'I wouldn't have had you down as the shortbread type,' she said as she watched Andy tearing clingfilm off the roll. 'It seems a bit . . . I don't know, girly?'

Andy laughed, smoothing it down on to the worktop. 'Try telling that to Robert the Bruce. Anyway, I did some shifts at Peggy Porschen many moons ago, I'll have you know. And I had a lovely time making flowers out of fondant icing. If pastry chefs weren't an endangered species because swapping actual desserts for random splodges on plates is the easiest way to cut costs, I'd probably be doing it full time.'

A memory popped into Dee's head. 'I actually think my dad was a pastry chef when he and my mum met,' she said, picking the dough up and passing it to Andy: there were dents in the sides where her fingers had been digging in. 'I remember her telling me that he made her a millefeuille on their first date. So eighties.'

'It's a classic for a reason.' Andy dropped the dough on to the clingfilm and squared it off with his palms. 'Did you ever cook with him when you were growing up?'

Dee thought back. 'I don't think so, no. He lived in a few different places after he moved out and they all had shared kitchens. So we always just used to go out to eat when I was staying with him. The big Pizza Hut in Leicester Square was my favourite, I was an absolute demon for the salad bar. Couldn't get enough of it.'

'Ah, yes, the legendary bacon-flavoured sprinkles,' Andy nodded sombrely. 'Forever in our hearts. Probably literally, I dread to think what they were made of.' He brought the sides of the clingfilm up around the dough and did a series of complicated folds like he was wrapping a present. 'Is he still cooking? Your dad, I mean.'

'In Denmark. He and his wife have a sort of luxury

smallholding that people come and stay on – the guests help bring the crops in, things like that. The food's meant to be really good.'

'You haven't been?'

Dee shook her head 'No, we haven't seen each other for years. We were meant to do something around my thirtieth but he basically stood me up – I was sitting in a restaurant waiting for him and he never showed up. He's always been really unreliable and it was sort of the final straw.'

Andy shook his head sadly. 'Well, I'm obviously not defending the guy, but I hope he can find a way to make it up to you so you can see each other again before too long. You never have as much time with people as you think.'

He gave her a look she couldn't quite make out. Then he tapped the top of the clingfilm parcel, suddenly all business again.

'All right, you're meant to chill this for twenty minutes before you roll it out, but if you put it in the door of the fridge, which is the coldest part, you can get away with ten. My mum told me that. She's an amazing baker, and shortbread is the first thing I can remember making with her. She had this set of cutters that were shaped like dinosaurs, and we used to march them around the table making roaring noises at each other while we were waiting for the biscuits to cook. Hours of fun.'

'Can I . . . see a photo of her?' Dee asked. The thought popped straight out of her mouth before she'd had a chance to interrogate it.

Andy looked surprised, but pleased too. 'Sure, if you like. I've got some old ones on my phone, actually.'

He got it out of his pocket and held it out for her, scrolling through until he found the photo he was looking for. It showed a much younger version of him in chef's whites kneeling next to a restaurant table – sitting at it was a beaming woman with his hair and eyes holding a glass of champagne.

'I was seventeen there and I'd just been made a chef de partie, which means you look after a station in the kitchen, like vegetables or sauces,' Andy said with a smile. 'My mum came in to the hotel where I was working for lunch – it was honestly one of the proudest moments of my life. And now we go even further back in time . . .'

He swiped again. The next photo was of a skinny, very young Andy in shorts and a knitted sweater standing on what looked like Blackpool beach next to the same woman and a tall, red-headed man with a moustache, who was shielding his eyes from the sun.

'So, yeah. That's my mum, Evie.' Andy put a finger on the page. 'Evelyn Irene Davis. And that's my dad, who was called Sean Patrick Jones – two-thirds Irish, one third Welsh, just like his name.' He looked across at Dee. 'I always thought Evie would make a good . . .'

Baby name, Dee thought as the unfinished sentence hung in the air. That's what he'd been about to say.

'Andy?' she heard herself saying. 'There's something I really need to tell you.'

Her heartbeat was pounding in her ears. She couldn't look at him.

'See, the thing is, I . . . like you,' she went on, feeling the pressure in her chest building. 'I mean, I *really* like you. That's what I came to tell you earlier. And I know you don't feel that way about me, and I know that isn't what this is, but I can't keep lying to myself. And if that means we can't—'

'What?'

She forced herself to look up. Andy was staring at her like she'd gone mad.

'Dee, stop . . . you've got this the wrong way round.' He shook his head. 'When we were having dinner here, Minnie said – what was it? That you were "impervious to my charms". And you literally told me I wasn't your type when we were in Tesco, remember?'

'But I . . .' Dee was floundering. 'I didn't mean it. I mean, I hadn't even properly thought about whether you were my type or not. I just said it because you'd said that you didn't want to ask me out, and I was embarrassed. Attack is the best method of defence, I guess.'

Andy had been listening to this with a look of complete bafflement on his face.

'But Dee, I didn't say that I didn't want to ask you out. I said I *wasn't* asking you out. Big difference. And I only said that because I suddenly thought, what if she thinks I'm some kind of massive creep who's using this whole platonic co-parenting thing as a smokescreen? I was trying to make it really clear that I wasn't doing that.' He shook his head. 'Christ this is getting confusing. We've both got ourselves into a proper mess here, haven't we?'

The kitchen clock ticked in the silence. Somewhere in the past minute, Dee thought, she had missed something very important.

'Wait, are you saying you do . . . like me?'

Andy put his phone back in his pocket. Dee got the distinct impression that he was trying not to look at her.

'Liking isn't something you can really do if you're not getting anything back from the other person – well, I can't, anyway. And I didn't think you felt that way, so I never properly let myself feel it. That's why I hadn't told Carla anything before tonight – I knew if I started talking about you she'd see how I felt and call me out on it, and then I'd have to properly confront it.' He finally met her eye. 'But I do. Like you, I mean. That's why I left the hospital in such a hurry, and it's why I've been a bit quiet on WhatsApp too: hearing about your ex really bothered me, and I knew I needed to get a handle on it because I had no right to feel that way. I've got nothing to offer you, Dee, my life's a total . . .'

She put her hand over his. And then they were kissing.

As soon as it happened Dee felt it go all the way through her – a loud, clear, electric *yes*. This was right. Andy moved a hand to the small of her back and used the other to push her hair to one side so he could kiss her neck. She pressed herself against him hard and he pressed back even harder, until there wasn't even a millimetre of space between them. They stayed like that for a moment, holding each other, their breathing slowing together.

'What about the shortbread?' Dee murmured into his shoulder. Andy laughed.

'I think it'll be fine in the fridge for a while,' he said, kissing the top of her head. 'Come on, let's go somewhere a bit quieter.'

Chapter Eighteen

Dee woke up with the sun full on her face. She opened one eye, made a noise like someone letting the air out of a tyre, then prised the other eye open and took stock of the scene. Her curtains were wide open – they must have forgotten to shut them – and there were clothes scattered all over her bedroom floor, along with a pair of tumblers, the bottle of vodka Andy had originally brought round for the pasta sauce and a half-empty jar of olives. The sky framed in the window was blue and cloudless. It was already a beautiful day.

She felt movement and rolled over. Andy was awake, lying on his front, his face slightly creased from where he'd slept on it.

'Nice bed you've got here,' he said with a bleary smile. 'And I'm not just saying that because I'm currently sleeping on an inflatable single mattress on the floor of my empty old flat.'

There was the tattoo just below his shoulder that she'd seen for the first time the night before, an old-fashioned anchor that he'd had done in Morecambe as a teenager when he lost a bet. He'd told her the stories behind all of them, her head on his chest and him stroking her hair, and she saw how they mapped his life out. He'd shown her the fourth finger of his left hand too. For a while after he'd taken his ring off there'd been an ident where it had been, he'd said. But it was long gone.

'You never told me where you were living when you moved out of London, by the way,' she said, tangling her feet up with his.

'Oh. Guildford. Well, a village just outside.'

'*Guildford?*'

'What?'

'I just can't picture it, that's all. Surrey doesn't feel very you.'

'Maybe not. I went fully native by the end, though, I had my own set of golf clubs.'

'OK, get out. Actually, no, please don't – this bed's much nicer with you in it.'

As they kissed she noticed again how easily her body fitted itself to his. There was none of the awkwardness she normally felt, none of the worry that she was taking up too much room. She moved her head too quickly off the pillow and groaned. 'God, I can't believe we made martinis at midnight.'

'They weren't even real ones.' Andy stifled a yawn. 'They were what we in the trade call Speed Martinis – a chef's special. You get a bottle of vodka out of the freezer and wave it in front of some vermouth. Then you pour yourself a little bit and drink it. Rinse and repeat.'

'So it's basically just a really cold shot?'

'Basically.' He glanced at the carpet and grinned. 'You can add an olive if you're feeling fancy, which we clearly were.'

'*God*. Who does that?'

'Us, apparently.'

Us. Dee hugged the word to herself. They were an us. She was part of a plural.

'I wasn't lying, I genuinely had no idea you liked me,' she said, nudging her foot against his.

'Why wouldn't I? You're funny and caring and beautiful, and you've got great taste in 1980s desserts . . .' Dee gave him a kick, and he rested his forehead against hers. 'But I'd never have said anything if you hadn't been honest. So thank you for that.'

'You're very welcome.' She shuffled even closer to him. 'And honesty will be the policy going forward.'

'Agreed. Honesty and Viennetta.'

They kissed again, more deeply this time. Andy pushed her gently on to her back and she pulled him on top of her, tangling her hands in his hair and running her feet down the back of his legs. A whole series of images from the night before played out behind her eyes: him picking her up, her legs wrapped around him, him looking down at her, her looking up at him. She'd always found sex with new people deeply stressful – but Andy didn't feel new, and it hadn't been like that at all. It was incredible how not spending the entire time worrying what the other person was thinking about you meant you could just . . . let go. And she had.

'Hang on . . .' Andy nodded in the direction of the bedside table's open drawer. 'Before we get too carried away, you only had two left, remember? And we got through them last night.'

She remembered now. Before what had nearly been the third time, she'd held the empty box upside down and pretended to shake it, and Andy had burst out laughing, and then they'd looked at each other and it had felt like staring down from the roof of a tall building, pulled towards the street by gravity. The question was no longer, *Why should we do this?* It was, *Why shouldn't we?*

Andy sat up and propped himself on his elbows. 'Tell you what, how about I pull some clothes on and nip out to the chemist now, then pick up some food to cook for us on the way back here? Couple of rounds of bacon sandwiches?'

'Oh my God, yes please, that sounds amazing.' Dee kissed his shoulder; the ease with which the gesture came to her was another small, tender shock. 'Have you ever tried them with marmalade? Roo got me into having it with bacon instead of ketchup when we were at school. She says . . .'

She leaned out of bed to grab her phone off the floor, switched it off airplane mode and waited. Nothing. Neither Roo nor Minnie had messaged. Andy, who'd been watching, put his arm around her.

'Let's have food, then you can write a message to Roo and Minnie once we've eaten.'

Dee nodded; however gut-wrenching the conversations were going to be with Roo and Minnie, she knew she wouldn't be dealing with them alone. He kissed the top of her head, then swung his legs out of bed and reached for his jeans.

'Right, back soon,' he said, picking his jumper up off the floor and pulling it on. 'Message me if you want anything in particular, OK?'

'Don't forget the edible flowers . . .' He chucked a pillow at her. 'Thank you, Andrew.'

'You're very welcome, Diana.' She threw the pillow back. 'Mind if I take your keys with me? That way you can stay in bed until I get back – which is my strong preference, just so you know.'

Dee waited until the door had closed behind Andy before treating herself to a starfish stretch under her duvet. She remembered how optimistic she'd been when she'd bought it with her first Anvil salary payment, hoping it might mark the start of a new, more settled phase in her life. Now, even though things were still very far from perfect in so many ways, she felt like she was finally getting there.

Once she'd clenched then unclenched her toes and flexed the stiffness out of her legs, she shuffled herself upright. She was going to tidy up the mess they'd made last night before Andy got back, she decided. But first, she was going to make them coffee. She picked up her phone just in case and padded through to the kitchen.

The pot Ines had given her for her birthday was still in its box. Dee unscrewed it and heaped Hiro's good grounds into the funnel, before carefully filling the base with water and screwing it back together again. As she clicked the hob on and got two of the nicest mugs out of the cupboard, she found herself replaying a conversation she and Andy had had the night before.

Turns out we're actually really good at this, doesn't it?

Actually? Don't sound so surprised, Andy . . .

You know what I mean. It isn't always like this, is it?

No, you're right. We're good. Good together.

A good team.

She was pouring the coffee when she heard footsteps coming up the stairs. A key turned in the lock, and there was Andy, his hair sticking up from being blown about in the wind, holding a paper bag from Salvino's. She watched him carefully folding his coat over the back of the sofa and hanging her keys back up on the hook next to the light switch – they were such ordinary things for someone to do, but the ordinariness felt extraordinary.

'They saw me coming a mile off in the deli,' he said, putting the bag down on the table. 'I just paid thirteen English pounds for eight rashers of bacon, a very small loaf of bread and some orange juice. Luckily for them I'm in too much of a good mood to care about being absolutely fleeced. God, that coffee smells good, I'm prepared to overlook the fact you're out of bed.'

Dee crossed the room to meet him, slipping an arm around his waist and pressing herself against him. She looked into the bag and saw there was a pair of metallic boxes in there too.

'Two twelve-packs?'

'They were on two for one: I was trying to recover the cost of the bacon.' Andy kissed her cheek. 'Should see us through the rest of the weekend, anyway. Now, how would you feel about me putting Radio Two on? Claudia Winkleman does Saturday mornings, I believe.'

'I would feel embarrassingly enthusiastic about that.' Dee grinned, settling herself on the arm of the sofa. Andy turned the radio on and started cooking, humming along to Johnny Cash. They would eat, she thought as she listened to the pan sizzle over 'I Walk the Line', and then they would go back to bed. Maybe they would drag themselves out of it when it was dark again, get dressed in whatever they could find and go to the pub. More extraordinary ordinariness. She wished she could freeze time and stay in today forever.

Andy's voice broke through her thoughts.

'Oh, I've got some news – I was going to tell you yester-day but I forgot what with one thing and another,' he said, casually flipping the bacon with his coffee in the other hand. 'Angie emailed me, some family stuff's come up and she's decided to stay in the US for longer. Like, six months longer. She asked if I want to stay on too – she said I can hire some help and rewrite the menu if I want to.'

Dee shuffled around on the sofa so she was facing him.

'Really? I mean, that's amazing – I just thought you said you didn't want to work in a kitchen any more.'

Andy nodded, putting his mug down. 'I really thought that was how I felt. But I've been mulling over what Minnie was saying the other night, and maybe I *was* a bit hasty in turning my back on it all. The company was Carla's thing really, it made sense for us to do it together but my heart was never really in the work itself. I *have* missed cooking for other people, I can't pretend I haven't. And it would be nice to cook them my own food.' He gave the bacon one last flip and switched the gas off. 'And maybe this could be a good stepping stone to opening my own place eventually – the cafe's pretty well known, it would probably help me get back-ing. If I did end up doing that, the hours I'd have to do still wouldn't be amazing, but we can figure that out. Ultimately you've got the kind of job you could do part-time from home if you had to, right?'

Even though the cooker was on and it was a sunny day, the temperature in the kitchen suddenly seemed to have dropped by several degrees.

'Sorry, what do you mean?' Dee asked.

'I just meant that if we—' Andy stopped himself.

'Depending on what the future holds for us, you've got the kind of job where you can be a bit flexible. Which is great.' He looked away with a bashful smile and started transferring the cooked bacon to a plate. 'Sorry, I'm doing way too much thinking aloud here, this hangover's turned me into Minnie. Just ignore me: breakfast won't be a minute.'

Dee's hands felt clammy and her pulse had started to race. Her instinct was to do exactly what she'd always done when something like this happened, and pretend it hadn't. But this time, she knew she couldn't.

'Hang on, has this always been your plan? For me . . . I mean, for whoever you had a baby with to cut back on their work? Is that what you meant by wanting to do your own thing?'

Andy spun around. 'Oh my God, no. I don't have a plan, Dee – I was just thinking out loud. All I meant was that if I *did* hypothetically go back to cooking and we *did* hypothetically start a family, doing it that way might make sense, because mine isn't the most flexible line of work. That's all.'

She'd promised that she would be honest. And what she honestly felt like now was an old, cold dread. But before she could work up the courage to say that although doing things that way round might make sense to him but it certainly didn't to her, her phone lit up – Minnie's name was flashing across the screen. She snatched it up.

'Minnie, I'm so sorry – please, can I just—'

'It isn't Minnie,' the shaky voice on the other end said. 'It's me, darling. Your mum.' There was a sob. 'Ines has gone.'

Chapter Nineteen

Alice opened the door wearing Dee's – now Minnie's – mohair jumper under her dungarees, in floods of tears.

'Ines and I had a fight this morning,' she gulped as Dee rushed up the path after running from the station; she'd said a hurried goodbye to Andy as soon as she'd put the phone down, leaving him in the flat. The conversation they'd been having when Alice had called was still hanging over Dee – but that was going to have to wait.

Alice's face was pink and puffy from crying and her eyes were swollen. 'I went to the shops and Minnie popped out for a run,' she went on. 'When we got back Ines was just . . .' She was struggling to get the words out. 'Gone. She left a note saying she needed a break, that was all. And now her phone's off.'

'Oh, Mum . . .' Dee held her as tightly as she could, trying to keep herself together. If she let go, she thought, Alice would simply fall apart like a dandelion caught in the wind. She had never had that feeling here before, in this house. She hadn't had it for nearly twenty years.

The landline rang. Alice jumped.

'That might be her!' She shrugged Dee off and hurried into the living room, kicking the door closed behind her.

The hall felt horribly empty. The whole house did. Even

when Ines hadn't been at home Dee had always sensed her stepmum's presence. She couldn't feel it now. She touched the empty arm of the stand where Ines's coat had always hung and felt cold as she thought about the million and one ways in which she and Alice leaned on Ines. Of course she'd broken. The only surprising thing was that it hadn't happened years ago. Hadn't Ines said it herself, in the wedding video? *As far as I was concerned I was going to live there by myself and have a nice, quiet life. That was the plan.*

Ronnie padded out of the kitchen and set a course for Dee's legs. When he got to her he nudged them with his head, tickling the backs of her knees with his tail. Dee crouched down and braced as she tried to scoop the cat up into a cuddle, but Ronnie was having none of it: he wriggled in protest, did a surprisingly acrobatic flip out of Dee's arms and thundered back in the direction he'd come from.

'Come on, Ron . . .' Dee stood up. Then she stopped. Minnie was sitting at the top of the stairs in her Snoopy pyjamas, her knees drawn up to her chin.

'I realised that I never sent you this week's horoscope,' she said quietly. 'It says I'm a dickhead.'

Dee took a step towards her. Minnie shuffled down a step. They inched towards each other until Minnie was at the bottom of the stairs. And then they were hugging, clinging on to each other. Minnie's familiar smell – Silk Cut and her fruity perfume – made Dee's eyes swim.

'I've been trying to call Roo but she's not answering,' Minnie mumbled into the front of Dee's top, which was already damp from Alice's tears. 'Have you phoned her? I'm so sorry, Dee. This is all my stupid fault: I made you lie to her – I should never have done that.'

Dee shook her head. 'She told me not to call. I know she'll hate it if I pester her.' She brought a hand up to wipe her eyes on her collar. 'Is Mum all right? I mean, she's obviously not, but is she . . .'

'She's had a coffee and she ate a few bites of toast just now. I didn't tell her anything about yesterday, don't worry.' Minnie dabbed Dee's cheeks with her sleeve. 'Ines'll come back, Dee – people always do. Come on, let's go and check on your mum.'

Not always, Dee thought.

They opened the living-room door. Alice was sitting at one end of the sofa, clutching the crochet cushion and staring into the middle distance. She looked utterly lost.

'It wasn't her,' she said hollowly as they came in. 'It was a man asking if I'd been in an accident in the past six months. I told him to fuck off.'

Minnie sat down right next to Alice and put an arm around her. Dee hovered by the sofa, feeling like a stranger in her childhood home.

'All right, let's look at the positives,' Minnie said, rubbing Alice's back comfortingly. 'Ines took a suitcase but not her passport, which means she can't have got on a plane. That's good, isn't it? There's only so far away she can be.'

'Her phone's never off,' Alice whispered. She pulled the cushion against herself and burst into tears again. 'This is all my fault,' she sobbed into it. 'I push everyone away. I'm too much for people.'

'That's not true, Mum . . .' Even as the words were leaving

her mouth Dee knew they sounded totally unconvincing. Alice looked right at her.

'If it isn't then why can't I remember the last time we spent any proper time together?'

She buried her face in the cushion again. Minnie wrapped Alice in a hug, rocking her gently. Ronnie padded into the living room, heaved himself up on to the sofa on Alice's other side and settled in. He stared at Dee, as if to say: *Your services are no longer required.*

'Sorry,' Alice mumbled into the cushion's fabric, burying a hand in Ronnie's ruff. 'I'm sorry, you two. I'm just so worried, that's all. I love her so much.'

She had two options, Dee realised. She could do what she always did whenever Alice was upset: back away, sweep everything under the carpet. Or she could do the other thing. The thing that Andy, if he was here right now – the thought of their rushed goodbye, and how worried he'd looked, made her feel ill – would definitely be doing.

She caught Minnie's eye. Minnie understood.

'Why don't I . . . make us something to eat,' she said, standing up. 'There's bread on the side and I think I remember seeing some cheese in the fridge, right, Alice? How do toasties sound?'

Once she'd gone, Dee lowered herself into the spot Minnie had just left. She put one arm around Alice and then, a second later, the other. Her mum was so much smaller than she was. Alice looked up. Her blue eyes were wet and her bottom lip was wobbling.

'The fight we had was about you,' she said with a sniff. 'I mentioned that conversation I'd had with Nat's mum, and

Ines said I was putting too much pressure on you to find someone to settle down with. I lost my temper and told her to mind her own business. She said that you *are* her business, and that you have been ever since we got together. That put my back up because I thought she was saying that I . . .' She blinked as tears filled her eyes again. 'That I wasn't a good mother.'

The tissue Andy had given her the night before was still in the pocket of her dress. Dee pulled out the little folded square and passed it to Alice. 'Mum, come on, don't say that . . .'

'But I wasn't, was I?' Alice insisted. She blotted her eyes and took a gulping breath. 'You were so understanding about everything when you were little. You never complained or made a fuss, you just seemed to take it all in your stride – you made it easy for me to tell myself that you were fine. But I don't think you *were* fine, were you?'

Her own face was wet too, Dee realised.

'You were here though, Mum,' she said, dabbing at the tears on her cheeks with the sleeve of her dress. Alice, seeing this, passed her the damp tissue. 'Even if things weren't always . . . great, you stayed with me. Dad was the one that left, not you.' She glanced at Alice's drinks cart in the corner, and the casual way that Andy had sketched out their future life together swam in front of her eyes. 'He went to America to follow his dreams and you just had to fit in around that. I'm sure you'd have loved to have buggered off to the other side of the world with no responsibilities and worked in a bar, right?'

'No, I wouldn't,' Alice said with surprising vehemence. 'Having you was very hard, but it was the best thing that ever happened to me. It was like I'd spent nineteen years living in a flat world, and then suddenly everything was in 3D.' She looked up at the ceiling and sighed. 'That's probably why I've rabbited on at you so much about finding someone. Because as soon as I took the pregnancy test and it said you were on the way, I had the most incredible feeling of . . . well, companionship. I knew that whatever else happened in my life, I'd always have you. And I wanted you to feel like that too.'

Very slowly, Dee lowered her head so the side of it was resting on the top of her mum's.

'We used to talk, didn't we?' Alice's voice came from below her. 'We never talk any more. Not properly. What happened?'

Dee shut her eyes. 'I get really scared about something happening to you, Mum,' she whispered. 'About you . . . doing something. I'm always watching out for it, whenever I'm with you. I always worry that if I say the wrong thing or do the wrong thing, you might . . .' She let out a breath. 'I think about it all the time. Even now. And whenever I do the ground just sort of . . . opens up under me.'

Alice didn't say anything for a while. Then she reached up to touch Dee's hand with her thumb.

'What you've got to remember, darling,' she said quietly, stroking it, 'is that I've been very lucky. When you're depressed, you don't see the world as it really is. You find it very hard to hold out any hope. But then I met a really special person and she helped to change the way I think about everything.' She glanced down at Ronnie, who had somehow managed to fall asleep. 'Remember how jumpy this one was when he came to live with us? And now look at him. It's a little bit like that – someone has loved me every day for twenty years, and that's made all the difference. Well, that and multiple prescriptions.' She laughed; then the laugh turned into a sob. 'God, I miss her so much. It's only been two hours and I feel like I've lost an arm.'

Dee hugged her again. She could feel her mum's heartbeat through Minnie's jumper.

'Maybe we should go and check Minnie isn't burning the kitchen down,' she said, once it had slowed a little. Alice's eyes darted to the landline.

'I think I'll stay here,' she said. 'Just in case she calls.'

Minnie was standing by the cooker with a mountain of sliced bread and grated cheese on one side of her and two small, singed-looking toasties on a plate on the other. Dee put her arms around Minnie's middle and pressed her cheek against the cottony back of her pyjama top. 'I'm really, really glad you're here,' she whispered. 'Thank you.'

'Always.' Minnie wrapped her arms around herself so they were touching Dee's. 'Did Andy message you, by the way?'

Dee took a deep breath. 'So, he actually came round after you left last night . . .'

'And?' Minnie turned around, agog. 'What happened? What did he say?'

'He came to tell me that his wife was there because their divorce is being finalised next week. He brought the paper-work with him, he was telling the truth. He didn't tell me at the start because – well, there were lots of reasons, but it turns out that neither of us was being completely honest about how we felt. Anyway, we . . .'

'YOU DIDN'T!' Minnie squealed, grabbed Dee and

danced her around in a little jig. 'Oh my God oh my God oh my GOD, Dee, tell me everything! OK, fine, maybe not *everything* – but, like, seventy-five per cent of everything. Was it good? It was, wasn't it? It was! Dee!!!'

'It was, but . . .' The smile Dee hadn't quite managed to suppress faded.

'But what?' Minnie stopped doing the Netflix-Christmas-movie-happy-ending dance.

'We had a weird conversation this morning. Then Mum called and I had to go, so we didn't finish it.'

'Weird how?' Minnie frowned. 'Sex-weird? I find that nine times out of ten the answer to those is always . . .'

'No, no, nothing like that. He just started talking about how actually he's realised he does want to be a chef again, and it wouldn't matter if his hours weren't great because I could be flexible about my work. It was like he'd made this whole plan for his life without ever actually asking me what I wanted.'

'But you two have already talked about what you want, right?' Minnie looked puzzled. 'Wasn't that meant to be the whole point?'

'Well, yes, but . . .' Dee didn't even really know what she was trying to say. 'We hadn't got to the details stage. We hadn't made any decisions at all. But what he was talking about this morning absolutely isn't what I want my life to look like.'

'So just tell him what you *do* want.' Minnie shrugged. She sighed. 'Dee, you've always put the people you care about first because you want them to be happy. Maybe it's not impossible that Andy might do the same for you?'

Minnie made it all sound so simple. But even as she nodded, Dee knew she was wrong.

After they'd eaten and she'd washed up, Dee went for a walk. She left her mum and Minnie in the living room, watching Ronnie's favourite Bird TV YouTube channel under a blanket, with the cat between them emitting *honk-shoo* snores. Her mum seemed calmer, but her eyes were still pink and swollen.

Dee walked to Brent Lodge Park, and to her and Roo's tree. As she got closer to it she could so clearly picture Roo in her school uniform, frowning at the laptop she'd spent half a year saving up for. Eighteen going on thirty-eight. What was she doing right now? For almost the whole time they'd been friends Dee would have known the answer straight away. As students they'd shared their timetables, and when Roo had spent three months in Australia Dee had wound her spare alarm clock eleven hours ahead so she'd always know what time it was for Roo. But right now, even though they were only a mile apart, she had absolutely no idea. There would probably never be another form that Roo could fill in for her like she had their yearbook. Or that she would want to.

She climbed on to the log. She inhaled and let all the breath out as slowly as she could, trying to postpone the next thing for as long as possible. Then she video-called Andy.

'Dee?' He was sitting on her sofa. He'd carefully straightened out the throw over the back of it, and the sight tugged at her heart. 'I was going to call but I didn't want to bother you while you're at your mum's – how is she?'

'She's . . . OK, I think.' There was a lump in her throat that she couldn't shift. 'Minnie's with her, I've just come out to get some air.'

'That's good. Are *you* OK?'

Dee nodded. If she didn't say it now, she told herself, she never would.

'I'm OK. But there was actually something I was going to tell you this morning too,' she began haltingly. 'I've been offered a new job as well. It's with this online plant company – I'd get to be much more creative, and the money's good, too.'

'Wow!' Andy's face lit up. 'Congratulations, Dee! No more Mulchomatics! We should definitely . . .' He stopped and frowned. 'Hang on, you don't look very pleased.'

'No, no – I am.' Dee put her free hand on the tree's trunk, pushing her fingers under a loose piece of bark. 'I really am. But what you were saying just before my mum rang, about getting back into cooking – you looked so excited. And it made me realise I want that excitement too. For me, I mean. I want to see something I like the look of and just go for it without having to factor in anyone else. I want to do that with lots and lots of things. I've never put myself first before, and I really want to start doing that. I think . . . I want to do that before I do anything else.'

'Honestly, Dee, that was just hungover nonsense from me – I promise I wasn't assuming you'd be the one doing all the childcare or anything like that, I just wasn't thinking—' Andy was really frowning now. 'What are you saying?'

'Um, I don't know, I just . . . ' Dee swallowed. 'No, actually, I do know.' Her heartbeat was banging in her ears and all her muscles had tensed up. 'I know that I always had this idea that if I could just make a family for myself I'd never feel how I did when I was growing up again. But getting to know you has made me realise that what I actually wanted all along is . . . love.'

As soon as she'd said it she wanted to snatch it back, but she forced herself to carry on.

'I know that it isn't that I don't want to be a mum – I do. It's that I'm not ready right now. But right now might be all I have. And you want to be a dad as soon as possible. So if all that's true, then . . .' Her eyes had started to blur. 'You should probably look for someone who isn't me. I'm sure you'll get loads of offers.'

The piece of bark came away in her hand. She fixed her gaze on it, trying to keep the tears in. The silence made her feel like she was being pulled apart.

'Maybe I would.' There was a stiffness to Andy's voice that she'd never heard before. He paused – she looked up, and their eyes met through the screen. 'But would any of them put marmalade in bacon sandwiches?'

It took Dee a second to realise what he'd said – or rather, what he hadn't.

'I really do want a family of my own, Dee,' Andy went on. 'I want the silly traditions at Christmas, and shit beach holidays where you argue about where to put the towels, all of that. It's been such a long time since I properly had those things, and I can't imagine the rest of my life without them. But since we met I've realised that when I think about them, what I'm actually thinking about is . . .' He paused, and Dee saw that the tips of his ears had gone a very faint but unmistakable pink. 'Love. That's the most important thing.'

Dee stared at him. Time had gone skewed.

'Anyway, to quote what I said when we were in Tesco, I think we should talk more about this,' Andy went on. 'Not

303

least because it's the only one of Roo's questions we haven't got to yet. But maybe we could do it as, you know' – he raised his eyebrows – 'boyfriend and girlfriend. You can crack on with your very cool-sounding new job, I'll see what comes out of running the cafe. And we just . . . see how we go. If it turns out that starting a family is something we're going to find difficult, there are lots of options. I don't know how you or I might feel about those if it comes to that. All I know right now is that I want to be with you.'

It was like someone had muted the entire park around her.

'So . . . you're not breaking up with me?'

'No, Dee,' Andy said solemnly. 'I am doing the opposite of breaking up with you.'

He smiled at her, and as she bit her lip to stop herself grinning back at him like a lunatic, she felt the knot that she'd had in her stomach for as long as she could remember start to loosen. Then Andy cleared his throat.

'Anyway, it's a scientific fact that chefs explode if we talk about our feelings for more than a few minutes without reaching for some kind of narcotic, so just going back to Ines for a second – where do you think she's gone? Has she got any connections anywhere else? Friends, family?'

'Not really.' Dee shook her head. 'She was born in Argentina and lived in the Netherlands for a bit, but she didn't take her passport with her so she can't be in either of those places. And her whole life's in London; she's been here for forty years, ever since she moved from . . .'

Something stopped her in her tracks.

'Andy, can I call you back in a second?' She scrambled off the log. 'I need to check some train times.'

Chapter Twenty

It was raining in Brighton. The tourists waiting to get on to Dee's train were standing in puddles of water, shivering in clothes chosen for a sunnier day at the seaside. Dee hadn't brought an umbrella with her from London; as she went through the ticket barrier she wondered if she ought to buy one, but there was a queue for WHSmith and she didn't feel like she had any time to lose.

She stopped by the taxi rank outside to Citymapper the address she'd managed to find online, and saw she had a voice note. It was from her dad.

There was a short, square-topped concrete bollard to her left. After a couple of seconds' hesitation she sat on it and pressed play.

'Hey there, kiddo.' Karl sounded much less bombastic than normal. 'Look, what you said the other day really got to me, but that's no excuse for radio silence at my end. I'm meant to be the adult here – in theory, anyway. I just wanted to say that I know I'm probably the last person you'd call when things are tough, but I hope you know you always can if you want to. OK, then. Bye for now.'

Dee checked the time, then went into her inbox's trash folder. There was the email her dad had sent her when she was at the market with Andy.

Thought you might enjoy this photo of yours truly back in the day. I'll tell you the story behind it when we next see each other, which I hope will be soon. Dad x

There were two images attached – both of them were at a slight slant, as though they'd been scanned in. The first was a photo of her dad, smiling and looking very young with his dark curls and moustache, standing next to the battered cooker in a bedsit kitchen. He was wearing a crisp white dress shirt, a splashy floral tie and black trousers held up by primary-coloured braces. The matching jacket was slung over his shoulder, and he was striking a catalogue-model pose for the camera.

The second image was the back of the photo. It was covered in her mum's extravagantly looped handwriting.

'22 October 1987,' it read. 'On our way to meet Dee! K insists he wants to put on a suit before we leave for the hospital! HAPPY BIRTHDAY TO OUR LITTLE GIRL.'

Dee looked away from the screen, blinking back tears. She saved both the images to her gallery, went back into WhatsApp and messaged her dad.

Nice braces, Dad . . . How did you get that photo?

Karl immediately came online.

Karl Jensen:
Hey kiddo, I took it with me
when I left

Dee:
Mum never told me you got
all dressed up for my arrival

Karl Jensen:
Of course I did. I was
meeting someone very
important

I know I haven't always
made you feel important,
Dee. And I know I can't
do anything to change the
past. But I'm hoping I can
change the future a bit?

If this was a film, Dee thought as she clicked out of Whats-App and got to her feet, the rain would have stopped and the sun would have broken through the clouds. But it wasn't, and it hadn't. As she set off towards North Laine it got even heavier: fat droplets smacked her in the face, sticking her hair to her forehead and pooling on her phone's screen, blurring the map that she was trying to follow.

She spotted the building as soon as she arrived in Kemptown. As she got closer she saw the steps she remembered from the Polaroid, and her heart started to race. She ran up them, splashing through the puddles in the dips that had been worn by generations of feet, and pressed the buzzer marked 'Rainbow Holiday Rentals'.

'Hello?'

As Ines's voice came through the intercom, Dee realised she hadn't actually thought beyond this point; she'd been so focused on holding on to her hunch.

'Um, it's me, Ines,' she said. And then, pointlessly: 'Hi.'

There was a disbelieving pause.

'Dee? What are . . .' Ines was silent for a moment. 'I'll come out. Stay there, OK?'

Dee stood on the step, tapping her foot, trying to ignore the rain running into her eyes. Then the door opened.

As she stared at her stepmum Dee felt two decades' worth of memories rushing at her. There was Ines taking a photo of her eating an apple outside the dentist after her braces came off when she was fifteen. There was Ines sitting in the bathroom with her all night when she'd drunk half a bottle of Malibu after getting her A-level results, giving her water to sip when she threw up and making her laugh. Twenty years of Ines keeping a constant, watchful eye on the balance of life at Milton Road, adjusting the scales whenever they wobbled so there was never any danger of the whole thing tipping over. She wanted to throw her arms around her and never let her go, but she couldn't move.

'How did you find me?' Ines asked slowly. She was wearing jeans and a loose denim shirt that Dee had never seen before, and thick walking socks.

'It wasn't that hard.' Dee managed to wipe a raindrop off her nose with the sleeve of her jacket. 'You left your passport behind so I knew you had to be in the country. Then I remembered you talking about this place when I came round. So I found the listing online and it said it was booked for the next few weeks. They don't give the exact address on the website but there aren't that many buildings that look like this in Kemptown. I just . . .' More rain ran off her hair on to her face. 'I guess I know how your mind works. Or I thought I did, anyway.'

Ines didn't say anything in response to this. The paint around the door frame was peeling in thick flakes; Dee watched as her stepmum pressed her palm against one, flattening it against the wood. The relief of actually having found Ines was starting to wear off now, and another feeling was forcing its way to the front.

'How can you just stand there like nothing's wrong?' she demanded angrily. 'Mum's in pieces, Ines, I'm really worried about her.'

Ines took her hand off the door frame, and the paint flake sprang back. She sighed. 'Look, do you want to come in? You're soaked; we can put your jacket on the radiator to dry.' Dee stayed where she was. 'Dee, please. Come out of the rain.'

Dee allowed herself to be ushered inside. The echoey hallway was much nicer than the outside of the building had suggested and looked as though it had been recently redecorated: there were black and white tiles on the floor and a spiral staircase in front of them like something from a Regency ball. To their left was a door with a Rainbow Holiday Rentals plate on it, which Ines unlocked.

'Go through,' Ines said. 'I'm going to get you a towel for your hair from the bathroom, OK?'

Dee left her sodden shoes on the doormat, then peeled her socks off and left them there too. The door led into a whitewashed living room with high ceilings, floorboards and long shuttered windows that looked out over the street. There was an L-shaped sofa, a small round table with two chairs and a gleaming kitchenette with a rainbow-print tea towel over the oven's handle. She could hear the seagulls outside. Ines had only been here for a few hours but she'd already unpacked, Dee noticed as she draped her jacket over the radiator and sat down on the sofa. Ines's laptop was out on the table, her slippers were by the window and there was a pile of her books on the rug next to the sofa. Dee had never seen any of them anywhere that wasn't Milton Road, and yet they looked as though they'd always been here. In fact, they all seemed much happier now they weren't struggling to breathe among the chaos of Alice's things.

Ines came in with a fluffy white towel rolled up into a hotel-style sausage. She passed it to Dee.

'When I lived in this building the first time round I was all the way up in the attic,' she said as she sat at the sofa's other end. 'It's strange being down here on the ground floor. I sort of know where everything is, but not really. I keep looking for switches in the wrong places.'

The cushion's worth of space between them felt like miles. Dee drew her knees up against her chest, leaving the towel next to her. She didn't want to go along with anything by unrolling it.

'Mum honestly didn't mean what she said when you were arguing,' she said, trying not to sound as agitated as she felt. 'She's really, really sorry. And I am too, for leaning on you as much as I have done recently. And for making you feel like everything was on you the whole time in general.'

310

Ines gave her a look that felt almost pitying. 'Oh, Dee-Dee, that's not why I'm here – none of those things are . . .'

She sighed and leaned back against the sofa's cushions.

'I've done a lot of thinking since I found out my father was sick. About him, obviously, but also about me. When your parent is dying I think it's very normal to find yourself wondering how much time you have left, and asking yourself what you want to do with that time. I realised that I've made my whole life about taking care of other people, and I've never let anyone take care of me – not Al, not you, nobody. That's absolutely not your fault, I never asked you to. I did the opposite, actually.' She spread her hands and shrugged. 'I've spent the best part of forty years encouraging people to think about what they need, and I've never done that myself. I thought the answer was just that I need to be needed. I do, but that isn't all I need. And I'm sixty soon, so . . .'

'How long had you been thinking about . . .' Dee couldn't finish the sentence: the thought that she might have completely missed the signs that Ines was planning to leave made her feel profoundly sick.

'I hadn't been thinking about it, not consciously anyway. But when your mum and I were arguing this morning I felt like I was drowning – I knew I needed some space.'

Dee swallowed. She wanted to tell Ines that it was OK, that it made sense, that she understood. But a voice inside her was screaming that she needed to do the opposite. That this was her last chance.

'Does that mean you're not coming back?' she heard herself saying. 'Because if you're not . . .'

Ines looked at her and burst out laughing.

'Of course I'm coming back.' She shook her head, looking bemused. 'I just need to do some thinking about what the next bit of my life is going to look like. I haven't had a proper break in about five years, so I've taken a few weeks off work. And I was thinking I might go back to Argentina for a bit if my . . .'

Her voice trailed off. Dee shuffled up the sofa and reached for Ines's hand.

'You really can talk to me about that stuff if you want to,' she said, squeezing it. 'I can handle it, I promise. I'm not a teenager any more.'

Ines smiled. 'Thank you. I might well take you up on that. Now, how about a hot drink?'

'Deal.'

Ines got up to boil the kettle. As she watched her making coffee the way she had countless times before, Dee wrapped the towel around her hair and rubbed her scalp through it. Ines had left, but she hadn't *left*, she told herself, repeating the motion over and over again. She was coming back; they just didn't know when. And her mum was going to be OK. She remembered what Alice had said a few hours ago, about how meeting Ines had changed the way she thought about everything. Love really could do that. If you let it.

'I hope you don't mind me saying this, Dee-Dee, but you look like you haven't slept a wink . . .' Ines came back with two identical steaming mugs. She gave one to Dee, put hers on the table, then sat down again and tilted her head in mock-innocence. 'Is there anything you want to tell me? Or *anyone* you want to tell me about?'

Dee pulled the cushion out from behind her and chucked it at Ines's feet. 'Oh my God, you're worse than Mum! I've changed my mind – I actually don't want you to come back.'

Ines laughed and kicked the cushion away. 'Is that a yes?'

'It's a yes.' Dee chewed her lip. 'So . . .'

She told Ines the whole story: about her test results, Nat, her agreement with Andy and everything else. Ines took all of this new information remarkably calmly.

'Well, if I've learned anything from my job it's that couples don't talk nearly enough about what they want at the start of relationships,' she said once Dee had finished. 'Or they do talk, but they just say 'I want X or Y', when what they actually mean is 'I want to feel a certain way' or 'I want to avoid this experience'. But nothing ever gets spelled out, and that's where the problems start. You and Andy have done your talking before even becoming a couple, so you're already miles ahead – more people should take a leaf out of your book, really.' She smiled. 'You look very happy.'

Dee pictured Andy sitting on her sofa; he was still there, in the flat, waiting for her. 'I am. I never . . . well, I guess I never thought anyone would actually choose me.'

Ines gave her a funny look and tucked her legs up on the sofa.

'Remember the day we met? You came home from school when your mum and I were sitting in the kitchen with the chessboard out. And you asked me whether I got paid twice. You really reminded me of myself as a teenager; I'd hated being tall too. And you seemed so worried about everything. I could tell straight away that you were scared, and

313

I didn't want you to ever feel like that again if I could help it.' She gave Dee a smile. 'I never knew my mother, and I certainly never thought I'd be one. I wasn't even looking for a serious relationship. But I knew as soon as I met you that I wanted you to be my family – so I chose both of you. You *and* Al.'

Dee looked down at the floorboards. As she stared at the whorls in the wood she felt the map of her life rearranging itself.

'Mum said you'd told her I'd always been your business,' she said.

Ines nodded. 'Yes, you have been. So you're stuck with me, I'm afraid.'

Dee let her gaze drift past Ines to the window. While they'd been talking the rain had stopped. She watched as a shard of blue appeared in the clouds.

'How would you feel about fish and chips?' she asked, looking back at her stepmum.

'I was just thinking that, actually.' Ines smiled. 'Let me get myself together, OK? Two minutes.'

Once she'd gone, Dee got her phone out. She went into her gallery and found the video she'd made after her mum and Ines's wedding, and fast-forwarded through the frames until she reached the point she'd stopped it at earlier that week. There was Minnie asking Alice and Ines if it had been love at first sight, and them replying that it hadn't.

'It crept up on me too.' Alice slipped her arm under Ines's jacket so she could put it around her waist. 'And you know what, girls, I think that's one of the reasons it stuck. We didn't even call it dating in those days, but I always found *going out with people* such hard work, I could never just relax and get to know them. With Ines I could because we started out as friends, so I didn't put any pressure on myself.'

'This from the woman who was wearing a new lipstick every time we saw each other.' Ines laughed, holding Alice. 'Anyway, we got there in the end, didn't we?'

On the way to the seafront they passed a pet shop.

'That might be nice for Ronnie,' Ines said, stopping to point at a fleece-lined bed in the window. 'Don't you think? He's getting so creaky in his old age, and this one has memory foam in it.'

The shop's manager came out with a dustpan and brush. 'We recommend that model for small to medium-sized dogs,' she said, following their gaze as she shook it on to the pavement. 'Perhaps a spaniel.'

Dee and Ines's eyes met. Dee bit her lip.

'We'll take it,' Ines said with an impressively straight face. 'Thank you so much.'

At four o'clock Captain's was quiet, becalmed between lunch and dinner. Dee and Ines crunched their way across the shingle on the beach and went to order from the hatch.

'Cod and chips for me, please,' Ines said, swapping the bag with Ronnie's new bed in it into her other hand. 'Oh, and a Dr Pepper if you've got any.' She glanced at Dee. 'Haddock, chips and peas with extra scraps, right?'

'Thanks. Here, let me take that.' Dee relieved her of the bag. Behind the till there was a wall of customer photos – and right at the top was the green of Ines's wedding suit, and Alice's red hair.

'Dr Pepper?' she said, turning back to her stepmum. 'You think you know a person . . .'

Ines winked. 'I contain multitudes.'

The wind had dropped and the sea was still. As they waited for their food on the beach, Dee and Ines watched a group of swimmers in rubber hats and goggles taking big crane-steps over the pebbles. They inched into the water, gasping as they splashed their bare skin with it. Then one by one they pushed off the bottom and glided into the distance. Dee and Ines smiled at each other. Neither of them spoke.

'One cod, one haddock?'

A man in a Captain's baseball cap and polo shirt was standing behind them with a brown paper takeaway bag.

'I hope you don't mind me saying this,' he twinkled as he handed it over to Ines, 'but you two look so alike. I expect you get that all the time, don't you?'

Chapter Twenty-One

The train that Dee had planned to catch was about to leave when she got to Brighton station. As she swiped through the barrier with her box of leftover chips she heard a whistle – she was about to break into a run when something stopped her.

It was fine, she thought to herself. There would always be more trains.

She watched it pulling away from the platform, feeling uncharacteristically peaceful. A man in a Thameslink uniform strolled past, whistling and jigging his ticket machine.

'This one's for London too,' he said, unlocking the doors of another train and climbing aboard. 'Leaves in ten minutes. It goes round the houses a bit, but it'll get you home.' He jerked a thumb towards a set of sliding doors further up the platform. 'You can sit through there in First if you like – it's never busy. Free Wi-Fi too.'

The carriage was empty. Dee chose a foursome rather than a pair of seats and stretched her legs out, clicking her ankles left and right. Her clothes were still slightly damp and she felt heavy with exhaustion. When she got back to the flat, she decided, she was going to run herself an extremely bubbly bath and spend a full hour in it, topping up the hot water as many times as she wanted to. Then she was going to sleep for a very long time.

She put her chips on the table and her bag on the seat next to her, then got her phone out. She had an email and a WhatsApp. The email was a reply from Morag to the message that she'd written with Ines's help while they'd been eating their dinner.

> I am absolutely MADE UP we're going to be working together again, Dee. Margaritas all round! I'll get HR to call you on Monday to discuss your start date. Thank you for saying yes. I think you've made a really great decision. M x

The WhatsApp was from her mum.

> Darling, just letting you know that I've spoken to Ines and I'm going to go down to see her next weekend, it's my turn to look after her now. Everything is fine here so don't worry, Ronnie kept squeaking for lasagne and Minnie gave him some, VERY naughty of them both! Mum xxx

Dee video-called her. Minnie picked up.

'You found Ines!' she cried; she was sitting on the bed in the spare room with her hair in a towel. 'Forget plants, your next job should be with MI5!'

Behind her on the carpet Dee could see a mountain of clothes and shoes. 'Are you and my mum just using each other's phones full time now? That's not weird at all . . .'

Minnie stuck her tongue out. 'I told her to leave it here so she wouldn't spend the whole evening checking it. Honestly, it's glued to her hand. Like mother, like daughter.'

She adjusted her towel and then glanced back at Dee, looking almost nervous.

'So, if it's all right with you, I was thinking of asking your mum if I could stay here for a bit longer. I really love hanging out with Ronnie, and if I was paying rent that would take a bit of the pressure off Ines with money, wouldn't it? Also, Jonas asked me out today, and if we're going to start seeing each other I *definitely* need to move – you've got to preserve a bit of mystery at the start, haven't you?'

'I think it might be a bit late for that.' Dee grinned. 'That sounds like a really great idea, Minnie. For everyone. And I'm looking forward to the two of you moving to Kent in due course.'

'I'll be leaving London on the Twelfth of Never.' Minnie suddenly looked mischievous. 'Now, I've got someone here who wants to talk to you . . .'

Dee was expecting her to duck out of the shot and reappear holding Ronnie. But Minnie stayed where she was.

And suddenly, there was Roo next to her on the bed.

'Right, I'm going downstairs to check on your mum – I'll leave you two to it,' Minnie said with exaggerated tact, handing Roo the phone.

Dee could feel the pressure of a held-in breath building inside her chest. Roo's expression was impossible to read. They stared at each other.

'Minnie Deliverooed me an entire chocolate fudge cake,' Roo said eventually. 'And Ealing's ten minutes on the train from Hanwell, so I couldn't really fob her off when she messaged me asking if we could talk . . . For someone who

can't keep a secret she's basically a criminal mastermind.'
She paused. 'She told me about Ines. I'm so sorry, Dee, you
must have been going through hell – I wish you'd said. If I'd
known . . .'

'I know. I know you would have.' The words seemed to
be sticking to the roof of Dee's mouth. 'I've missed you so
much, Roo,' she managed to say. 'I know it's only been a day,
but I . . .' She swallowed. 'I went to our tree in Brent Lodge
Park today. I wish we could just go back to the way things
were then.'

'Well, I don't,' Roo said bluntly. Then she softened her
voice. 'I think we're both much better off now than we were
then, don't you? You're not moping around after Nat any
more and I don't look like Wednesday Addams.'

'Oh, Roo.' Dee swallowed painfully. 'I really hurt you yesterday. I don't think I'll ever forgive myself. I'm so, so sorry.'

'You did – but you didn't mean to. And I was hurting
anyway, that part wasn't your fault.' Roo shook her head.
'And I've been thinking a lot about what you said. I honestly
don't know what I'd have done if I'd been in your shoes with
Minnie, Dee. Probably exactly the same thing.'

She looked down at the bed for a moment.

'Remember when we were in my bedroom looking at university prospectuses, the day after your mum broke up with
North Face Richard? You said that Alice was all you had, and
I said that wasn't true – I promised I'd always look out for
you. I really meant that, Dee. I've hated watching you get
hurt by people who don't deserve you and not being able
to stop it happening. When you started talking about the
whole platonic co-parenting thing it sounded like it could

get so messy . . . I just didn't want that for you. But what *I* want and what *I* think is right for you are completely irrelevant at the end of the day. The only thing that really matters is what *you* want.'

Dee tried to speak but she couldn't. As she flailed around for the right words she watched the beginnings of a smile spread across Roo's face.

'Anyway, it turns out it was a good thing we never got round to opening any wine last night.'

She ducked out of view. When she came back she was holding a pregnancy test. There were two pink lines in the window.

'When did you . . .' Dee had always pictured herself throwing her arms around Roo when she broke the news and the two of them jumping up and down like they had when they'd got their A-level results. But now it was actually happening, and they were miles apart. All she could do was stare.

'This morning.' Roo's smile grew. 'I just woke up feeling very . . . odd. I can't explain it. I actually took three more, just to make sure – the rest are at home, but I wanted to keep one in my bag – so I could keep checking I hadn't imagined it, I think.' She shook her head and the smile faded, a serious expression taking its place. 'I mean, look, it's really early days still. I'm trying not to get too excited. But the second line's strong, which is meant to be a good sign – it means the pregnancy hormone levels are high. Or that I'm having two.'

Dee couldn't help laughing. 'Twins would really be taking overachieving to the next level. And you did always say you wanted them. That would be incredibly on brand for you.'

'It really would.' Roo laughed too. They looked at each other. 'So . . . what else did I miss, apart from you launching a search-and-rescue mission and Minnie moving into your old bedroom?'

A smile tugged at the corners of Dee's mouth. 'Well, your theory about Andy was correct. His divorce is being finalised next week. And I think we're going to try to make a go of it. Like, as a . . . couple.'

Roo's eyes widened. 'I think that's what's called a buried lede,' she said. 'Huh. Well, well, well. So are you and me going to be in the same NCT group, or . . .?'

Dee shook her head. 'We're not having a baby. At least, not right now. Andy's decided he wants to get back into cooking and I really want to focus on my new job. We'll see where we are once the dust has settled. And if we're still not ready . . . well, we'll cross that bridge if we come to it.'

'You could still think about IVF,' Roo said in her doctor voice. 'You'd probably need to do quite a lot of rounds, given your egg quality. Or you could always look into donor eggs . . .' She rolled her eyes at herself. 'But I'm sure you already know all that.'

Someone blew a whistle on the platform.

Dee grinned. 'Thanks, Dr Gill. My train's about to leave, I'd better go – speak to you tomorrow?'

'I'll call you then for a follow-up.' Roo gave her a wink. Then she paused. 'I love you, Dee. You know that, don't you?'

Dee's breath caught. 'And I love you too, Roo,' she managed to say. 'Always.'

Roo ended the call, and Dee's home screen came back into

view – the photo of her, Roo and Minnie on the roller coaster. A part of her family.

While she'd been on the phone Andy had messaged her.

I realised we never got round to baking that shortbread.
Let me know if you're coming back from Brighton tonight
and I'll put the oven on x

She ran her finger over his name, paused, smiled. Then she started typing a reply.

I am. And yes. Thank you x

Eleven Months Later . . .

The light in the flat seemed to change every hour of every day. Right now, three o'clock on a Saturday just after it had rained, was one of Dee's favourite times – the way the afternoon sun hit the tarmac on Camden Road made psychedelic patterns on the living-room walls. She watched them out of the corner of her eye as she stood by the hob, peacefully frying cubes of bacon.

Six months ago Andy had moved in: the two of them were renting the flat from Hiro together. With all of his and Poodle's clothes gone there was suddenly more than enough space for another person. Andy had taken his things out of storage, and the kitchen cupboards were full now – the cast-iron pan Dee was using right now was one of his. It sizzled, then spat a little as she stirred the bacon.

Dee pushed the sleeve of her jumper up out of the way, revealing the plaster in the crook of her elbow from the blood tests that she'd had done recently. The hospital-issue plaster had made her itchy, so Andy had carefully replaced it with a blue catering one. Behind her, the living room was full of plants, none of which, miraculously, were dead yet. When she'd started working at Prick, Morag had sent her home with a selection of low-maintenance greenery: three snake plants in Mexican pots; a trailing ivy to go on the shelf. The trick to not killing them, Dee was learning, was to leave them alone most of the time. You had to just trust that they'd be OK.

She glanced at the clock above the hob: ten past two. Andy would be getting a tray of something sweet out of the oven at the cafe, ready for the teatime rush. He started work early but he didn't close, and he and Dee had the evenings together. And it wasn't forever.

The bacon was done. Dee popped over to the cupboard, then the fridge, and got the rest of the ingredients out. The Philadelphia was Garlic and Herbs now, but the pasta bows had stayed the same. She put the packet down next to the bowl, fork and spoon she'd already laid out. As she shut the fridge door she smiled at the two Air New Zealand tickets that were stuck to it: proper paper ones, date-stamped for December. She and Andy were going for a fortnight, to visit his mum over Christmas. It was going to be the first time that Dee had met her, and the first holiday either of them had taken in years. Next to them was a printed copy of the photograph her dad had sent her of him in his suit on the day she'd been born, along with one of the two of them that he'd asked Andy to take when they'd gone to Denmark together over the summer.

Dee scooped a third of the tub of Philadelphia into the bacon pan and loosened it up with a splash of milk, then grated in some Parmesan. Once she'd turned it into a sauce she switched off the gas and put a lid on the pan, then grabbed a pen and paper. 'Starter', she wrote at the top, then drew an arrow towards the six pack of beers on the kitchen windowsill. 'Main: Philadelphia carbonara'. Then she got two miniature Snickers out of the box of Celebrations that Jay had sent in an attempt to get her to come back to Anvil, arranged them on the paper and wrote 'Dessert' underneath.

The journey to Ealing from here took less than an hour – she still had plenty of time. She sat down on the sofa and flicked the TV on. She and Andy had been watching *Dragon Quest* the night before, and the Netflix episode card was still on the screen. There was Lulu in the dungeon, next to the chiselled, curly-haired actor who'd got the part of Olric Longblade instead of Nat (his character had been carried off by a troll in a battle scene during the first five minutes).

'Are you afraid, my lord?' Dee said out loud in a passable imitation of Lulu's upper-crust accent. Then she switched into a booming man's voice. 'Of dying, you mean? No, Agnes. I have no fear of death – only gratitude for the life I have lived.'

She snorted, then turned the TV off and picked up her phone. Her hand crept to it less these days – she found it easier to be alone with her thoughts now. But it was still where (almost) all of her favourite people lived.

Hiro had posted a wedding photo to Instagram, a month on from his and Poodle's big day: there they were in full Victorian steampunk regalia, kissing outside the gates of Highgate Cemetery. Underneath it, Minnie had cross-posted one of her TikToks from her @minnieandronnie account, which featured her tunelessly serenading the cat. In this one, which Dee saw had racked up nearly a million views, Ronnie was flopped across Minnie's knees.

Minnie sang:

> *If you've got a ca-at on your lap*
> *And you wa-ant to get up*
> *Don't even tryyyyy*
> *Cos that is illegal*

Right on cue, Ronnie looked up at Minnie and glared. Dee burst out laughing. She took a screenshot and sent it to the Milton Road group. It was made up of her, Minnie, Alice, Ines (who had finally caved in and downloaded WhatsApp; it had been too expensive to send texts while she'd been over in Argentina) and Jonas. Jonas didn't actually live at number 67 – much to the disappointment of the entire street – but he was a regular visitor. His contributions to the group chat were limited to the occasional random thumbs-up and fitness memes that nobody understood.

Minnie replied straight away.

Ronnie says thank you and
talk to his agent (me). Have
fun with Roo, Dee! Send
them my love!

Jonas:
👍

Roo was at a table outside Reineta in Ealing with the Bugaboo next to her. She waved to Dee and mouthed, 'SLEEPING'. Dee pretended to tiptoe across the cobbles.

'Your goddaughter exhausted herself earlier so she's having an extra-long nap,' Roo whispered. 'That means tonight is going to be hell on earth, but I'm too tired to do anything about it right now. I actually said "Excuse me" to a bin on the way here because I thought it was a person.'

Dee hugged Roo as she sat down next to her, then peeped into the Bugaboo. Sara Gill-Brennan was cocooned in pastel-yellow wool, her chest rising and falling under the blanket that Sam's mum had knitted and the puffy layers of her sleepsuit. Dee's eyes brimmed as she took in her determined expression and the shock of thick, dark hair sticking out from under her duck-print hat. At three months old Sara had lost her fragile newborn look – her cheeks seemed to have filled out even more every time Dee saw her. Above her, attached to the handle of the buggy, was a furry crab: it had been a present from Minnie, who'd been so convinced that Roo's baby was going to be a Cancer that she'd bought her crustacean-themed everything (Sara was actually a Gemini).

'I got you something,' Dee said, handing Roo a gift bag. 'Well, it's for Sara really.' She watched as Roo unwrapped a soft toy rhino. 'Sophie the giraffe is so last season – it's all about endangered species now, apparently.'

Roo stowed the rhino carefully in the bottom of the Bugaboo, then straightened up and very gently ran a finger down Sara's nose. Sara sighed in her sleep. 'She's ahead on all her developmental milestones,' she said proudly, smiling down at her daughter. 'The health visitor came yesterday; she couldn't believe she was already copying sounds she hears. They're not meant to do that until four months. She's doing so well.'

'A high achiever, just like her mum.' Dee laughed. 'And how are you doing? I mean, how are you *doing*?'

Roo hesitated. 'Still terrified quite a lot of the time, to be honest,' she said after a pause. 'I really thought I'd be good at this bit – it's what I did every day at work, isn't it? Watching people really carefully, making sure they don't die. But it turns out it's quite a lot more stressful when you can't clock off at the end of a shift. Also, my patients very rarely vomit all over me.'

'I think that's a pretty normal feeling when it's your own child.' Dee put a hand over Roo's. 'You're doing amazingly, trust me.'

Roo put her hand on top of Dee's to make a sandwich. 'They call this bit the fourth trimester,' she said, her eyes flicking back to the Bugaboo. 'They're too little to be out in the world really, but whoever's in charge of these things decided it really wasn't practical to keep them in longer. For which, can I just say, I am extremely glad.'

Roo's birth plan, which had existed in laminated form since her twelve-week scan, had not gone to plan. Ten days before Sara's due date she'd been doing a *Yoga with Adrienne* video at home when her waters had broken. Annoyed that things were running ahead of schedule, she'd finished the video then taken the bus to Ealing Hospital. When she got there she was told that she was actually much further along in labour than she'd thought, and also that the only anaesthetist working that day was stuck in surgery at Northwick Park – and no, she couldn't give herself an epidural. In the end she'd had to get by on gas, air and bites of chocolate from the waiting-room vending machine.

'How are you feeling about your appointment later to get your blood test results?' Roo asked now.

'Oh, fine.' Dee shrugged. 'It's not a big deal, we're . . .'

'Just talking.' Roo winked. 'I know, I know. Will you let me know what they say?'

'Of course.' Dee glanced at the Bugaboo, which had a car seat, a cupholder and a wireless charger built into it. It was basically an armoured personnel carrier, defending Sara against the world and its uncertainties. 'It's so good that Sam's going to be at home full time when you go back to work.'

Roo nodded. 'I know. Who'd have thought his company would be so progressive? He's so excited – I think he really just wants to be a stay-at-home dad. My salary isn't going to stretch to that obviously, but . . .' She smiled. 'And to think I only married him because he knew how to stack a dishwasher.'

A snuffling sound came from the Bugaboo. Two dark eyes – Roo's eyes – were taking them in from its depths. Then Sara yawned, wriggled in her swaddling and went straight back to sleep.

'I reckon we've got ten minutes before the Kraken properly awakes,' Roo said with another smile, smoothing her hair down. 'Want to split a tortilla with me?'

The blue plastic chairs in the Whittington's Obstetrics and Gynaecology waiting room were just as uncomfortable as they had been the last time Dee had been there. The rack of copies of *Gurgle* was still there too, but there was a different issue on it now: the baby on the front of this one was sitting up and looked startled, as though it had crawled into the studio by mistake on its way somewhere else.

As Dee was taking a copy down the doors opened and Andy walked in – he'd showered and changed at home into jeans and his rainbow-striped jumper. It was getting colder so the parka had come out too. Dee waved at him. He grinned and waved back.

'Thanks for tea, you,' he said, bending to kiss her. He smelled of his minty shower gel and, more faintly, caramelised sugar. 'Your best yet, I think – Garlic and Herbs Philadelphia was an inspired addition.'

'I try. Good day?' she asked as he sat down next to her, reaching for his hand. Even after nearly a year together, the everyday magic of them simply being able to touch each other like this whenever they felt like it hadn't worn off.

'Yeah, really good. Busy.' He glanced down at the magazine on Dee's lap. 'Ah, the latest issue, I've been on the edge of my seat waiting for this . . .'

'Dee? Andy?'

A doctor was standing in the doorway. He smiled at them.

'Are you ready?'

Thank you to . . .

My agent-in-a-million Emma Finn, for your unending support, thoughtfulness and care: you are a remarkable and inspiring person and I am so grateful for you every time I sit down to write. Thank you also to Saida Azizova at C&W – your emails are always a joy to read – and Hillary Jacobson at ICM, whose notes strengthened this enormously.

My brilliant editor, Emily Griffin: without your heroic patience, enthusiasm and kindness this book simply would not exist. Thank you for bearing with me, Dee and the rest of the gang as we got ourselves together. A huge thank you also to Katya Browne, Sania Riaz, Claire Simmonds, Hope Butler, Laura Brooke, Amy Musgrave, Sophie Melissa, Klara Zak and everyone at Penguin Random House who has worked so hard on both of my books.

My Roos and my Minnies: Alex Peake-Tomkinson, Alicia Grimshaw, Andrew Pirrie, Anthony Harte, Emma Underwood, Florence Wylde, Freya Coote, Ianthe Cox-Willmott, Izzie and Rollo Crichton-Stuart, James Harlow (and Fogarty), Jenny Stevens, Johanna Derry-Hall, Kate Hutchinson, Leonie Cooper, Leila Latif, Lara Tyrrell and all of Fancy Lunch Club, Peter Attard Montalto, Rach Adams, Sophie Orbaum and everyone at QV, and Yassine Senghor.

And my Andys . . . You know who you are, gents.

The group-chats, for the celebrations and commiserations, the scandalous voice notes and the sanity checks: Laura Kay,

Lily Lindon, Bethany Rutter, Lizzy Barber, Caroline Khoury, Sara Jafari and Vicki Rendall. The very best thing about being a writer is getting to be friends with other writers.

All the other brilliant authors whose kind words and generosity on and off the page have made such a difference: Daisy Buchanan, Sophie Cousens, Sophie Irwin, Felicity Cloake, Helly Acton, Abbie Greaves, Kate Sawyer, Laura Jane Williams, Katherine Heiny, Bethany Clift, Phoebe Luckhurst, Justin Myers, Laura Price, Sian Meades-Williams, Sophia Money-Coutts and Mhairi McFarlane.

The booksellers all over the UK and beyond who have championed my writing, and been so welcoming when I've visited – if you're reading this I'm probably outside the shop with a Sharpie (sorry).

Bre Graham, whose wonderful newsletter *Just To Delight* Andy got his pasta sauce recipe from.

Patricia Touton-Victor, for being my home from home.

Jessica Gunn and all the team at *Waitrose Food*, for not just tolerating but embracing the chaos of this writer's life and feeding me so well on my office days. I still think about the chocolate trifle.

Oliver Carter-Wakefield, for the Marmite pinwheels and much else besides.

Claire Strickett and the one and only Peggy Sue, for sofa snugs, podcast-length voice notes and treatos galore.

Anna Sulan Masing, the hardest-working person I know, for listening to all my stories, trusting me with yours and always being there with a much-needed strong drink and snacks. I treasure our morning coffee downloads.

Julia Beck, forever my first and best reader, for enthusiastically receiving every single version of this book (even the early ones we don't talk about), taking me to the Wetland Centre and always, always being in my corner. I am impressed by you every single day.

Edward Williams, the C-3PO to my R2-D2 and the other half of my brain, for being there during laughter, tears and everything in between. I cannot imagine my life without you, Pat, and nor do I wish to. Good day!

The irreplaceable Hugheses: Iain, Claudia, Edward, Hannah, River and Doris. I love you all so much.

Finally, the biggest thank you goes to all of you, for buying, borrowing and reading this – you're the best.

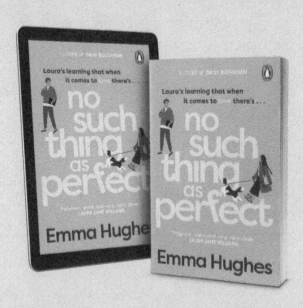

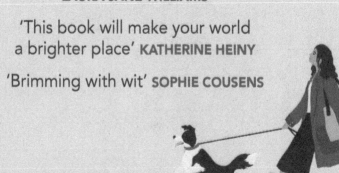